*The*
# NAMELESS THING

" We found Druce dead!"

[Page 12.]

# *The* NAMELESS THING

BY

MELVILLE DAVISSON POST

**WILDSIDE PRESS**

# CONTENTS

*" Behold the night is of great length, unspeak-*
*able, and the time for sleep in the hall is not yet;*
*tell me, therefore, of those wondrous deeds."*—HOMER.

# THE NAMELESS THING

## CHAPTER I: *The Mystery*

IT is the most mysterious thing that ever happened."

The coffee had been brought in; Judge Flint had declined and was lighting a cigar; Father Jerome was sipping at his cup. Dr. Lennard had been speaking. He was a man in middle life, hard and sunburned. He stood by the table, near the lamps, a cigarette in his fingers.

"You mean the manner of his death," said the priest.

"Not only that," continued the doctor "— and it was the strangest death that any man ever died — but also the manner of his life."

"It was strange," said the priest, musing over his cup, "but I had little opportunity to know. He saw me often, but he never spoke to me in his life."

"Never spoke to you in his life!" cried the judge. "Why, man, you are the beneficiary of his will!"

The lean figure of the priest lifted in astonishment.

"He left a sum of money to me?"

" He left everything to you."

The pale, intellectual face of the priest was serious and perplexed.

" For what purpose? " he said.

" For no purpose that the will names," replied the judge. " It is drawn in a dozen lines, and bequeaths everything to you, absolutely, without a condition."

The priest sat for some moments erect, motionless.

" Then he feared God," he said.

" He feared something," replied the doctor.

The lawyer went on. He was astonished to discover that Father Jerome did not know the man. This fact had snuffed out a light which he had expected to find burning.

" I do not know either how this man lived or died," he said. " When I heard the bare fact that he *was* dead, I wrote Dr. Lennard that we held the man's will, in which he was named as the executor, and you as the beneficiary. He at once telegraphed me to come here, and I have just arrived." He was looking at the priest. " We drew the will entirely by correspondence, and sent it to him to be executed. It was executed and returned in proper form, but it was accompanied by a letter, to be opened at his death, and I thought you would be able to explain this letter."

" What sort of letter? " inquired the doctor.

2

.

"A most incredible, a most amazing letter," replied the lawyer. He got a sheet of paper out of a leather pocket case, and read it:

"'I do not know how I shall die, but I do know the design that will accomplish my death. Therefore, if I am found dead, it is my desire that no inquiry be made. It could serve no purpose, except perhaps to implicate innocent persons.— Wilfred Druce.'"

"Now," said the judge, "what did the man mean by this extraordinary note?"

The doctor and the priest exchanged an enigmatic glance, and the doctor shook his head.

"That note," he said, "leaves the whole thing in even greater mystery. The man was surely living in some deadly fear, and he died as no living creature ever died in this world."

"How did he die?" inquired the judge.

"I will tell you that," replied Dr. Lennard. "But, first, I want to tell you how he lived."

He went over to a window and drew aside a curtain. A white moon illumined the world. Below the doctor's gabled, red-tiled house, there stretched fields and meadows down to a lake; and, beyond, on the summit of a hill, bare of trees, stood a great stone house, fantastic and shadowy under this moon. It was a country of beautiful hills, enclosed by the bow

3

of a wooded mountain range, that hemmed it in like a wall.

" I have often thought," continued the doctor, as he turned back from the window, " that Wilfred Druce chose this community in America because it resembled England more than any other; the lie of the hills, the big country houses, the gardens and the parked lands, gave him the atmosphere of England. A man cannot get the scent of his native land out of his nostrils. If he goes into a new country he will build a house like the one he was born in, and keep the old names. That house on the hill is the exact replica of an English country house."

Dr. Lennard paused. " Remember," he said, " I do not know that this man was English except by what you would call circumstantial evidence — his name, his personal peculiarities, and the like. He purchased the house from an agent and came here. That was seven years ago. The colony here called on him, as he seemed a gentleman, but he sent his card by a servant in return. We overlooked that, and asked him to dinner once or twice, but he made excuses, and presently we gave him up. This marked him as, to say the least, peculiar. He had horses, and he rode and drove about the country, and sometimes he had a game of golf, but always alone,— in the afternoon usually, when no one was on the course, or early in the morning. At first the man went about alone, and then, later he was always accompanied by a servant. At first he rode a good spirited horse, and through the loneliest wooded roads, then he came to ride the very quietest horse he could get, and only on the open roads. This was curious because the man was an excellent horseman."

The doctor paused, then he went on.

"Another thing he did that nobody could understand was this: There were some splendid old trees about his house when he bought it, and some capital shrubs. Well, he cut these trees down, cleaned out the shrubs, and made the place as bare as your palm, down to the foot of the hill. Then he began to take precautions to guard the house. That was perhaps not extraordinary, because burglars come out to these country colonies during the season, and crooks always get enticing ideas about persons of apparent wealth who are eccentric. But it was extraordinary to make a house into a fortress, and that, practically, is what Wilfred Druce did. He put iron bars over the windows, and rigged the house up inside with all manner of locks and bolts."

The doctor got another cigarette.

"None of us had been in his house, you know," he continued, "but workmen and servants gossip, and such things get about. Besides, since this thing happened, I have tried to find out everything I could. The next thing the man did was gradually to get rid of all of his servants and his horses, until, during the last year, he came to live in the house with a single servant, and to ride a saddle horse that a schoolgirl would have scorned."

"That servant?" said the judge, with his practical instinct for a leading point.

The doctor nodded. "Yes, he came here with Druce, and we were sure he could clear the mystery up when we got at him. But he could not. His story was that one night he was sleeping on the embankment in London. He had been a butler in a good family, but his appetite for liquor had driven him out, and he was on the town. He was awakened by hearing a man walk past him. He had an eye out for a 'bobby,' but the man was this chap Druce. He was going for the Thames, and there was something about him that alarmed the old butler.

"At any rate, he sprang up and caught the man by the arm. He says that when the man turned, his face was 'awful'— I never could get any other word out of him, 'awful' he continued to say. . . . And that's all he knows. Druce took him to a hotel on the Strand, and, in a few days, brought him along to America. . . . I put the old fellow through what you lawyers call the third degree, on what his master's peculiarities meant, and he says the man was afraid. But he does not know what he was afraid of any more than we do. I suggested some enemy, but he shook his head. ''Ow could an enemy make a rotten branch to fall on you, sir, or your 'orse to come a cropper, or an elm tree to crush you, or lightning to strike the 'ouse? Now, I ask you that, sir?' ... 'And, yet, sir, the master was always armed, and there was the manner of his death,' and he continued to shake his head. 'If a man's afraid of one thing, 'ow could he be afraid of everything?' "

"But, Lennard," interrupted Flint, "are not these clear evidences of insanity? Is not the delusion of persecution, and secret enemies, a common mania?"

The doctor sat down.

"Let us consider that a moment," he said. "If one takes elaborate precautions against a danger that does not exist, we call him mad, but if he takes these precautions against a danger that does exist, we call him prudent. The former is evidence of insanity, but the latter is evidence of the soundest common sense. If nothing had happened, I should have pronounced the man mad, but, by heaven, Flint, something did happen!"

"But was death the only thing that the man was taking precautions against?" said the lawyer. "It seems to me not entirely. Now, that my attention is directed to it, I observe this tendency to caution in the investments which we managed for him. At first he bought the usual market securities, and then he gradually became more and more careful, until bonds of the government were the only securities that he would put his money into. Now, what did that mean?"

"What does it all mean?" said the doctor.

The priest, who had been silent, now spoke.

"Perhaps," he said, "the thing which this man feared was something that menaced him at every point."

"But what sort of thing could that be?" said Dr. Lennard.

The priest seemed to consider before he would undertake to reply. He stroked his lean face with his white, emaciated fingers. And in the interval the attorney interrupted.

"Gentlemen," he said, "before we begin to speculate, let us have all the evidence before us. You were speaking, Doctor, of this servant."

"The suggestion is sound," replied Dr. Lennard, "there is this evidence yet." And he opened a door in the writing table, lifted out an iron box, and set it beside the lamp. It was a heavy square box of curious Japanese workmanship. It looked very old, as though it was some ancient heirloom that descended

8

from father to son. The metal was bright except for a dull brown stain that bordered the bottom of the box, for perhaps a quarter of an inch. He laid a sealed envelope beside the box.

"One moment, Lennard," said Flint; "the testimony before the exhibits. Go on with your story."

"Ah," replied the doctor, "our professions differ there in handling a mystery. We examine the exhibits first. Let me see, I was on the butler. Well, there was truth in one element of the man's story, at any rate. He was a drunkard. Servants about the colony say that the man was never entirely sober. At any rate, he was drunk on the night that Wilfred Druce died." The doctor paused. "He must have been drunk! A thing that he asserts simply could not have happened. . . . True, the whole thing looks impossible, but this one thing is downright impossible. He says that as he fled from the house in terror, he saw that the cement walk by the library windows was covered with bloody footprints — covered!"

"But if it was night," interrupted Flint, "how could he know that it was blood?"

"I screwed him down on that," continued the doctor, "and he swore to me that he slipped in it as he ran, and that the whole place was wet. And he sticks to it. True, he was capitally full of liquor that night, and no question, those who found him thought he had delirium tremens, and that is the reason no one went to the house until morning. He was wading around in the pond at the foot of the hill, and screaming like a woman."

"But the cement walk itself," cried the judge, "the footprints would be there. . . . That would tell you."

The doctor shook his head.

"No," he continued, "it did not tell us a thing. The whole country had been dry, as dry as a bone, but just at daybreak there was a thunder storm and a tremendous rain. But, mark you, it was as dry as powder when the thing happened. Father Jerome knows."

"Yes," said the priest, "I had prayed for rain. My people's little crops were withering, but the rain did not come until dawn. Some of my people brought this man to me at two o'clock in the morning, and the rain did not fall until five. Then, there was a deluge as from God's door."

"Of course, that rain scrubbed the cement walk as clean as your hand," Dr. Lennard continued. "Outside there was nothing; but inside, by Heaven, there were things to confirm the creature's story. He had heard a very hell of cries in the library where Druce spent his evenings, and a perfect fusillade of shooting, as though the man were fighting like a demon, in some deadly fear. And he fled the house with his hair on end. He says the thing came on like a flash. He had come down from his room to get a nightcap of liquor, and the house was as quiet as a grave. Then, as at the snapping of one's finger, the row began. The creature was in pajamas, and barefoot when they found him.

"Father Jerome sent for me and we went up to the house as soon as the storm was over. The man said that the house was protected against burglars, but we did not expect to find it a fortress. The library, which was on the ground floor, especially was secured like a jail — the windows were protected by a grating of two-inch iron bars set into solid masonry, and solid oak shutters that locked on the inside. These windows had not been opened, but the shutters were splintered and riddled with shots — every one of them fired from within the room — every one, — we could tell that from the splintered holes.

"We got into the house, expecting to find the door to the library open, but, by Jove, it was as fast closed as the shutters! We couldn't budge the door. It was solid oak, and the man said it was secured on the inside by bolts and an iron bar. We were pretty certain that Druce was dead. And our theory was that he had admitted someone, who had killed him, and was, himself, perhaps dead. At any rate, we could not get inside. The room was as impregnable as a cell. The windows were simply out of the question, and we had to go at the door. It took a dozen workmen three hours to force it, working with every tool we had.

"Well, we found Druce dead! But our theory!" he stopped and snapped his fingers. "I haven't any, theory any longer. . . . The room was in great confusion, chairs were broken, articles on the table overthrown, a corner of the bookcase thrown off its support, as though someone had lurched against it, its glass doors broken, and the fragments of glass on the carpet. The panes of glass had been shot out of the windows. Druce was lying in a corner of the room, a big calibre automatic revolver gripped in his hand. There was a pool of blood on the floor, and he was stone dead. There was no sign of blood in any other part of the room. And there was only one wound on Druce, and that was a deep gash on the top of his head that fractured the occipital bone. There wasn't a mark, a scratch, or a bruise on the man. I think he was killed by a single blow, and that the creature that killed him never touched him until it struck him down. There had been the very devil of a fight. The carpet was strewn with shells from Druce's weapon. He had continued to reload it as he fought; the magazine was half filled when we picked it up, but the barrel was foul with shots. There was a curious thing about these shots,— every one of them had been fired into the windows. There was not a bullet hole anywhere in the room. The three window panes and sash were literally shot to fragments. We went over every inch of the room — wall, floor, ceiling, and there was no place that an assassin could have entered. The throat of the chimney was not broad enough to admit a cat; the iron bars over the windows had not been tampered with. . . . Yes, we were careful about it, we went over these windows with a glass. The bars had not been tampered with; the rust remained where they were cemented into the solid stone, every bar was sound as on the day it was forged; and the door could not have been entered.

"I thought Druce might have first admitted the assassin, and then bolted the door. But, if so, how did the assassin get out and rebolt the door behind him? The bolts were all on the inside, and the iron bar was up across it. No, Druce could not have fastened that door after the assassin had gone out, because that blow crushing the skull must have killed him instantly. He did not move after he was struck down. The shooting was all in a single direction, the windows. That meant that the man was menaced from the direction of the windows only. I should have believed that the thing, or things, that killed him had not been able to enter the room at all, except for the fact that the man had been killed in a corner of the room farthest from the windows, and he was apparently struck down by some *tall* creature, some sort of creature much taller than the ordinary man, because the wound showed a blow made directly downward on the top of the man's head with some implement. Now, if that blow had been given by an ordinary man with any sort of weapon, the wound would have shown some slant. It must have been dealt by some sort of creature that towered over him. . . . No, there is no theory. Three steps along any theory that you can imagine, brings one up sharp against the sheer wall of the impossible, and iris bubbles of the fancy only get well on their way until they collide with the sharp edge of a fact, and puff out."

The judge had listened with the greatest attention.

"Lennard," he said, "the way you relate these facts, this thing is downright impossible. No one ever heard of such a case."

The doctor shrugged his shoulders and spread out his hands.

"I have stated the evidences exactly as we found them. Father Jerome knows."

"It is all precisely the truth," said the priest.

"Of course," continued the doctor, "I have used the words 'thing' and 'things,' 'creature' and 'creatures,' and the like, because I don't know how else to speak of the agency that killed Druce. The facts surrounding his death seem to preclude any agency that we know anything about. And, at the same time — what is incredible — these facts seem to establish that the man was killed by some physical agency. Of course, there is a solution. But the thing resembles those problems of physics, like the atomic theory, in which, to get a working hypothesis, you must begin by postulating an impossible base. And, like those problems, any theory will do if you simply force a single impossible gap in it. Granted that Druce killed himself, and you can work the thing out. But no living man could have dealt himself that blow, and besides, there is his letter to you, the fact of his desperate resistance, and the innumerable evidences that he was in constant fear. Granted that the agency that killed him could have entered the room, and it works out — but no living creature could have entered the room! . . . Pull the problem any way you like, put the pieces down on the table and edge them up, move them about, join them, fit them until you are mad, and you always find exactly the same thing, namely, that you must fit in an impossible piece in order to make a design. The thing simply will not go together without postulating the impossible. . . . But the impossible does not exist! We know that. It is perhaps the sole physical fact that we do, unquestionably, know. So, there we are!

" A man is killed by assassins, but no trace of them can be found, either within or without the house. The whole country has been searched. No strange person has been seen or heard of. Everything about the premises has been literally scrutinized under a glass. The only thing is what this butler says, and he was drunk! And, yet, here is the fact of a desperate resistance, and the further fact that Druce died with an expression of terror so stamped into his face, that the lips were drawn back from the teeth, and the eyes protruded. I have seen faces of men killed in all sorts of fear, but I never saw a human countenance so indentured with deadly terror. The man saw something awful, and he fought it in a very hell of fear. . . . That much is certain! "

The doctor indicated the steel box on the table.

" I fancied that the box was the object of the attack on Druce because it was sitting on the floor beside him, in the pool of blood, as though he had retreated into the farthest corner of the room to defend it. But, if so, why was it not taken? It could not have been opened because we found the key in a leather case among some jewels, which Druce had left at the village bank. Of course, the assassins might have had a duplicate key, or they might have abandoned the box in alarm. But, again, if the thing that killed Druce could have been frightened off, that hell of shooting would have done it."

" The contents of this box ought to clear that up," said the judge. " Was there any sort of treasure in it? "

" I'll show you what is in it," replied Dr. Lennard. He tore open the envelope, got out a little curious flat key, inserted it into the lock, and opened the box.

CHAPTER II: *The Strange Data*

NOW, Flint," said the doctor, " you see that the contents of this box only make the mystery more impenetrable. The thing was dark enough, believe me, but the articles in this box make that darkness Stygian. Father Jerome and I have puzzled over this thing from all points of view, and every advance we make is only a step in the fog. It is inconceivable that common assassins would make a deadly assault on Druce to secure what that box contains. And, as Father Jerome has just pointed out — a thing I had forgotten — nothing could have been taken out of the box by the assassins because there was a seal over the keyhole, and this seal was covered with dust. We had a high-power lens on it, and we are certain that the seal was old, and had not been tampered with. There is the fancy — I can't call it anything more than a fancy — that the killer of Druce imagined this box to contain a treasure of some sort. But you must concede, even to the most abandoned cutthroats, a grain of common sense, and what assassin, not sheer mad, would attack an armed man in a fortified room, and wage a desperate encounter like this one, on the mere fancy that this box contained something valuable? The idea is absurd!

"On the other hand, if the agency that killed Druce, knew what this box contained, how is it possible to believe that they would have entered into this terrible encounter to secure it. True, a sort of theory branches off here, that the box may have at one time contained something removed from it in later years. But if that was the moving idea of Druce's assailants, they would not have gone away without making sure, and this they could not have done on account of the seal over the keyhole. So this way leads only into confusion. The only thing we know is what the box contains now. And these contents, as you observe, Flint, fall into three distinct classes, one having no apparent relation to the other, and no one of them connected with any other fact that we are in possession of.

"First, here are these eight photographs in the bottom of the box. They are all of one size, and evidently taken by the same photographer; and, from the character of the work, I should say that they were not more than ten years old. They are the pictures of eight men. Every mark on these photographs has been carefully erased. There is nothing here to guide us but the pictures themselves. The men are young, and, one would say, English — the sort of sturdy fellows one would see in a cricket match any-where. And, there, all that we know about these eight photographs halts abruptly.

"Second, here are a lot of memoranda in Druce's hand that seem to be descriptive of something that took place on Nelson's flag ship, the *Victory*. This memoranda is fragmentary. It appears to be notes, jotted in pencil, to confirm or describe some story that ran parallel with it, but until we have the story, we simply cannot make head or tail of it. But there is here a certain fact, and that is this reference to the *Victory*. That looks like a moving candle in this darkness. But when you try to follow it, you are immediately lost. It has been one hundred and seven years since the *Victory* was Nelson's flag ship! Druce was about thirty. These photographs and the dress of the men show them to be near Druce's age, and to have been living within the last ten years. So neither Druce, nor any one of them could have been with Nelson on the *Victory*. Nor is it possible that Druce or any one of these men could have had any-thing to do with what occurred a century ago on the *Victory*.

"Now, the only other thing that the box contains is this mass of newspaper clippings. There are hun-dreds of these clippings, cut from all sorts of papers, and they fill the box. But no one of them refers to

Druce, or to the *Victory*, or to these eight men; nor do any two of them refer to the same event. But they do all have some relation to the general idea of retributive justice, that is to say, that the criminal, in the end, is discovered and punished, and that no degree of ingenuity, or care on his part, is sufficient to prevent this result. These clippings illustrate the variety of precautions which criminals have taken, and the variety of events and agencies that have accomplished their ruin."

The doctor stopped and relighted his cigarette.

"Now, Flint," he said, "the whole evidence is before you. I have stated it, I think, completely and accurately. What is your opinion?"

The judge did not at once reply. He had been carefully going over the contents of the box — the eight photographs, Druce's scribbled notes, and the piles of clippings. He had listened with the greatest attention to every word. Now he arose.

"Can I get New York by telephone?" he said.

"Certainly," replied Dr. Lennard, "you have not made an adventure into Darkest Africa." He rang for a servant, and bade him show the guest to the telephone.

The judge was gone for perhaps twenty minutes. When he returned, he replied to the doctor's question.

"Gentlemen," he said, "I believe this to be the most extraordinary case that ever occurred. Frankly, as the matter stands, I have no opinion. And I believe it useless to speculate on the data which we now possess — one's fancy would simply go to riot. My experience is that one can hardly ever arrive at the truth if he permit himself to entertain a theory before he has collected and examined every fragment of evidence that it is possible to obtain. I have set some inquiries afoot that may uncover something of this man's history. Only one thing seems precisely certain here, namely, that Wilfred Druce was in constant dread of some agency which he feared would destroy him. The evidence seems to establish this, I think, conclusively. From the letter accompanying his will, it seems permissible to believe that he knew what thing or things menaced him. But the expression which he uses is vague, ' I know the design that will accomplish my death.' Now, this expression does not necessarily imply that he knew the agency that would make use of the design, nor yet the means which that agency would use to carry this design into effect. Strictly construed, this word, as used here, means ' purpose ' or ' intention.' "

The judge put his cigar down on the table and continued.

"I want to try to pull this thread out of the skein.

Let us, then, abandon all the other threads, and admit at once that from this data we can have no rational idea whatever, of how Druce was killed, or who killed him, or the reason for it. . . . Now, he knew the 'design,' the 'purpose,' the 'intention,' which would accomplish his death. But did he know in what manner, or at what time, or by what means this design, purpose, or intention, would be put into effect? We cannot be certain here, but it is permissible to believe that he did not. The variety of his precautions tend to support that conclusion. . . . Then, did he know the agency behind this design?

"I feel that we cannot answer that question. I at first thought that these newspaper clippings might be evidence upon this point, but they seem rather to bear upon the preceding point. They appear to be a mass of data upon the variety of ways in which retributive justice overtakes the criminal agent. Now, if we are to conclude that this man had committed some crime, for which he feared a visitation of retributive justice, but was ignorant of either the means, or the agency, or the date of its visitation, then this great volume of data comes into the light. It means that the man was endeavoring to find out all he could upon that very point."

"Father Jerome and I," said the doctor, "have arrived at about the same general conclusion as the one you suggest — that Druce had been involved with something which he feared would follow and destroy him, and that these newspaper clippings were evidence upon the man's state of mind. But whether they were assembled to throw light upon the thing that menaced him, or the means or agencies which it might employ, I am not certain."

The priest had not spoken. He had been sitting with his thin fingers locked together, his face introspective and in repose. Now he entered the conversation.

" I think this data is equally upon the two points," he said. " This man has gathered here a great mass of evidence to prove that the criminal cannot escape the Providence of God, and that its methods are inscrutable; that vengeance is the Lord's; that He will repay; and that all human precautions against the hand of His Providence are idle and useless."

" Taking this data as evidence of Druce's state of mind," said the judge, " it does not appear to me that the man believed in what the Church calls the Providence of God. This data seems rather to establish that there is in all human affairs what the Greeks called an *inevitable necessity* to establish justice, and this impulse causes punishment to follow crime, as reaction follows action, or as the upward swing of the pendulum is followed by the downward swing;

that this impulse or necessity is universal in all human affairs, as gravity is universal in all matter, and the operation of it can be no more avoided, than the operation of any other natural law. Matthew Arnold attempted to formulate the idea when he said, ' There is a power not ourselves that makes for righteousness,' that is to say, an impulse or tendency. Now, Goethe says that man never will know how anthropomorphic he is, and, consequently, it is natural that this impulse should have taken form into a sort of Nemesis that follows and punishes the criminal agent."

" For my part, Flint," said the doctor, " I cannot agree with either Father Jerome or you. The data is upon the point that one who perpetrates a criminal act is discovered and punished. And I agree that this is usually true, but not for the reasons which either Father Jerome or you assign. The reason lies in the incapacity of the human mind. It is not possible for any man to foresee the involved and intricate order in which future events will arrive, consequently no man can take a sufficient precaution to foreguard himself at every point. The criminal will always neglect or overlook something, or fail to foresee something that, in the end, leads to his detection and punishment. And this is inevitable, because the human mind is too feeble to grasp all the multiple ramifications of an event, or the infinitely intricate manner in which it is related to innumerable events that precede and follow. But that there exists in the universe an Authority that will punish, or a tendency or impulse in nature to do so, I deny. The whole universe is a physical machine, in which man dwells at his peril, and in which he is able to exist only by adapting himself to its inexorable laws. It is wholly and eternally indifferent to him."

" Now, that conclusion," said the priest, " results from a study of things instead of a study of men. Science studies the body, and it has ascertained the forces that affect the body; but the Church studies the soul, and it has ascertained the forces that affect the soul. Now, it is the soul of man that is moral or immoral . . . crime is a transgression of the soul, not the body. Therefore, the agency that overtakes and punishes crime is something which the Church, and not the dissecting-room, has discovered."

" The opinion which I indicate," said the judge, " is drawn neither from science nor metaphysics. If one will examine the record of criminal cases, he will be impressed that events and human agencies seem to combine to effect the ruin of the criminal. And this happens so constantly, and in such a variety of strange and incredible ways, that one is impelled to the conclusion that only some tendency or impulse, inherent and universal in all human affairs could produce it. Now, if one must be anthropomorphic, he might call this thing a Nemesis, but he could not call it a Providence."

"But, my dear Flint," interrupted the doctor, "the very number of these cases in which events have taken an unforeseen turn, go to prove how inadequate the human mind is, and how little it can foresee, and nothing more."

"Pardon me," said the priest, "if I venture the opinion that because events and human agencies seem so strangely to combine to punish the criminal, is because the Providence of God has seized and moved them to that end. Now, if there was no strangeness or unusualness about the manner in which criminals are brought to justice, one might believe that the thing worked out through some tendency or impulse in nature. But so often an incredible combination of circumstances arises that only a power independent of nature could have put together, that we can only explain it upon the theory of God's Providence. I have in mind an extraordinary illustration."

The priest paused and lifted his thin, intellectual face.

"It was in the autumn in Virginia. An hour before sunset the man, who had been at work all day, turned out of the cornfield. He crossed to the rail

27

fence, with the hoe in his hands. At the bars leading into the field a squirrel rifle, with a long wooden stock reaching to the end of the barrel, stood against the chestnut post; beside it lay a powder-horn attached to a pouch of deerskin containing bullets. The man set his hoe against the fence. He wiped his hands on the coarse fox-grass growing in the furrows, examined the sun for a moment, then took up the rifle, removed an exploded cap from the nipple, and began to load it.

" He poured the black powder into his palm, and bending his palm emptied it into the barrel. The measure of powder was a sufficient charge, but he added to it half the quantity again, emptied into his palm from the horn. Then he took a handful of bullets out of the pouch, selected one of which the neck was squarely cut, and placing a tiny fragment of calico over the muzzle of the rifle, drew out the hickory ramrod and forced the bullet down. He got a percussion cap out of a paper box, examined it, placed it on the nipple, and gently pressed it down with the hammer of the lock.

" When the gun was thus carefully loaded the man threw it across his shoulder and, taking the horn and pouch in his hand, left the field. He went along a path leading through a wood to the valley below. Midway of the wood he stopped and con-

cealed the horn and pouch in a hollow tree.  Then
he continued on his way with the rifle tucked under
his arm.

" The country below him was one of little farms,
skirted by trees lining the crests of low hills.  The
man traveled for several miles, keeping in the shelter
of the wood.  Finally, he crossed a river on a fallen
tree and sat down in a thicket behind a rail fence.
Beyond this fence was a pasture field and a score of
grazing cattle.  In this field, some twenty paces from
where the man sat, the earth was bare in little patches
where the owner of the cattle had been accustomed to
give them salt.

" The sun was still visible, but great shadows were
beginning to lengthen across the valley.  Presently
an old man, riding a gray horse, entered the field
from the road.  When he came through the gate,
the man concealed in the brush cocked his rifle, laid
the muzzle on a rail of the fence, and waited, with
his jaw pressed against the stock.  The old man
rode leisurely across the field to the place where he
had been accustomed to ' salt ' his cattle.  There he
got down, opened a bag which he carried across the
pommel of his saddle, and began to drop handfuls
of salt on the bare patches in the pasture.  From
time to time he called the cattle, and when he did so
he stood up with his back toward the fence, looking

at the bullocks approaching slowly from another quarter of the field.

"There was a sharp report. The old man turned stiffly on his heels with his arms spread out. His face was distorted with amazement, then it changed to terror. He called out something, in a thick, choked voice; then he fell with his arms doubled under him.

"A thin wisp of smoke floated up from the rail fence; the horse, however, did not move; it remained standing with its bridle-rein lying on the earth. The cattle continued to approach. The man in the brush arose. The dead man had called out his name 'Henry Fuget.' Of that he was certain. That he had distinctly heard. But of the other words he was not so certain. He thought the old man had said, 'You shall hear from me!' But the words were choked in the throat. He might have heard incorrectly. He looked carefully about him to be sure that no one had heard his name thus called out; then he took up his rifle, crossed the river on the fallen tree, and returned toward the cornfield.

"He was a stout, compactly-built man of middle life. His hair was dark, but his eyes were blue. He was evidently of Celtic origin. He walked slowly, like one who neither delays nor hurries. He got the horn and pouch from the hollow tree as he passed, reloaded his rifle, shot one or two gray squirrels out of the maple trees, took them in his hand, and went down the ridge through the little valley, to a farmhouse. He had traveled seven miles, and it was now night."

The doctor had got another cigarette; the judge sat with his cigar in his fingers, a thin wisp of smoke climbing upward. Both men were listening with the closest attention. The priest continued.

CHAPTER III: *After He Was Dead*

AFTER the evening meal, which the laborer ate with the family of his employer, he went to his bed in the loft of the farmhouse. On this night Fuget ate well and slept profoundly. The stress which had attended his plan to kill Samuel Pickens, seemed now to disappear. The following morning he returned to his work in the cornfield. But as the day advanced he became curious to know if the body of Pickens had been found, and how the country had received the discovery. He had no seizure of anxiety. He had carefully concealed every act in this tragic drama. He was unknown in this part of the country. Pickens had not seen him before the shot. He had come here quietly, obtained employment as a farm laborer, under the name of Williams, located his man, watched, and killed him. True, Pickens had realized who it was who had fired the shot when the bullet entered his body, but he was dead the following moment, and before that he had believed Fuget in another part of the world.

" As Fuget remembered the scene, he found himself trying to determine what, exactly, it was that Pickens had said, after he had called his name. It seemed to Fuget that he must have heard incorrectly. He labored to recall the exact sounds that had reached him. If not these words,—' You shall hear from me,'—what was it that Pickens had said? And as he puzzled, he became more curious to know how Pickens had been found, and what the people were saying of the murder. Such news travels swiftly.

" As the day advanced, Fuget's curiosity increased. He paused from time to time in the furrow, and remained leaning on his hoe-handle. Finally he thrust the blade of the hoe under a root, broke it at the eye, and returned to the farmhouse, with the broken hoe in his hand.

" At the door he met the farmer's wife. She spread out her arms with a sudden, abrupt gesture.

" ' La! Mr. Williams,' she said, ' have you heard the news? Somebody shot ole Sam Pickens.'

" Fuget stopped. ' Who's Sam Pickens? ' he said.

" ' Bless my life! ' said the woman; ' I forgot you're a stranger. Sam Pickens? Why, he's a cattle-man that come over the mountains about two year ago. He bought the Carpenter land on the River.'

" Fuget had now his first moment of anxiety.

" ' I hope he ain't much hurt,' he said.

" ' Hurt! ' replied the woman. ' Why, he's dead. They found him a-layin' in his pasture field, where he'd gone to salt his cattle.'

" Fuget stood for a moment, nodding his head slowly.

" ' Well, that's a terrible thing. Who done it ? '

" The woman flung up her hands.

" ' That's the mystery,' she said. ' He didn't have any enemies. He was curious, but he was a good neighbor, folks say. They liked him. He lived over there by himself.'

" Fuget ventured a query.

" ' Did they see any signs of anybody about when they found him ? '

" ' There wouldn't be any signs in a pasture field,' said the woman, ' an' the person that shot him must have been standin' out in the pasture field, because he was a-layin' a-facin' the river. An' he'd been shot in the back. They could tell that for a certainty,' she added, ' because a bullet tears where it comes out, an' it carries in stuff with it where it goes in."

" Fuget made some further comment, then he held up the pieces of the hoe.

" ' I come in to get another hoe,' he said. ' I broke the blade on a root.'

" Then he went out to the log barn, selected a hoe from a number hanging in a crack of the logs, and returned to the cornfield.

" He had now a sense of complete security. Even chance had helped. The turning of the old man in

the act of death had diverted inquiry from the direction of the river, where some broken bushes might
have indicated his hiding-place. He worked the remainder of the day in the cornfield. He had the
profound satisfaction of one who successfully shapes
events to a plan. Nevertheless, he found himself
pausing, now and then, to consider what it was that
Pickens had said. The elimination of all anxieties
seemed somehow to have brought this feature of the
tragedy forward to the first place. It seized his attention with the persistent interest of a puzzle.

" That evening at supper the farmer related the
gossip of the countryside. There was nothing in this
gossip that gave Fuget the slightest concern. No
clue of any character had been observed, and there
were no conjectures that remotely approached the
truth. Fuget talked of the tragedy without the least
restraint. That anxiety which he had feared to feel
when the matter would come to be discussed did not
present itself. The old wives' tales of tortured conscience and the like, while he had not believed them,
had, nevertheless, given him a certain concern. They
were like tales of ghosts, which one could laugh at,
but could not disprove until one had slept in the
haunted house. He now knew that they were false.

" He went to bed with the greatest composure.
He was even cheerful. But he did not sleep. His

mind seemed unusually clear and active. It reverted to the details of the tragedy, not with any sense of anxiety, but with a sort of satisfaction, as of one who contemplates an undertaking successfully accomplished. He passed the incidents in review, until he reached the words which Pickens had uttered. And, keenly alert, like a wrestler in condition, his mind began to struggle with that enigma. He endeavored to compose himself to slumber. But he could not. He was intensely awake. His mind formulated all the expressions that might resemble in sounds those words which Pickens seemed to have said, but they were of no service. He turned about in his bed, endeavoring to dismiss the problem. But his mind seemed to go on with it against every effort of his will. He concluded that this sleeplessness was due to the coffee which he had taken at supper, and he determined to abandon the use of it. Now and then he fell asleep, but he seemed almost instantly to awaken. He was glad when the daylight began to appear.

" The following night he drank no coffee, and he fell asleep. But some time in the night, he awoke again to the besetting puzzle. He sat up in the bed, and determined to dismiss it. He had believed Pickens to say, ' You shall hear from me '; very well then, that was what he had said. And he lay down. But, instantly, upon that decision, there appeared another phase of the puzzle that fascinated his attention. Why had Pickens used that expression? Why should he say, 'You shall hear from me'? He was in the act of death when he spoke. He knew that. The realization of it was in his face. These words were inconsistent with a sense of death.

" He lay for a long time, intent upon this new aspect of the matter. Did the dying man intend this as a threat which he expected to carry out? But how could one hear from a dead man. And there arose a medley of all the tales that he had ever heard, relating to messages transmitted to the living from the spirit world. He dismissed these tales as inconsistent with the sane experiences of men. But the effect of them, which he had received as a child, he could not dismiss. Moreover, how could one be certain that, under some peculiar conditions, such messages were not transmitted? Learned men were, themselves, not absolutely sure.

" And intent upon this thing he remembered that those about to die were said sometimes to catch glimpses of truths ordinarily hidden. Men plucked from death had testified to a supernal activity of mind. And those who had watched had observed the dying to use words and gestures which indicated a sight and hearing beyond the capacities of life.

" He reflected. When Pickens had said, ' You shall hear from me,' it was certain that he meant what he said. Men did not utter idle threats when they were being ejected out of life. The law, ordinarily so careful for the truth, recognized this fact. He had heard that the declarations of those who believed themselves in dissolution, were to be received in courts of law without the sanctity of an oath. It was the common belief that the dying did not lie. Then, if he had heard correctly, this business was not ended. But had he heard correctly? And here the abominable thing turned back upon itself. And he began again on this interminable circle, as a fly follows the inside of a bowl, from which it can never escape.

" In the realities of daylight, he was able to assail this thing, and, in a measure, overcome it. The dead did not return, and their threats were harmless. But in the insecurity of darkness, it possessed him. In the vast, impenetrable, mysterious night, one could not be so certain. One seemed then on the borderland of life where things moved that did not venture out into the sun, or in the sun became invisible. And, under the cover of this darkness, the dead man might somehow be able to carry out his threat. This was the anxiety that beset him. And in spite of his disbelief and the assurance of his reason he began to expect this message. And he began to wonder from what quarter it would approach him, and at what hour, and in what form. This thing appalled him: that one, whom he did not fear from the activity of life, should thus disturb him from the impotency of death.

" Fuget was preparing quietly to leave the country when, about a week later, the farmer inquired if he wished to go with him, on that morning, to the county seat. It was the day on which the circuit court convened,—' court day,'— and by custom the country people assembled in the village. The farmer had been drawn on the grand jury.

" ' The judge will be chargin' us about the Pickens murder,' he said. ' You'd better go in an' hear him; the judge is a fine speaker.'

" It was the custom of these circuit judges to direct the attention of the grand jury to any conspicuous crime, and they usually availed themselves of this custom to harangue the people.

" That curiosity which moved Fuget to seek the earliest news of the murder now urged him to hear what the judge would say, and he went with the farmer to the village. The court-room was crowded. Fuget remained all the afternoon seated on one of the benches. After the assembling of the grand jury, the judge began his charge. He reviewed the incidents of the assassination. Fuget found himself fol-

4          39

lowing these details. Under the speaker's dramatic touch the thing took on a more sinister aspect.

" It could not avail the assassin that no human eye had seen him at his deadly work. By this act of violence he had involved himself with mysterious agencies that would not permit him to maintain his secret. It was in vain that human ingenuity strove against these influences. One might thrust his secret into the darkness, but he could not compel the darkness to retain it. These agencies would presently expel it into the light: as one could cast the body of the dead into the sea, but could not force the sea to receive it; it would be there when he returned, ghastly on the sand. And the hideous danger was that one never could tell at what hour, or in what place, or by what means, these mysterious agencies would reveal the thing which he had hidden.

" While the judge spoke, Fuget thought of the strange words which Pickens had uttered, and he felt a sense of insecurity. He moved uneasily in his seat, and the perspiration dampened his body. When the court adjourned, he hurried out. He passed through the swinging doors of the court-room, and descended the stairway into the corridor below. As he elbowed his way through the crowd, he thought someone called out his name, ' Henry Fuget,' and instinctively he stopped, and turned around toward the stairway.

But no one in the crowd coming down seemed to regard him, and he hurried away.

"He was now alarmed, and he determined to leave the country at once. He returned with the farmer. That night, alone in the loft of the farmhouse, he packed his possessions into a bundle and sat down on the bed to wait until the family below him should be asleep. He did not cease to consider this extraordinary incident. And it presently occurred to him that if someone had, in fact, recognized him, and he should now flee in the night, his guilt would be conclusively indicated. And side by side with that suggestion, there arose another. Had he, in fact, heard a human tongue call out his name? He labored to recall the sounds which he seemed to have heard, as he had labored to recall those which Pickens had uttered. The voice had seemed to him thin and high. Was it a human voice?

"He rose, unpacked the bundle, and went over to the window. The night seemed strange to him. The air was hard and bright, thin clouds were moving, a pale moonlight descended now and then on the world. There was silence. Every living thing seemed to have departed out of life. He thought of all the persons whom he had this day seen alert and alive, as now no better than dead men, lying unconscious, while the earth turned under them in this ghostly light. And it seemed to him a thing of no greater wonder, that the dead should appear or utter voices, than that these innumerable bodies prone and motionless, should again reënter into life.

"The following morning the farmer reassured him. No witness had come before the grand jury, and the prosecuting attorney had no evidence to offer.

"'I reckon nobody will ever know who killed ol' Pickens,' he said. Then he added, 'The grand jury's goin' to set pretty late, an' I may have to stay in town to-night. I wish you'd go in with me, an' bring the horse home.'

"Fuget could not refuse, and he returned to the village. Again he sat all day in the crowded court-room. Loss of sleep and fatigue overcame him, and occasionally, in the heat of the room, in spite of his anxiety, he would almost fall asleep. And at such times he would start up, fearful lest some word or gesture should escape him. And always, when the judge turned in his chair, or an attorney spoke, he was anxious. And when anyone passed the bench on which he sat, he appeared to be watching something in the opposite corner of the court-room, or, by accident, to screen his face with his hat.

"But as the day advanced, he became reassured, and when the court adjourned he went out quietly with the crowd. On the stairway and in the corridor below, he was anxious lest he should again hear his name called out. But when it did not occur and he approached the exit of the courthouse, his equanimity returned. On the steps, in the sun, he stopped and wiped his face with his sleeve. He seemed to have escaped out of peril, as through a door. He was glad now of the good judgment that had turned him back from flight, and of the incident that had brought him here to face the thing that he had feared. He came forth, like one who had braved a gesticulating spectre and found its threatening body to be harmless and impalpable.

" He descended the long stone steps leading down from the portico of the ancient courthouse, with that sense of buoyant freedom peculiar to those who are lifted out of danger. At the street, as he was about to walk away, someone touched him on the shoulder. He turned. The sheriff of the county was beside him.

" ' Will you just step into the Squire's office,' he said.

" Fuget was appalled.

" ' Me!' he stammered. ' What does the Squire want with me?'

" But obedient to the command, he followed the sheriff into the basement of the courthouse, and through a corridor into the office of the justice of the

43

peace. Here he found himself come into the presence of the prosecuting attorney, the justice, and a little man with sharp black eyes, and a thin, clean-shaven face. He remembered having seen this man enter the court-room, on the first day, while the judge was speaking. He had carried then a pair of saddle-pockets over his arm and had seemed to be a stranger, for he had stopped at the door and looked about, as if the court-room were unfamiliar to him. Fuget had observed this incident, as with painful attention he had observed every incident occurring in the court-room during these two days of stress. He had not seen this man again. But he now distinctly recalled him.

" The justice of the peace sat at a table. Before him lay a printed paper, certain blank lines of which had been written in with a pen. He put his hand on this paper; then he spoke.

" ' Is your name Henry Fuget? ' he said.

" Fuget looked around him without moving his head, swiftly, furtively, like an animal penned into a corner. The eyes of the others were on him. They seemed to know all the details of some mysterious transaction that had led up to this question, and of which he was ignorant. He felt that he had entered some obscure trap, the deadly peril of which these men had cunningly hidden that he might the more

44

easily step into it.   Nevertheless, he realized that he could not remain silent.

" ' No, sir,' he said, ' my name's Silas Williams.' Then he added, ' I work for Dan'l Sheets, out on the ten-mile road.   You can ask him; he'll tell you.'

" The justice continued, as though following a certain formula,—

" ' Did you know Samuel Pickens? '

" ' No, sir.'

" The justice seemed to consult a memorandum in pencil on the margin of the written paper.

" ' Were you not convicted of arson, on the testimony of Samuel Pickens, and sentenced to the penitentiary; and have you not repeatedly threatened to kill him when your term of penal servitude should have expired? '

" Fuget was now greatly alarmed.   How did these exact facts come to be known in this distant community?   Here Pickens alone knew them, and he was dead.   He saw that his security lay in denying that he was Henry Fuget.

" ' No, sir.'

" ' And your name's not Henry Fuget? '

" ' No, sir.'

" The justice turned to the stranger.

" ' This man denies that he is Henry Fuget,' he said.

"Then it was that the words were uttered that dispossessed the prisoner of composure, and cast him into panic.

"'If the communication which I have received from Samuel Pickens is true,' said the stranger, 'Henry Fuget has the scar of a gunshot wound on his right arm above the elbow.'

"The muscles of Fuget's face relaxed. His mouth fell into a baggy gaping. Then he faltered the query that possessed him.

"'Did *you* hear from Sam Pickens?'

"'Yes.'

"'After he was *dead?*'

"The stranger reflected. 'Yes,' he said. 'Pickens was dead then.'

"Fuget's mouth remained open. A sense of disaster, complete and utter, descended on him. The dead man had carried out his terrible threat. He began to stammer, unconscious that he was completing his ruin.

"'That's what he said — that's what he said when I shot him — but I thought I'd hear,— I didn't think somebody else would hear.'

"He caught hold of the table with his hand, and lowered himself into a chair. But he continued to regard this sinister stranger. And presently he spoke again.

" ' How did he tell you ? ' he said.

" A crowd had begun to gather at the door and at the windows,— a rumor had gone out.

" The stranger put his hand into his pocket, and drew from it a folded paper.

" ' I will tell you,' he said.   ' I am an attorney at law; my name is Gordon, and I reside in Georgia. On the third day of November, I received this paper, inclosed in an envelope, and addressed to me.   It was dated in October, but when I got it, Pickens was dead.'   He unfolded the paper and began to read in a thin, high-pitched voice: —

" ' In the name of God, Amen!   I, Samuel Pickens, do make, publish, and declare this to be my last will and testament.   I hereby appoint Horatio Gordon my executor, and I direct and charge him as follows, to-wit: Henry Fuget, a convict about to be discharged from the penitentiary of Georgia, has repeatedly threatened my life.   I have come here to avoid him, but I fear that he will follow and kill me.   Now, therefore, if I should be found dead, be it known that Henry Fuget is the assassin, and I direct my executor to expend the sum of one thousand dollars in order to bring him to the gallows.   Fuget is to be known by a scar on the fleshy part of his right arm where he was shot in an attempt to escape from the

47

penitentiary. The residue of my estate, both real and personal, I bequeath to my beloved daughter, Selina Pickens, now Mrs. Jonathan Clayton, of Jackson, Miss.

" ' Given under my hand and seal, Oct. 14, 1850.
" ' SAMUEL PICKENS. (Seal).'

" The stranger looked up from the paper.

" ' When I heard that Pickens was dead,' he said, ' I came here immediately. The circuit court was sitting when I arrived. It occurred to me that the assassin might be present in this crowd of people. To determine that, I placed myself at the head of the stairway, and as the crowd was going out, I called the name. This man turned, and I knew then that he was Henry Fuget.'

" Fuget sat with his hands on the arms of the chair, his big body thrown loosely forward, his eyes on the stranger. Slowly the thing came to him. The atmosphere of ghostly and supernatural agencies receded. He saw that he had been trapped by his own fancy. The hand that had choked this confession out of him had been born of his own flesh; the bones of it, the sinews of it, he had himself provided.

" And a madness seized him. He sprang up, and rushed out of the door. The crowd gave way before the bulk of this infuriated man. But the corridor

48

was narrow, and as he fought his way, persons began to seize him. He staggered out into the courtyard. The crowd of people wedged him in, clung to him, and bore him down. He rose. Under the mass of men who had thrown themselves upon him, the bones of his legs seemed about to snap; his muscles to burst; his vertebræ to crumble. For a dozen steps he advanced with this crushing burden, but every moment it increased, and finally he fell."

The priest concluded his story.

" Father Jerome," said the doctor, " your example case is a striking illustration of the inability of the human mind to foresee the relation of events. It does not prove the interposition of any divine influence. It proves only to what a limited extent we are able to understand the intricate relation of one event to another."

The priest looked at the doctor in astonishment.

" The hand of God is clearly to be seen in it," he said.

The judge now spoke.

" I think," he said, " that this case is clearly on fours with the idea of which I have just suggested. All the events seem to move here to a single purpose. The workings of the criminal's mind, the physical acts about him and the incident which destroyed him.

The moving of these events from diverse points to a single purpose would indicate that they were forced thereto by a common impulse, determined on justice. This idea seems so clearly to be indicated that I would like to follow Father Jerome's illustration with an equally curious case that came under my observation.

" You will picture a girl standing on the stone steps of a jail. The city was full of sunlight. Winter was departing. April was about to possess the world. In the park across the square the buds were beginning to swell, the sap to move, the grass to appear; and the gray squirrels, colonized in this urban forest, held noisy carnival to the welcome of summer. The crests of the great office buildings rising here and there out of the city were gilded. Along the cobble-paved street, opposite the stone courthouse and the great red-brick jail, the windows of the attorneys' offices shone like reflectors and their gold letters glittered in this brilliant sun.

" The girl was slender; the contours of her body were not yet filled out. She was under twenty. Her cloth dress was neat and clean, but it was old. It impressed one that if another spot should be removed, if another seam should be ironed, the worn meshes of the fabric would give way. She wore a little fur piece, but along the collar the fur was gone; and the lining beneath, once silk, had been replaced with some cheaper material. The girl's face was a beautiful oval, her eyes big and gray, her mouth delicate. She dabbed her face with a handkerchief that was already wet.

" There was a little iron grating over a wood panel on the jail door. This panel was opened and the jailer spoke to the girl through the grating. His voice was not unkind.

" ' If I were you,' he said, ' I'd go over and see the prosecuting attorney; you might find out something.' He did not wait for a reply, and when the girl turned the grating was closed.

" She put the wet handkerchief into her pocket and went down into the street, crossed the square paved with flagstones and entered the courthouse. The advice of the jailer seemed worth while. It occurred to her that if she could see the prosecuting attorney she might at least learn what he intended to do.

" The ground floor of the courthouse was occupied with the offices of court officials. It was badly lighted and persons stood about or hurried from one room to another, as in a railway station.

" The girl entered the prosecuting attorney's office. No one gave her the slightest attention. The place was filled with persons evidently representing every variety of distress. The chairs along the wall were occupied with this audience of misery. There was a door marked ' Private ' going from this room into another, but no one of the persons seated about the wall was permitted to enter it.

" A little old man, who seemed to have been designed by Nature and fitted for life into the position of an office boy, heard and dismissed these forlorn visitors. Now and then he went with some message through this door, but usually he got rid of the person without that trouble. Occasionally others — clerks, officials or those evidently not of an impoverished genus — entered this office and, without paying any attention to the old man, went directly through the door marked ' Private.'

" The girl, who had a chair near the door, occasionally heard how these persons were greeted by the official beyond. She sat for some time, oppressed by the atmosphere of this wretched chamber. Then she spoke to the little old man, but he indicated by a gesture that he was hearing visitors in the order of their arrival; and she went back to the chair patiently to await her turn.

" Persons continued to come in and to go out, and to these she paid no attention. But presently a man entered who brought the blood into her face. He was about forty and might have arrived here from a fashionable club. All those things that shopkeepers could add to him were of the best; but in a certain conspicuous manner they seemed but to falsīfy the man. He was pink and fat; there were tiny blue veins along his nose; and his eyes, hard and cruel, seemed to swim in a sort of yellow liquor. He glanced at the girl as he crossed the room, but he evidently did not recall her, for she heard his voice as he entered the private office of the prosecuting attorney. It had a peculiar gurgle which she distinctly remembered.

" ' Say, Henderson, you've got a snap; who's the peach by the door.'

" The girl arose, her face flaming, and hurried out.

" As she passed, the little old man spoke to her.

" ' If it's bail,' he said, ' go and see Dickerson; he's in that business.' Then he added: ' The other side of the bridge.' "

## CHAPTER IV: *The Fairy Godmother*

THE girl went out of the courthouse. She stood for a moment in the sun like one who has emerged from some subterranean chamber where the air was foul and damp. She seemed bewildered by this brilliant light. For some minutes she walked up and down aimlessly in the square, then she went over to the park and sat down on one of the benches. She sat so quietly that a gray squirrel drew near, climbed on to the bench and approached. She put out her hand and tried to caress the little friendly animal, but it fled chattering. Her mind, under the pressure of disaster, seemed now in a sort of stupor. She looked at the people passing in the park with the vague interest of those steeped in misery — at the carriages with their polished panels, the glittering harness of the horses and the men on the box, formal and elegant. She observed those who rode and those who walked in this thin, vitalizing sunlight. And she wondered how all these persons could maintain this air of unconcern and this appearance of comfort — and by the fortunate possession of what secret they had managed to escape the flying arrows that Destiny loosed from her steel bow. She was moved to stop some one of them — some gentleman who walked thus at leisure as though secure in this immunity, or some lady who drove in her carriage — and to inquire at what place and by what means they had obtained this secret.

"Presently a vehicle approached that drew the girl's attention. It was a common hack, such as one takes at any stand for a small fee. As it passed the bench on which the girl sat a woman leaned over into the hack window and with her fingers struck the ashes from a cigarette. This woman was not past the common measure of life, but she seemed to the girl to be very old. Her face, puffy and swollen, was of the color of some ancient manuscript; and her bearing and the gesture which she had made indicated the relaxed muscles of extreme age.

"The presence of this hack among the elegant carriages and of this hideous woman among the attractive protégées of Fortune brought the girl to her feet. She stood watching the hack move through the line of carriages until it turned out of the park and entered the street leading to the bridge.

"This direction awakened her memory. The old man had said: 'Dickerson — the other side of the bridge.' And, without any hope that this man would help her, she determined to visit him — and she set out in the direction that the hack had taken. The pressing needs of her own situation had now returned and possessed her.

" In ten minutes she had reached the stone bridge spanning the river that bisected the city. She crossed it, walking swiftly. At the farther side, close to the abutment, was a small one-story frame building with a very large glass window. Across the brow of this building a sign extended: ' James Dickerson, Real Estate Agent.' And the window was covered with white-enamel letters repeating the sign and enumerating the other varieties of business in which the proprietor was engaged: ' Rents collected. Loans made on real estate and personal property. Fire insurance. Notary public ' — as though, from the rubbish of all legitimate business, this man maintained here a sort of junkshop.

" The hack which had passed before her in the park stood now at the door; but she entered without observing it.

" The man who sat within before his table was dressed like a country lawyer — a shiny frock coat, a black string tie, a standing collar cut away in front and through which his prominent larynx protruded. His hair was parted in the middle and brushed up to curling edges. But the thing about the man that repelled and dispossessed one of any confidence in him

56

was a manner at once mincing and voluble. Beside him, in an attitude of extreme languor, was the woman of the hack — a cigarette burned in her fingers, her head had fallen to one side. Before them on the table was a roll of bills inclosed by a rubber band. They were evidently casting up accounts and had fallen on a disagreement, for the man was presenting profuse explanations with a variety of arguments; and the woman, in a voice of extreme fatigue, monotonously repeated the same words over and over again — the tone ending in a sort of dreary retrospection:

" ' You're a thief, Dickerson — a thief — a thief ! '

" The man looked up when the girl entered.

" He made a gesture with his hand, as though to silence the woman.

" ' Do you want to see me ? ' he said.

" The girl was undecided. ' Yes,' she replied doubtfully.

" He got a map of the city from a drawer of his desk and opened it out on the table.

" ' Where do you live ? '

" ' At 1735 North Market Street.'

" With a quick gesture Dickerson put his finger on the map.

" ' Impossible ! ' he said. ' The police wouldn't let you.'

" Suddenly the woman in the chair beside the table laughed.

" ' Dickerson, you're a fool — a fool — a fool! '

" The voice drooled off into that tone of gentle contemplation with which she had said ' A thief — a thief — a thief! ' as though these were the words of some soothing refrain that pleased her.

" The man scrutinized the girl with a glance that traveled to her feet; then he gave his body a quick, expressive jerk.

" ' What do you want? ' he said.

" The girl explained in a dozen words.

" Dickerson made a sharp gesture with his hand, the palm extended toward the girl, as though to dismiss her.

" ' No homicide cases,' he said. Then he swept the map from the table and returned it to the drawer. But as he arose an idea flashed on him. He sprang up and called to the girl, who was turning through the door.

" ' Have you an attorney? '

" ' No.'

" ' Ah, then I can be of some service to you.'

" He got a card from his table, wrote something on the margin in pencil and handed it to the girl.

" ' There,' he said, ' is the very best firm of attorneys in this city. Give them this card.'

" The girl thanked him and went out into the street. There she stopped to read what he had given her. The card bore the name of a firm of lawyers which she remembered to have seen in the newspapers often connected with criminal trials; and below were the words:

" ' Sent by James Dickerson, Esq.'

" The address was one of the office buildings on the cobble-paved street before the courthouse. This definite direction to a firm of good attorneys from one evidently known to them — and perhaps not without influence — encouraged the girl; and she set out to return over the bridge. She walked rapidly, the card in her hand.

" Meanwhile, the woman of the hack arose. With a visible effort she moved to the door and stood looking after the girl. Then she asked a question without turning her head:

" ' How much rake-off . . . those sharks give you, Dickerson?'

" The firm of attorneys to which James Dickerson had directed the girl was not difficult to discover. They occupied the entire second floor of a small office building opposite the courthouse. The girl went up the steps from the street; there she found herself in a hall that, for economy of space, had been fitted into a waiting room; the frosted-glass panel of every door opening into the hall bore the name of a member of the firm. One or two persons were before her — an actor, a gambler — and some women, over-dressed, painted and reeking with perfume, came out as she entered.

" She gave the office boy the card that she bore and sat down. Presently she was conducted through one of the frosted-glass doors. A big man standing before a table turned about as she entered. He had the card in his fingers and indicated a chair with a gesture. The man's face was heavy; his jaws were massive and square and his eyes the color of cold tallow. He was thick, without giving one the idea of fat.

" ' What's your name ? ' he said.

" ' Mary Randolph,' replied the girl.

" ' What other names ? '

" The girl did not understand.

" ' Mary Eldridge Randolph,' she said.

" ' Is that all ? '

" ' Yes, sir.'

" The man wrote the name on the card; then he went over to his table, thrust the card on a spike such as banks use to file checks, and sat down.

" ' What's the trouble ? ' he said.

" ' It's about my father,' the girl replied; ' I want to get a lawyer to defend him.'

" The man repeated the name.

" ' Randolph! ' he said. ' Ah! Richard Randolph? ' Then he touched a bell concealed somewhere about his table and a clerk entered, a thin youth with a jaundiced face. When he was in the room the man called to him:

" ' Bring me the clippings on the Fanshaw case.'

" The clerk returned in a moment with a big manila envelope. The attorney opened it and took out several folded newspaper sheets. He examined these clippings for some time in silence. Then he spoke to the girl:

" ' Are these facts correct? Your father, Richard Randolph, had at one time a considerable fortune by inheritance. He spent it and was forced to work at some trade. He had a certain mechanical turn and was employed for several years by the Empire Tool Company; then he became a freight engineer. One night, on a southern division, he ran through a block and a gate at a crossing, struck a passing freight, knocked a car clear out of the train and was ditched. The fireman was killed; your father escaped. He was discharged. The company held that he was drunk.'

" The blood mounted to the girl's face.

" ' But my father was not drunk,' she said. ' It was very cold and there was a heavy fog. My father was having trouble with the injectors and he did not see what was ahead.'

"The attorney looked up from his paper.

"'Not drunk, eh? — when he ran through a block, a gate and into a passing train! I guess he was drunk all right.'

"The girl's eyes kindled.

"'My father was not drunk,' she said. 'The injectors were giving him a lot of trouble and he was working with them. The very week before a defective injector had caused the boiler of one of the big passenger engines to go dry. It blew up and killed the engine crew. My father helped clear the wreck and after that he was always watching the injectors. He was not drunk.'

"The attorney made a gesture as though to dismiss a controversy.

"'Anyway,' he said, 'your father was drunk a-plenty after that.'

"'Yes, he was,' she said. 'The terrible accident affected my father. He felt that his inattention had caused the poor fireman's death. He began to drink then.'

"The attorney went on: 'Your father continued to drink and you became very poor; the house in which you live was mortgaged to its full value. Finally he obtained this position of chauffeur with

Miss Fanshaw. As the old woman had a steam car, she got the notion that only a railroad engineer could drive it — and, as she did not know your father's habits, she employed him. He received fifty dollars a month. That was on the first day of September last. He continued in this position until the sixteenth day of November. Right?'

" ' Yes, sir.'

" The attorney again referred to his newspaper sheet:

" ' Miss Henrietta Fanshaw was seventy-three years old. She lived alone, except for her nephew who occasionally visited her. She resided in a big old-fashioned house on Oakland Avenue. This house was connected by a covered way with a smaller one in the rear, which at one time had been occupied by negro servants. When the old lady purchased this motor car she converted the negro quarters into a garage and it continued to be connected with the main residence by this covered way. In this private garage the steam car which your father drove was always kept, and in going to the house to receive the old lady's directions he always used this covered way. Is that correct?'

" ' Yes, sir.'

" ' It is stated here that Miss Fanshaw never kept any money or other valuables in the house in which she resided; but, as she was a woman who valued personal adornment, she had always near her jewels of considerable value. What do you know about that?'

"'My father told me,' replied the girl, 'that Miss Fanshaw was a very foolish old woman who painted her face and loaded her fingers with rings.'

"The attorney bobbed his head.

"'So the rings caught his eye — eh?'

"'He mentioned them, sir.'

"'Did he ever say anything about their value?'

"'No, sir.'

"'Well, I guess he knew, all right.'

"He returned to his newspaper clippings:

"'On the morning of November sixteenth Miss Fanshaw was found dead in her bed. She had been this night alone in the house. Her servant, a middle-aged negro woman, had gone on the afternoon before to her daughter's, in a neighboring village. Miss Fanshaw had been killed by a blow from some blunt instrument. Nothing in the house had been disturbed, except that rings and personal ornaments to the value of about five thousand dollars were missing. These jewels Miss Fanshaw was accustomed to drop into a green vase that stood on the mantel when she retired for the night.' The attorney paused. 'Have the newspapers got these facts straight?'

"'Yes, sir,' said the girl; 'I think that is right.'

64

" ' The fact,' continued the attorney, ' that nothing in Miss Fanshaw's room had been disturbed — no drawers opened, no article moved from its place — indicated that the criminal agent was acquainted with Miss Fanshaw's habits and knew exactly the place in which she was accustomed to conceal these rings and jewels. This single incident led the police strongly to suspect that the crime had been committed by some inmate of the house or someone on intimate terms with the deceased. This definition could include only three persons. I will name them in their order.'

" He paused, held up three fingers of his right hand and continued:

" ' Chatfield Fanshaw, the nephew; Jane Johnson, the negro servant, and Richard Randolph. The police played no favorites; they set about to discover where these three persons were on the night of the fifteenth of November — and this is what they found out: On that night Chatfield Fanshaw gave a dinner at the Saturn Club, which continued until four o'clock in the morning; at that hour the guests left the club, except those who lived there permanently. Fanshaw did not go out with any of these persons. He went from the table directly upstairs to the club red room. There, with four of his companions, he remained until daylight; then he went down into the basement of the club, took a Turkish bath and at seven o'clock came up into the breakfast room.'

" The lawyer now doubled one of the three fingers into the palm of his hand.

" ' That is the history of the night of November fifteenth, so far as Chatfield Fanshaw is concerned; and it is so definite, so certain and so complete that it eliminates Fanshaw.' "

## CHAPTER V: *The Ghost*

HE remained with his elbow on the table, his forearm raised, the two fingers extended. His left hand held the sheets of newspaper clippings.

" 'Now for the negro — Jane Johnson. She left the house at four o'clock on the afternoon of November fifteenth and did not return until the evening of November sixteenth — after she had heard of the death of her mistress. The police know where she was and what she did during every hour of that time. Her daughter's husband, a miner, had been killed by a fall of slate and on this night she sat up with the body — attending the funeral on the sixteenth. . . . Now the fact that this woman was an old and trusted servant and that the event taking her from the house was of such a nature as to preclude any premeditated design to be absent indicates that Jane Johnson had nothing to do with this homicide.'

" He doubled the second finger into his palm. A moment the third finger remained; then he clenched his hand and struck it heavily on the table.

" 'This brings us to Richard Randolph,' he said.

' And from eleven-thirty until daylight no one knows where he was.'

" The girl began to cry quietly.

" ' Why, yes, sir,' she said; ' we know where he was. He was in the engine house down at the power plant.'

" ' Who saw him there ? '

" ' No one saw him; but I know he was there, sir.'

" ' How do you know it ? '

" ' My father told me he was there ! '

" The attorney made an exclamation of disgust.

" ' He told you — eh ? '

" ' Yes, sir; and it wasn't his fault. Mr. Fanshaw had no right to take him into the club that evening and give him whisky to drink. He had promised me not to drink again and he had kept this promise. . . . Then he was ashamed to come home.'

" ' On the preliminary examination,' continued the attorney, ' Fanshaw said that he regarded your father not as an ordinary chauffeur but as a gentleman in reduced circumstances, and that his invitation into the club was a mere act of courtesy — that he did not know your father's habits.'

" ' I don't think that's quite true, sir,' replied the girl, ' for he had been making inquiries about my father only a few days before.'

68

"The attorney returned to his newspaper clippings:

"'That's unimportant anyway. The important thing is that, after going from one saloon to another, your father left the Palace Poolroom about midnight, saying that he was going home — and he did not go home. . . . Do not interrupt me. . . . That is not all  The police now carefully examined the garage and this covered way leading to the house. They found bloodstains on the wall of this covered way, near the door of the house, as though one groping his way out in the night had touched the wall with his hands.  They removed the entire board containing these stains.'

"He read from a newspaper:

"'"An effort was made to identify the lines appearing in these stains according to the rules of the Bertillon system, but the result was not satisfactory. These were not direct prints, as when one grasps an object, but they were smears, rather, as when one wipes his hands on a smooth surface."

"'And that is not all.  In searching for the implement with which the deed was done the police examined the automobile toolbox; there appeared to be some stains on a heavy wrench, although it had apparently been wiped with a cloth.'

"Again he read from the newspaper:

69

" ' " It is interesting to observe how modern science has come to the aid of justice. It used to be taught in the schools that, although a bloodstain could be detected, no one could be quite certain whether it was human blood or that of some animal, for the reason that unless it was quite fresh the difference in dimensions of the red blood corpuscles was too slight to be definitely ascertained. But modern biological chemistry has developed methods so exact and elaborate that measures to the extent of one twenty-thousandth gram are easily established. With these so-called ' anti sera ' the chemists of this city have been able to say that the automobile wrench submitted to them bears red corpuscles of human origin." '

" The attorney thrust the papers over into a corner of the desk and leaned back in his chair. His eyebrows contracted into a bushy ridge across his forehead, the muscles of his heavy jaw protruded.

" ' There's your case,' he said, ' and the man who takes it has got his work cut out for him.'

" The recital of this evidence revived and freshened the girl's distress. She sat dabbing her eyes with the damp handkerchief. The attorney gave her no attention. He began to walk about the room, his thumbs thrust into the pockets of his waistcoat. Presently an idea struck him and he turned abruptly on his heel.

" ' Is this case set down for trial?'

" ' Yes, sir,' replied the girl; ' on next Thursday.'

" The man made an exclamation of astonishment.

" ' Why didn't you get an attorney sooner?'

" ' An old friend in Virginia, a Mr. Lawrence,' replied the girl, ' promised to defend my father; but to-day we got a letter saying that he could not come.'

" ' Had you paid him a retainer?'

" ' No, sir.'

" ' Humph!' The man began again to walk through the room. Finally he stopped directly before the girl.

" ' There's only one chance,' he said, ' and that's to prove an alibi. We must find some witnesses who were with your father from eleven-thirty until daylight on the sixteenth day of November.'

" ' But there are no such persons.'

" ' They can be found for the price,' continued the attorney. ' Now, listen! This thing's going to cost money. You had better bring all the stuff down here and turn it over to me. The newspapers have probably over-valued it, but the junk ought to be worth a couple of thousand dollars — and it will take every cent of that.'

" The girl arose. ' I don't understand you,' she said.

" The lawyer looked her steadily in the face, his tallow-colored eyes unmoving.

" ' Oh, yes,' he said; ' you understand me perfectly.'

" ' You mean — you mean,' she faltered, ' that I have these jewels? '

" ' Yes,' he said; ' that's it exactly. And, what's more, you've got to come down with them.'

" ' But how can I give them to you when I haven't got them? '

" ' Nonsense! Of course you've got them. Now, look here; I suppose you tried that game on your Virginia lawyer, but you can't work it on me. Get that right out of your head! '

" The girl was thoroughly frightened. She began to step backward toward the door. The man followed her, his face menacing and ugly.

" ' But my father is innocent,' she said. ' My father didn't kill Miss Fanshaw.'

" The man's mouth snapped like a dog's.

" ' Bosh! ' he said. ' Of course he killed her.'

" The girl was in terror. She feared that this person would take hold of her, tear her clothes, search her for the jewels. She put her hand behind her, touched the doorknob, seized it and flung the door open.

" She sprang through and fled down the steps.

The man followed her into the hall. She caught a glimpse across her shoulder of his repulsive face thrust over the banister at the top of the stairs. And she heard him answer to some query, with an oath:

" ' Sure! Didn't Dickerson send her? '

" When the girl was in the street she did not cease to hurry. She crossed the cobblestones and the paved square to the bench in the park that had been her first asylum. There she flung herself down, buried her face in the hollow of her arm and gave herself up to the despair that possessed her. Her body did not move; her arm rested on the back of the bench and her face was covered by the bend of the elbow. She seemed only to be resting in the sun. And the world passed, giving her no attention.

" Finally the bitterness of this cruel adventure wore itself out. The clock on the courthouse began to strike an hour of the afternoon, and she sat up, put back her hair and turned her face resolutely toward the street from which she had fled. Surely somewhere on that street, among so many lawyers, there must be one to whom she could go who would believe what she said! Surely the leading men in this profession, as in any other, would be honorable gentlemen! She would go to one of these. She vaguely remembered to have seen certain names in the newspapers and she began to search the street, hoping to discover one of these names on some of the lettered windows.

"In the line of office buildings of every variety there arose one in white stone, of perfect architecture; and on a window of it the girl saw a name that she remembered. It was a great name, associated with great affairs. She arose and, ignorant of the difficulties that would attend obtaining an audience with so important a personage, she determined to go and see him.

"As she approached she noticed the hack that had passed her in the park a few paces below the building. The driver had gone away and a thread of smoke arose from a corner of the window. And, without being able to formulate the idea, this dilapidated hack, like some subterranean thing crept here against the white marble of this clean place, which it was not permitted to enter, encouraged the girl. She went into the building, took an elevator and ascended to the floor occupied by the great attorney.

"She went along a narrow hall and entered the waiting room. A woman with light straw-colored hair was standing at a window, looking down into the street. A young man was beside her; by his dress and manner he might have been transported at that

74

moment from the athletic field of some university. The woman with the straw-colored hair came forward when Mary Randolph entered.

" ' What is it? ' she said.

" Her attitude was that of one who bars the way.

" The girl began to explain. The woman interrupted her after the first sentence.

" ' He doesn't take criminal cases,' she said.

" ' Then I can't see him? '

" ' No.'

" The word was like a door closed firmly before one's face. The girl remained motionless, stunned by this swift, this ruthless, decapitation of her hopes. And there, motionless in the sunlight, her eyes wide, her lips parted, the beauty of the girl strikingly appeared.

" The young man at the window looked at her, his head thrust forward, his thick under lip falling away from his teeth. Then he turned abruptly and went through several rooms of busy clerks to one near the elevator. The door of this room bore the name of the great lawyer, followed by the abbreviation of the word ' Junior.' He threw back the door and sat down by a mahogany desk, on which there was an open novel. A moment later, when Miss Randolph came along this hall, he beckoned to her with his finger. When she entered he spoke:

" ' How about a little dinner at Keator's to-night and a jog in the bubble? '

" The girl stood for a moment as though she did not understand — as though these words reached her as mere sounds from some remote distance; then, without a sign that she had heard, she went out of the room and with slow steps into the elevator.

" In the street below she began to wander about like one bewildered. The sun lay in the street; the air was soft and warm. Persons passed her, but she no longer paid any attention. She moved aimlessly like one in a sort of somnambulism. Energy and hope had gone out of her. She seemed borne along by the current of some evil fortune, to which she now abandoned herself as to a thing inevitable.

" Presently she passed near the hack standing in the street by the curb and a voice spoke to her. She turned. The woman whom she had seen was looking at her from the hack window — her elbow on the sill; her chin resting in the hollow of her hand, as though she had been there always, looking out thus from some eternal window. The woman dropped her hand and pointed to an office in the basement of a building that had once been a residence.

" ' Go in — see Burton,' she said. Then she made a gesture as though to indicate the whole street.

" ' He's drunk — most — time; but he's — only

76

honest one.' In her extreme physical languor the woman omitted the small words in her speech as though from an economy of effort.

"The girl went down the steps into this office. A man whose hair seemed prematurely white sat reading a newspaper; a crooked cane was hanging on his arm; his hat lay on the floor beside the chair. There was an old couch in a corner covered with dust; a few ancient books in a case that appeared never to have been opened, and a broken rolltop desk on which one seemed to have emptied a waste-paper basket full of rubbish. The man was one of those attorneys to be found at every bar and called in the vernacular a ' ghost.'

"The woman followed the girl. She sat down on the dilapidated couch.

" ' I want you — take — case, Burton,' she said. Then to the girl: ' Tell him.' And she leaned back to inhale the cigarette that seemed eternally in her fingers.

"The weak face of the man was not unkind and the girl related the story, omitting no detail. He was sober and he listened.

"The woman seemed asleep, although her eyes were not closed; but she was not asleep. She had followed every word, as her subsequent action indicated; for presently, with a visible effort, she arose.

A window level with the street looked out on the square before the courthouse. A big white motor car stood in the street before this square. A man coming through the courthouse door had paused to speak with some persons who knew him.

" The woman indicated this man with a gesture toward the window.

" ' That Fanshaw ? ' she said.

" The girl looked after the pointed finger, to recognize the pink person who had spoken so flippantly of her to the prosecuting attorney.

" ' Yes,' she said; ' that is he.'

" The woman went out of the office, up the steps and across into the square. She walked as though every muscle were relaxed and with her knees bent. In the square before the courthouse, as the man approached the car, the woman seemed to stumble. She lurched against the man and caught hold of him. A moment her hand clung to him; then he flung her off and she fell. He went on; and presently she arose, getting up slowly on her hands and knees like a child. Some persons helped her to the hack; they called the driver from a near-by saloon and the hack departed. It took the way around the square into the park; then it crept into the line of carriages and disappeared.

" When the woman fell the girl would have gone

78

to her assistance, but the ' ghost ' stepped before her into the door.

" ' You must not be seen with that woman,' he said.

" ' Why not ? '

" ' If you do not know,' he replied, ' so much the better.'

" ' But she is hurt; let me pass, please ! '

" ' No,' and he continued to bar the door.   Then he added:   ' She's not hurt; they all fall like that. Their muscles are loose — you can push one of them over with your hand.'

" The girl was incensed; the blood was in her face; the nails of her fingers bit into her palm.

" ' The beast ! ' she said.   ' The beast — to fling her down ! '

" The ' ghost ' was undisturbed.   ' Well,' he said, ' no man cares to have a woman like that catch hold of him in a public street.'

" The girl turned on him.

" ' What do you mean ? ' she said.   ' What is wrong with her ? '

" The ' ghost ' made a sweeping gesture.

" ' Oh ! ' he said.   ' Everything !   Everything ! '

.     .     .     .     .     .     .     .     .

" The woman of the hack had secured a seat in the court-room on the first row of benches behind the rail. She had not obtained this desirable place without some difficulty. The court-room had been crowded from the first day. When she came the bailiff had stopped her, and she had passed him only by saying that she was a relative of the prisoner. This was false, but it obtained for her the seat that she wished.

" She had gone in and out upon this pretext, but in spite of it she came near to being excluded on the afternoon of the last day of the trial. There was a pressing crowd and she had loitered in the hall until the prosecuting attorney and Mr. Fanshaw came to enter the court-room; then she had crowded into the door and endeavored to thrust Fanshaw to one side in order to make way for herself. She had put her open hands against his breast and pushed like a petulant child vexed with the crowding. Fanshaw was angry and the bailiffs would have forcibly removed her; but she claimed the right to enter, and the prosecuting attorney, hearing what she said and unwilling that a relative of the prisoner should be excluded, permitted her to go in.

" He did not stop to reflect on this obvious untruth: All sorts and conditions of men were of the family of criminals; and it was a courtesy of Justice to award them a place beside their kinsmen when she judged him for his sins.

" The woman got her seat again on this afternoon and she sat in it in a sort of heap, resting her arms against the rail, and from time to time, from long and constant habit, bringing her fingers to her lips — although the inevitable cigarette from necessity was absent.

" In some respects this was a pathetic trial. As it advanced, one looking on became unhappy. The prisoner, pale from his long confinement, and the miserable girl, who kept so brave a face beside him, made one hope — even against justice — that the case might take some favorable turn. But when it continued, hour by hour, more clearly and more inevitably to involve the prisoner, one gave up that hope.

" And, though one did not see how a substantial defense could be maintained before the evidence, one came to resent the unequal matching of the prosecuting officer against the attorney for the prisoner. This liquor-shaken, prematurely white old man was so visibly in a situation beyond him! He was like some decayed actor who, having long haunted the theater as a place of memories, is called on some night of license to play a leading part. He had brushed up for the part — this ' ghost.' He was cleanly shaven, his clothes were pressed and he was sober; but these conspicuous attentions could not rehabilitate him with the solidities of life.

" Everything that he did, every method that he

used, every trick that he relied on, every argument that he advanced, was of the nature and after the manner of a ghost. It was in vain, in this pressing need, that he endeavored to take on the aspect and assume the offices of life. There was no weight in his hand and no authority in his voice. When the prosecuting officer challenged the statement of a witness, or urged a conclusion upon the facts, the aspect and the manner of the man compelled the attention of the court. But when the attorney for the defendant essayed these attitudes of conflict, in spite of every effort he was only a gesticulating wraith.

"The proof of this was everywhere. It was a case of circumstantial evidence, with those joinings of the piece that defending attorneys are accustomed to assail. But under this man's hand the wedge — even in a crevice — rebounded.

"The board containing the finger-prints, which the police had removed, had been set up on a sort of easel before the jury. A lay figure, clothed with the garments of the deceased, had been brought into the court-room and the implement with which the deed was accomplished had been introduced in evidence. The witnesses had spoken and upon each of these the attorney for the prisoner had tried the stock tricks of cross-examination. But, where other men were accustomed to obtain a doubtful expression or a qualifying phrase, he got only a greater assurance.

"'Doctor, the microscope is not a perfect device?'

"'No, sir.'

"'And even the most skillful biological chemist is not infallible?'

"'No.'

"'Then, sir,' raising the wrench with a dramatic gesture, 'how can you swear, with that degree of certainty which would justify this jury in depriving a fellowman of his life, that these are bloodstains?'

"And the only effect was that the expert again explained the scientific method by which he had arrived at his conclusion so exactly that no man could doubt it.

"With the chief of police, upon the platitude that having found a crime the police will always find a criminal to fit, he came off no better.

"'You have taken a good deal of interest in this case?'

"'Yes.'

"'And you have been pretty active in it?'

"'Yes.'

"'Now, sir, why are you so anxious to fix this crime on the prisoner?'

"And the chief had replied: 'Because I believe him to be guilty.'

"The things out of which another might have

made capital for the defense only turned to nothing in his hand. The fact that no one of the articles taken by the assassin had been found on the prisoner or about his premises; the fact that Fanshaw was the sole heir of the deceased and thus the one to gain by her death; that his life had been dissolute, and that he needed the estate he would inherit; and also the further possibility, however remote, that the evidence had been manufactured by the real criminal — items that another would have avoided until the argument — this man flung headlong at the witnesses and got them explained away.

" It was the custom of criminals, every police officer said, to conceal the booty until public interest in the crime had waned. And the prosecuting officer had met the second suggestion so fairly that no force remained in it. He himself would have considered this thing but for the physical impossibility that attended it — no man could be in two places at one time.

" With pains and with care the prosecuting attorney had shown by testimony that was incontrovertible exactly where Fanshaw was every hour of that memorable night. And with every witness and at every point he had called upon the prisoner's counsel to indicate any doubt that could be inquired into. The deed had been perpetrated in the night, but there was no hour of the night, no moment of the night, that Fanshaw was not in the company and before the eyes of disinterested witnesses who knew him.

"Upon the theory of fabricated evidence he was quite as fair. That, with the alibi, was a stock defense in desperate cases; but if the prisoner's counsel could indicate one point, however insignificant, that suggested a design in any item of this evidence he would go with him to any length upon that theory. It was not a victim that he sought — it was the truth that he was after. And this outspoken method, albeit a thing of sheer policy in the prosecutor, disarmed and stripped and devitalized these doubts before the hour at which they could have served the prisoner.

"The counsel for the defense caused the witnesses to repeat their evidence; and, as he lacked the skill to draw them into contradictions, the effect was that their testimony only the more impressed itself upon the jury. In his examination of Fanshaw this was especially marked; and by his insistence he brought Fanshaw clean out of suspicion.

"He had been with his aunt on the afternoon and until the evening of November fifteenth. She was happy and quite well. It was her custom to retire at ten, and sometime after that the deed had been done.

" ' And where were you, sir? '

" And Fanshaw had shown again and again where he was from the hour that he left his aunt, on the evening of November fifteenth, until the following morning — until there remained no doubt that it was physically impossible for Fanshaw to have committed the crime on this night.

" Then, when the state rested, the prisoner's counsel had made the culminating blunder. He refused to permit the prisoner to testify in his own behalf. This move in criminal defenses is heroic. Only in desperate need do the most skillful masters hazard this perilous finesse. It is the law that one charged with a crime may keep silent if he likes; and it is the law that no inference of his guilt shall be drawn therefrom — and a judge will so instruct a jury. But no direction of a presiding judge can remove from a juror the ultimate conviction that, if one remains silent, there is something that he wishes to conceal. It is a weapon that one will take down from the arsenal of defenses only when he has an eye forward to a conflict with a bench of judges who regard the technicalities of the law.

" Before the jury and before the court-room it helped the prisoner that he contended against this decision of his counsel. The court waited while the argument went on in whispers. There could be no doubt about the good faith of this resistance. One could see how deeply in earnest the prisoner was — but the attorney possessed the insistence of the weak; and in the end he had his way.

" The prisoner's face went gray then, and the girl beside him wept. The hope of sympathetic persons in the court-room that this man, when he took the stand, might be able to exculpate himself, departed.

" In hazarding this desperate move the ' ghost ' went upon the theory that, if Randolph remained silent, no one could be absolutely certain where he was on the fatal night and in his argument he could amplify this doubt. It is an academic theory, not without value in certain cases; but here, where Randolph stood convicted upon the circumstantial evidence — where his guilt was indicated and where explanations were required — the thing was ruin.

" In this feeble manner the case had been conducted and now the counsel for the prisoner was about his argument. What he said were platitudes that lie in the very nooks and corners of a criminal court-room — vaporings upon the presumption of innocence and reasonable doubt. These are substantial doctrines of the law and where proper evidence is absent they prevail; but, where all the circumstances of time, place, motive, means, opportunity and conduct concur in pointing out the accused as the perpetrator of the crime, it is idle to concern oneself with these presumptions.

" Moreover, the conduct and manner of the man emasculated these defenses; his thin voice and his devitalized gesticulation weakened what he said. He stepped about, drank from his glass of water and declaimed; but when in his case there was a real fact or a genuine emotion that might have moved the jury, this advocate, by his manner, made it hollow. He was but the shadow of a man and he could not present the reality or the solidity of life.

" It was near the end of his address, when there was no longer any doubt about the issue of the trial, that the court-room was aroused by an exclamation impossible to describe. It was the 'Ah!' of a cab-driver in Paris, who, after laboring to understand the direction of some foreign tourist, finally has a flash of comprehension. The unrestraint of it aroused the court like the sting of a lash. The attorney stopped in his argument and the judge flung himself forward on the bench. Below him, now upon her feet, holding to the rail with her hands, stood the woman of the hack."

CHAPTER VI: *The Trivial Incident*

THE judge was indignant.

"'How dare you,' he said, 'interrupt this trial?'

"The woman was not looking at him and she did not now turn her head. Her eyes were fixed on the board containing the finger-prints that had been introduced in evidence. The woman did not directly reply. She raised her hand and pointed to the board.

"'Somebody made those finger-prints — purpose!'

"The whole court-room, dulled and wearied by the insipid argument of the attorney for the prisoner, now flashed into life. The judge looked from the woman to the board and back again to the woman. It was evident that something moving and vital lay behind this extraordinary act.

"'What do you mean?' he said. His voice was severe, but the threatening note had gone out of it.

"The woman rose. She came around the rail into the space before the jury.

"'I'll show you,' she said.

"She took up an inkstand from the table and went over to the board; there she wet her hand with the ink and touched the board a number of times, as one might do if he were groping with his hand.

"'See, if — accidental,' she said.

"Then, continuing to wet her fingers with the ink, she touched the board an equal number of times below the other.

"'See, if — purpose,' she said.

"The great truth that this woman had discovered now sprang into view before the court-room. Everyone saw instantly what she meant. The ink marks accidentally made by touching the board with a wet hand were at first heavy, but they gradually became fainter. Those made by design — by continuing to wet the hand — were all equally heavy; and, like these latter marks, all equally heavy were the original finger-prints on the board.

"Every man saw it now. If the assassin by accident had touched this board with his wet hand, as he groped his way in the night, the first marks would have been heavy and those that followed fainter, for the hand would have been gradually cleaned by contact. And only by the design of one who had gone there for that purpose, intent on getting all the prints on that board that he could, was it possible for the last finger-print there to be as heavy and as well marked as the first.

"Fanshaw spoke hurriedly to the prosecuting attorney and that official arose. He began to object. He said that the evidence was in, that the case was closed, that such an interruption of a trial was unheard of and irregular. It was clear now that his attitude of fair dealing had been a pretense.

"The judge silenced him.

"'We are here to convict the guilty,' he said, 'and to acquit the innocent. Anything that will help us to perform this duty correctly I will permit and I will hear!'—and he addressed the woman: 'Go on!'

"But the woman of the hack did not reply. While the judge and the prosecutor were in this controversy she had been looking at the lay figure clothed in the night garments of the deceased.

"'Are these things on — figure correctly?'

"The judge beckoned to the chief of police and he came forward.

"'Yes,' the chief said; 'exactly.'

"'Sure?'

"'Yes.' And he explained how carefully he had observed and marked the position of each garment in order that the lay figure might be clothed precisely as the deceased was when the police found her.

"The woman turned slowly. She spoke like one pronouncing a conclusion.

"'That's what I thought,' she said.

" The judge's voice was no longer severe.

" ' What, exactly, do you mean? '

" The woman replied as though she spoke a thing obvious to everybody:

" ' Why, that — Fanshaw — did it himself! '

" Every person in the court-room seemed to move in his seat.

" Fanshaw seized the arm of the prosecuting attorney; his pink face was moist with a spray of perspiration. The attorney arose; he got out his objection before the judge could stop him.

" ' Impossible! ' he said. ' We know — accurately, definitely, conclusively — where Mr. Fanshaw was every hour of that night.'

" The woman remained looking up at the judge. The only evidence that she was in the least affected by this situation of stress was that she no longer omitted the little words in the sentences that she uttered.

" ' It was not done in the night,' she said. ' It was done in the day! '

" The judge put the query that was on every tongue:

" ' How do you know that? '

" The woman indicated the lay figure.

" ' That nightcap's on wrong part before! ' she said.

" The girl, who had been straining forward in her chair, her tear-stained eyes wide, her arm close around her father, sprang up and stooped over the lay figure. The jury, forgetting the etiquette of the court-room in this compelling interest, left their seats and crowded round her.  A moment the girl remained scrutinizing the headdress — then she began to cry and laugh in hysteria.

" ' Oh, it is true ! ' she cried.  ' It's on wrong ! '

" Then the severe decorum of the court-room went to pieces.  Everyone saw how conclusive this thing was.  No woman who had gone quietly to bed would put her night garments on wrong part before.  The deed had been done in the day and the garments put on to deceive the police into the belief that it had been done in the night.  Fanshaw's careful alibi covered the night only — not the day; in fact, by his own testimony he stood convicted of being the last person alone with this woman in the day.

" He stood now, his back against the rail, his hands clenched, his sweat-sprinkled face as white as plaster.

" The woman of the hack advanced toward him. She pointed her finger at him.  Her eyes kindled in her dull, swollen face.

" 'Hand over the rings ! ' she said.

" The man's voice became a whisper.

" ' I haven't got them.'

93

" ' You are a liar ! ' said the woman. ' They are sewed up in your waistcoat. I felt them ! '

" Then terror possessed him and he turned to fight his way to the door; but the police seized him and dragged him struggling before the bench. They ripped open his waistcoat and the stolen rings tumbled out on to the floor.

.        .        .        .        .        .        .        .

" In the tumult that followed — in the congratulations to the prisoner — in the revulsion of feeling that now lifted into a public idol the girl who yesterday had been disregarded — in the sobbing, the hysteria, the confusion — the woman who had accomplished this result disappeared from the court-room. Someone sitting in the window saw a hack enter the park and melt away into the line of carriages — a thin wisp of smoke ascending from the window."

" Ah ! " said the priest, " you have indeed shown how mysterious and inscrutable are the ways of Providence. An abandoned and profligate old woman is made the instrument of Divine justice. The case is a rebuke to the egotism of man's intelligence. It shows how feeble human reason is when compared with the Divine wisdom of Providence."

" It certainly proves how feeble human reason is," said Dr. Lennard.

"But the march of events in it," said the judge, "all towards a single, central idea. Does it not prove that the criminal is menaced by an intention in nature to destroy him?"

The doctor laughed. "But, my dear Flint," he said, "nature, as you call it, destroys those who are not criminals with an equal determination, as you would say it, or as I would say it, with an equal indifference. Now, how would you and Father Jerome interpret the idea of justice included in this case? I shall endeavor to follow your excellent method of presenting a detached picture to the eye."

The doctor paused, remained a moment silent, then he began.

"On a morning of early April, Adolphus Wyatt was crossing the meadow lying between his residence and the one long street of the village. The air, warmed a little by the sun, was still crisp. The buds were showing. The fields were green. The robins hopped about. Everywhere were evidences of that joy in life which is the charm of springtime. A little path wound through the meadow to the street, over a brook crossed by a hewn log, and, now and then, under a sugar maple.

"Wyatt walked with a comfortable stride, swinging his cane. Occasionally he stopped, planted his

95

legs wide apart in the path, thrust the cane behind his back, held it there with both hands, drew his under lip into his mouth over his teeth and looked out across the meadow to the village. On this morning Wyatt was profoundly satisfied with life. The newspaper which he carried in his right hand with the cane had mentioned him as a leading citizen of the village of Clarksville. It seemed to Wyatt that this term placed a correct estimate on his life, that it constituted a sort of title which he had laboriously earned. He had been about the labor of earning this distinction for all that he could remember of sixty-five years. He had made in that time whatever sacrifices this ambition required. He had remained unmarried. He had lived a careful, sedate, exact life. He had even foregone those harmless recreations in which his neighbors indulged, that he might all the more be regarded as substantial.

" Industry, frugality, patience had not failed of their result. Wyatt had accumulated a little more property than any other man in the village. He owned the local bank. He passed the hat in the village church, and occupied a certain fixed bench-end, well forward. The position which he held in the village was reflected in Wyatt's manner. His movements were deliberate. He seemed to weigh carefully what he said, and when he spoke he always contracted the muscles of his mouth, as if thereby to add a certain firmness. The newspaper which had named him as 'a leading citizen' was the local one of the neighboring county, and, for that reason, he felt that this estimate of him was without bias, and could be taken to define the opinion of the community.

" Beyond the brook, under the shade of a sugar maple, a little negro boy was squatting in the grass beside the path. He was, perhaps, three years old, round, plump and sturdy. There was about him all the softness, the filled-out lines of a well-nourished little animal. The grass near the child was crowded with wild, blue violets, and he was engrossed with a game familiar to country children. He would take up a violet in either hand, hook the heads together, and draw the stems slowly apart, until one of the flowers decapitated the other. It was a contest of strength between the flowers, which the child conducted with the greatest care and fairness. When one of the violets prevailed over the other he dropped the headless stem and selected a new flower out of the grass. He accompanied this act with a sentence, monotonously repeated:

" 'Heah comes anuder champeen up to be killed.'

" As Wyatt approached the child his face softened,

97

as one's face unconsciously softens when he meets with a fluffy little animal at play. That impulse which moves one to put out his foot and turn over a puppy moved the man. The child squatted by the path, with his face toward the village and his short, chubby back toward Wyatt. The man paused, smiled and drew near, walking delicately. When he arrived on the path beside the child he put out his cane to tap him on the tightly-drawn seat of his breeches. At this moment the child turned sharply to select another violet, and the iron ferrule of the cane struck him on the cheekbone, below the eye. The constant hammering of the cane on the flagstone walks of the village had caused the soft iron to flatten around the end of the ferrule into a sharp edge. This edge, even under the slight tap of the cane, striking on the cheekbone, cut through the skin, and the blood began to flow. The child arose, crying, and set out running to his home, a shanty on the border of the meadow, some fifty yards away. As he ran he rubbed his face with his fists, and thereby daubed himself with tears and blood.

" Wyatt, alarmed at the accident, followed to explain. The child's mother appeared in the door of the shanty as he approached. When she saw the blood she rushed out, demanding to know how he had been injured. Wyatt endeavored to explain.

The mind of the excited negro seized on the one fact that the man had struck the child, and rejected everything else.

" She turned angrily on Wyatt. ' You, a growed-up man, hittin' a little chile! ' she shouted.

" The boy cried louder and the woman wiped his face with her apron. The blood appearing on the apron increased the woman's fury. She refused to hear any explanation, caught up the boy and carried him into the house.

" At the door she turned and shook her clenched hand at Wyatt. ' Mine what I tell you! ' she shouted; ' I'll have the law on you fur this, you, a growed-up man, hittin' a little chile! '

" Wyatt, greatly annoyed, resumed his walk to the village. The last words of the woman particularly disturbed him. Standing alone, those words charged him with an act conspicuously reprehensible. He felt that, unaccompanied by an explanation, they did him a glaring injustice. The child's father was a blacksmith. His shop, a mere shed, was on the outskirts of the village, some dozen paces from the point where the path through the meadow entered the street. Wyatt walked slowly across the meadow to the path; when he came to the street he turned down to the shop. The woman was already there, carrying the boy in her arms. The child's face was streaked and daubed where the woman had half wiped it with her apron.

" When Wyatt approached the man took the child from its mother and came out into the road. Wyatt began to explain how the thing occurred. ' He turned around just as I went to tap him with my cane.' The man, like the woman, cut through this explanation to the main fact:

" ' What did you want to hit him fur ? '

" Wyatt was perplexed for a reply to this question. The motive which had moved him was wholly innocent, but it was illusive. He labored to find some words which would make it intelligible to the man — some plain, ordinary terms that the man could understand.

" Finally he said: ' It was only for fun, just fun.'

" The man did not say anything, but the woman came to the door; her face was hard and sullen. ' It's mighty cur'us kine of fun,' she said; ' a growed-up man hittin' a little chile.'

" Wyatt saw that he had failed to make them understand, and he turned to walk back to the village street. He began to realize that his explanation was not convincing. The ugly, naked fact, as repeatedly stated by the woman, seemed to demand some further justification — some justification of an equal proportion to it. Wyatt began to review the incident, and he was smitten with a sense of profound injustice. He had not been moved by the slightest unkind impulse; on the contrary, the impulse had been sympathetic and appreciative, yet the incident bore an aspect of malice. His efforts to remove that aspect from the incident had signally failed. He had not been able to justify what he had done, and yet he was wholly innocent of wrong, and he felt as if he ought to be able to make that justification appear. He reflected carefully, and he was greatly perplexed. The exact truth, while sufficient in his own mind, seemed to lose its virtue when presented to another — to become a totally different thing, and, instead of justifying his act, to convict him of wanton cruelty.

" It was Wyatt's custom to go in the morning to his bank, and, if the day were bright, to take a splint-bottom chair and sit on the street before the door. He held here a sort of court, conversed with his neighbors, and conferred with his cashier as to the solvency of persons who came in to borrow little sums of money. He knew every man in the county, and exactly how his financial affairs stood.

" All the morning, in the sun before the bank, he continued to review the incident of the meadow. When he came to think of it, he was surprised that the slight blow of the cane should have caused such injury to the child. He began to practice with the cane, in an effort to reproduce the tap which he had given. There was a hitching-rack for horses before the bank, and Wyatt, sitting forward in his chair, struck the locust post of the rack over and over again, endeavoring to reproduce the exact blow. He was so engrossed with this labor that the cashier had to come to the door and call him whenever he required his advice.

" The storekeeper opposite observed this and called his customer's attention to it.

" ' Ther's somethin' botherin' Dolph,' he said.

" As Wyatt was on his way home to dinner at twelve o'clock, the justice of the peace came out to the gate and called him. The justice was a shoe-maker. He worked on the porch of his house, and also conducted there the duties of his office. He wore a patched ' hickory ' apron. His spectacles were tied around his head with a shoestring. The justice of the peace leaned over his gate, and moved the spectacles up into his gray hair.

" ' That woman,' he said, ' come in here to git a warrant ag'in you, but I wouldn't give it to her.' Then he added: ' You didn't hit the little nigger, I reckon?'

" ' I didn't go to hit him,' Wyatt replied; ' it was accidental.'

" ' Of course, of course,' said the justice; ' I

knowed a man like you wouldn't hit a child a purpose. It's fine spring weather we're havin'.'

" Wyatt remained a moment to comment on the probable fruit crop and went on. But his annoyance over this matter increased. The words ' hit a child a purpose ' particularly disturbed him. It was the old, ugly, malicious fact turning up again. He was glad that he had thought to say ' accidental '; it was, in a way, accidental; he had not meant to do the child an injury. But he was also glad that he had not been required to explain how the accident occurred.

" Then he suddenly thought: ' Suppose the warrant had been issued?'

" He stopped in the street and the perspiration dampened the palms of his hands. He stood for some time without moving; then he went on to his house. But all the afternoon he considered this possibility, and passed the matter in review. He tried to recall each detail in the situation, and exactly how each event arose; and, unconsciously, he continued to practice with the cane. He struck at almost every object he passed: the dandelions, the trees, the hitching-posts along the street. In the afternoon, in his chair before the bank, he fell into the same perplexing effort to reproduce that exact tap of the cane.

" Wyatt's preoccupation did not escape idle persons about the village. They discussed it with the storekeeper.

" Finally one of them said: ' I wonder if there's anything wrong with the bank.'

" The storekeeper's wife, who was weighing out sugar, heard the remark. After that she watched the man who sat before the bank, tapping the hitching-rack with his cane. About three o'clock she spoke to her husband, and he went over to the bank, when the cashier began to put up the shutters, and drew out his deposit.

" That night Wyatt did not sleep very well. His mind did not seem able to put down the worry which it had taken up. He was accustomed to eight hours of profound slumber, and, for this reason, the one restless night affected him far more than it otherwise would have done. In the morning his face, and especially his eyes, bore that decided evidence of fatigue which marks the first interruption of long-established habits of life.

" On his way to the bank he met the storekeeper's wife, who had set out to deliver a basket of groceries.

" ' You look kind a dauncey,' she said. ' Are you sick?'

" Wyatt replied with some trivial excuse, that he had caught a cold, or the like.

" ' It ain't cold,' said the woman; ' it's your blood. You ought to take the three bitter barks.' Then she began to explain how this tonic was compounded out of dogwood, poplar and wild-cherry bark, steeped in whisky. ' You cut off the rough outside bark with a drawin'-knife,' she said, ' and then you scrape the inside bark up.' When she got back to the store she said to her husband:

" ' Mind what I tell you, things ain't goin' right with old Dolph.'

" Wyatt took up his accustomed place in his splint-bottom chair before the bank. He felt dull and listless, and he nodded in the sun. He rested his hands on the head of his cane, and occasionally, half asleep, his head went down on his hands. Not the slightest detail of the man's movements escaped the woman across the street. Every now and then a customer would come into the store and she would make some remark, directing his attention to Wyatt. These remarks were always suggestive.

" ' I've knowed him now goin' on forty years, an' I never seen him carry on like that.'

" About two o'clock in the afternoon the deputy sheriff came up the street to where Wyatt sat, stopped, spoke to him, and jerked his thumb over his shoulder toward the inside of the bank. The two men went through the bank to a little back room.

There the deputy sheriff took a folded paper out of his pocket and handed it to Wyatt.

" ' I've got a suppeeny fur you,' he said.

" Wyatt opened the paper and read it. It was a summons in an action at law for damages, brought by the blacksmith. The grave aspect of the paper affected Wyatt. The legal terms appeared formidable. ' State of West Virginia, County of Madison, to-wit. . . . Trespass on the case. . . . Damages ten thousand dollars.'

" Wyatt carried the paper to the window, as though he needed a better light in which to read it.

" ' What lawyer has he got? ' he said.

" ' Asbury Sheets,' replied the deputy sheriff.

" Wyatt folded the summons and creased it along the fold with his fingers. Then he opened it and read it through. Again he folded and creased it, and again he opened it. Finally, he put it into his pocket. Even the name of the notorious pettifogger whom the deputy sheriff had mentioned did not reassure him.

" ' If you are walking back to the courthouse,' he said, ' I will step along with you.'

" The two men went out of the bank together. Wyatt was excited, and he walked a little in advance of the deputy sheriff.

" This incident had not escaped the storekeeper's

wife. She now came out from behind the counter, and began to wipe her hands on her apron.

" ' I'm goin' to run around to the mill,' she said.

" About half an hour later, the miller, who was the woman's brother, slipped into the bank, made some excuse to the cashier, and drew out his deposit.

" The office of the clerk of the circuit court was on the right of the door as one entered the court-house, between the battered plaster walls. The clerk was sitting at a long table in the middle of the room. Before him, on this table, was a pile of legal papers, done up in blue and red wrappers. He was writing the rule orders on the backs of these wrappers. The papers in blue wrappers were suits in chancery; those in red, actions at law. The clerk looked up when Wyatt and the deputy sheriff entered.

" He nodded to Wyatt. ' Have a chair,' he said.

" Wyatt picked up a chair, the splint bottom of which had been replaced by a board nailed across the rounds, carried it to the table and sat down beside the clerk. He leaned over, rested his arm on the table and spoke.

" ' Andy,' he said, ' I've been sued.'

" There was a certain overdone intimacy in Wyatt's manner, as though, in the lawsuit, he hoped to attach the clerk to his side. The clerk put out his hand, searched through the pile of papers, finally took up a very thin one in a red wrapper, ripped off the rubber band and opened it. He leaned back in his chair, and held the unfolded wrapper between the thumb and forefinger of his hand.

" ' An action in case,' he said; ' summons issued returnable to these rules.' Then he began to explain. ' You don't have to appear now,' he said. ' When the docket's called at the next term your lawyer'll demur to the declaration, then the judge will pass on the demurrer, an' if he overrules it he'll set the case for trial.'

" ' Yes,' said Wyatt. His voice was husky. The legal terms, and especially the word ' trial,' alarmed him.

" The clerk continued: ' You'll want to git up your defense. Where was the little nigger?'

" Wyatt moistened his lips with his tongue. ' He was in my meadow.'

" ' Um! ' said the clerk, ' trespassin'?'

" ' Yes,' said Wyatt.

" ' Was there any cattle or horses in there that might have hurt him?'

" Wyatt reflected. ' There is a run,' he said; ' he might have fallen in that.'

" ' Trespassin', an' in a dangerous place,' said the clerk. ' There's your defense.'

" Then he laid down the paper and put the tips of

his fingers together. He spoke with deliberation.

" ' The infant plaintiff was trespassin' on your land, an' in a locality where he was likely to come to harm, an' you chastised him in order to make him go home. That's a good defense.'

" Wyatt was profoundly relieved. To him the clerk was a great expert on such matters. His opinion ought to be conclusive. And here, available to him, was a complete defense that carried conviction.

" He began to repeat it: ' I was comin' along the path, I saw the little nigger playin' by the run in my meadow, where he had no right to be, I thought he might fall in and be drowned, so I tapped him with my cane to make him go home out of danger.'

" ' Exactly! ' said the clerk. Then he snapped the band over the red wrapper and tossed the papers on to the pile before him. ' No jury will ever find against you on that defense.'

" Wyatt was now wholly relieved. He felt that the clerk had done him a great kindness, and he wished to say something to please him. He remembered that the clerk had been elected by a rather unusual majority. He began to smile and nod his head.

" ' You'll be runnin' for the legislature next, I reckon,' he said; ' a man that carries the county in his pocket like you.'

" ' Oh, I don't know,' replied the clerk, as though the arriving of a political distinction were to him merely a matter of selecting it.

" Wyatt went out of the courthouse door; there he stopped to read the notices of judicial sales, cut out of the local newspaper and pasted against the wall. He continued to smile. He even began to whistle softly under his breath. He tapped on the wall with his fingers while he scanned the notices. He experienced that sense of exalted confidence which one takes from the favorable opinion of an expert.

" Presently, he heard the deputy sheriff speak to the clerk.

" ' I don't believe that was the reason old Dolph hit the little nigger.'

" ' Why don't you? '

" ' Because there ain't water enough in that run to drown a cat.' "

CHAPTER VII: *The Peril*

WYATT remained for a moment motionless. He had not foreseen this possible contingency. He endeavored to recall how the little stream appeared, and especially that portion near the sugar maple where the negro boy had been squatting. He went down the steps engaged with this memory. It seemed to be the hinge upon which everything turned. He determined to look at the brook at once, and he hurried, walking rapidly. As he came up to the bank window the cashier beckoned to him. When he entered the cashier said:

" ' There's a jug of tree molasses behind the door, that Benny Bean brought you the other day; I've been forgettin' it.'

" It was a two-gallon stone jug in a grist-mill sack. The end of the sack was tied in a knot. Wyatt picked it up and went out of the bank. He carried the sack in one hand, his fingers around it, below the knot. It was heavy, and he stopped occasionally to shift it from one hand to the other.

" The storekeeper's wife, who had been keeping her eyes on the bank, saw Wyatt enter it hurriedly and come out with the sack. She spoke to her husband, who was at the door putting out a box of timothy seed:

"'What's he carryin', you reckon?'

"'I don't know,' replied the storekeeper; 'it looks heavy.'

"''Tis heavy,' replied the woman. And she continued to watch Wyatt, changing the sack from one hand to the other, until he reached the end of the village street.

"Wyatt hurried along the meadow path to the sugar maple, put down his sack and advanced to the brook. There was not a great deal of water running, but at this point there was a little pool, with perhaps twelve inches of water. At one time this pool had been two or three feet deep, but it was now partly filled up with soft clay from the bank.

"Wyatt stood for some time regarding this pool, then he picked up the sack and went on to the house. That evening he turned his horse into the meadow. After supper he went out into the garden, got a hoe and started down toward the meadow with the hoe in his hand, but he stopped at the gate and set the hoe against the fence. Then he sat down on the steps. When it began to get dark he got up, went to the gate, picked up the hoe and crossed the meadow to the brook. There he carefully cleaned out the little pool, dragging out the soft clay and piling it up in a sort of dam below. He worked for some time and it was quite dark when he had finished. As he knocked the mud off the hoe he said:

" 'There, now, there'll be plenty of water for Barney.'

" The next morning the negro boy who swept out the store, and who lived in one of the shanties on the border of Wyatt's meadow, said to the storekeeper's wife: 'Pap saw ole Dolph diggin' in his medder las' night.'

" The woman sat down in a chair, smoothed out her apron and put her fat hands on her knees. She sat perfectly motionless for twenty minutes; then she went out. A little later word passed rapidly from one house to another in the village that Wyatt had been sued for 'thousands an' thousands' and had taken all of his own money out of his bank and buried it.

" There is no place in the world that a secret rumor can be so swiftly spread, and, at the same time, so carefully guarded, as in a country village. The community becomes at once a close society, including everyone but the person maligned. By twelve o'clock this rumor was known to every individual in the village but Wyatt and his cashier. They were excluded. The rumor moved everywhere about them, but it was as scrupulously guarded from their knowledge as though every man, woman and child had bound himself with an oath.

" There began now what in cities is called a run on Wyatt's bank; but, unlike the manner of cities, it was conducted here with the greatest stealth, and attended with an infinite variety of ingenious subterfuges. A young man would drop into the bank with a catalogue of Cincinnati buggies, show it to the cashier, ask his opinion, discuss with him the various types of vehicles, finally decide upon a certain one, make a pencil-mark on the picture of it, and draw out his deposit. Or an old woman would come painfully into the bank, with a begging letter from some fictitious, destitute relative, which she had laboriously forged, get the cashier to write her a letter in reply, put her money into the envelope, address it to the pretended relative, and even put on a postage-stamp, then she would start out to the post-office, with the letter in her hand, complaining bitterly.

" Every variety of business transaction, including the passing of money, was rehearsed before Wyatt and his cashier, and invariably concluded with a payment drawn out of the bank. The street before the bank became a market-place where all sorts of articles were bought and sold, but especially horses and mules. The trading in these was unprecedented. This trading was never ' even '; ' boot ' was always given, and was in amount exactly the sum which one or the other trader had on deposit to his credit. The skill, the ingenuity, the minute attention to detail with which these subterfuges were presented would have deceived the elect.

"However, the fact that deposits were being steadily withdrawn could not be obscured. Wyatt began now to visit, as by accident, those persons who used to be his largest depositors, in an effort to discover why they no longer put their money into the bank. He had never the slightest difficulty in bringing this topic into the conversation. Invariably, these persons mentioned the subject themselves, and presented so apt and convincing an excuse that their course seemed normal and unsuspicious. The efforts of his cashier to induce the several horse-dealers and the like to leave the 'boot' on deposit, to their credit, were likewise ingeniously met. They owed a 'little' store bill, or they had borrowed a 'little' money last winter, or certain members of their family were 'doctorin',' and so forth.

"The slow, steady drain on the bank began to give Wyatt the greatest concern. To the anxiety of the lawsuit was now added this additional, nearer anxiety. He could not tell whether this run on the bank was a concerted, intentional thing, or merely incidental to a peculiar business inactivity.

" He endeavored to surprise the secret out of the children on the street, but in this he never succeeded. They met his questions with instinctive cunning, repeating glibly the excuse which they had heard their parents rehearse: ' Pap's goin' to buy Sis an organ,' or ' Ma's goin' in yander to Uncle Lige's fur Easter.'

" All plans contemplated an expenditure of money.

" This exasperating riddle pursued Wyatt day and night. He no longer slept with any regularity. Sometimes he lay awake the whole night, summing up the evidence on one or the other side of this issue.

" When, some days later, the local doctor was passing the bank, Wyatt called him, and took him into the back room.

" ' I ain't been sleepin' very well, Doctor,' he said. ' Could you give me somethin' for it? '

" The doctor, who, like all country ones, depended on only those drugs from which he could get a pronounced result, gave Wyatt a box of little white pills, with the direction to take one at bedtime.

" That night, after taking the pill, Wyatt slept profoundly, but the next day he felt stupid. He continued to take the pills at bedtime. It seemed to ' cure ' the sleeplessness, and he did not connect

the increasing daily languor with the remedy. A
week later he went again to the doctor.

" ' I feel generally no account,' he said. ' I s'pose
I ought to have a little medicine.'

" ' How do you sleep now? '

" ' I don't have any trouble to sleep,' said Wyatt,
' but I feel sort of wore out.'

" ' You'd better take a little whisky,' the doctor
suggested.

" ' Why, Doctor,' said Wyatt, ' I never tasted
whisky in my life. I wouldn't like to take whisky.'

" The doctor was familiar with this prejudice
against whisky, and knew how to circumvent it.

" ' All right,' he said, ' I'll fix you up some bitters
at the drug-store; drop in and get it on your way
home.'

" The druggist told Wyatt to take a wine-glassful
of the bitters before meals, and to bring the bottle
back when it was empty, and he would refill it. The
stimulant made Wyatt feel better. He continued
to take it with regularity. When the bottle was
empty he took it back to the druggist. He took also
the pill-box, which was nearly empty.

" The condition at the bank, presently, became
critical. Wyatt did not keep a very large supply of
currency. The steady withdrawals were rapidly re-
ducing his reserve, and Wyatt found it necessary to

look about for cash. His loans were almost wholly
to the country farmers, who could meet their notes
only at one season of the year, when their harvests
were marketed. He took his commercial paper and
began to visit the banks of the neighboring counties,
but, as he had never been on very friendly terms
with other banks, he found his mission particularly
difficult. Wyatt's bank was a private one, and the
regular banks were accustomed to refer to it as a
' shavin' shop '— that is, a place where notes were
' shaved ' or discounted at an excessive rate. These
banks regarded Wyatt as an outsider, and they refused his notes except at a ruinous discount. He
went from one to another, but he met, everywhere,
with the same reply:

" ' We couldn't handle your notes unless you cut
'em in two.'

" The pressure of extreme need forced Wyatt to
negotiate one or two of these notes at this extortion-
ate rate, and he would return with the money in the
hope that he would not be required to make another
sacrifice. The strain on the man began to tell. He
looked much older and thinner. The withdrawals
steadily continued, and Wyatt was again and again
forced to borrow cash at this fifty per cent. discount.
He borrowed each time the smallest sum that would
prevent immediate suspension, and, consequently, he

was seen to leave the village every few days, riding
his old horse, Barney, with a few of his notes in his
pocket, and his saddle-bags, filled with corn for the
horse, across the seat of his McClellan saddle.

"This mysterious activity of Wyatt moved the village to conjecture. When a man began thus to
travel, one of two things were indicated: he was
either courting a wife, or he was looking for new
lands in which to settle. The village rejected the
first explanation, but the second seemed consistent
with its theory of Wyatt's affairs. It became generally known that Wyatt was 'a-goin' to move away.'

"This addition to the current gossip added activity to the run on the bank, and Wyatt's trips became more frequent and his loans larger. He was
coming to the opinion that the whole country had
entered a condition of great financial depression,
when one night, on his way to the drug-store, he
overheard some conversation issuing from the porch
of the justice of the peace.

"'Ten thousand would buy Sheets a heap of good
drinkin' liquor.'

"Somebody laughed. There was a moment's silence, and then a slow, deliberate voice, evidently
that of the justice, replied:

"'An' it would break old Dolph.'

"This remark opened to Wyatt the closed door

as with a key. It was this lawsuit that had affected his credit, and caused the withdrawals from the bank. Clearly, then, if he could win this suit, confidence in him would be restored, and the withdrawals would cease. His integrity was not impaired. He was known to be upright and reliable. With this suit out of the way he would rapidly regain what he had lost. If, then, he could keep the bank going until this suit was tried, all would come out right. When his negotiable paper was exhausted he gave deeds of trust on his property for short loans. Meanwhile the term of the circuit court arrived."

# CHAPTER VIII: *The Sign*

WHEN the attorney for the blacksmith began his cross-examination of Wyatt almost
the entire village was present in the courthouse. This attorney was one of those pettifoggers
to be found at every bar, who live one knows not
how, whose office is a chair before the courthouse
door, and whose plan of life is to draw some unwary
person into a legal proceeding and then, by a series
of imaginary expenses, extract from him petty sums:
two dollars for ' calling up ' the case, fifty cents for
' making up the issue,' a dollar for ' settin' ' the case
for trial, and so forth. They are constant spectators
in the court-room, and so, in a way, are familiar with
the routine of trials, and by copying the papers in
a similar action they are able to get their cases
into court. They have usually a certain fluency,
and a certain skill in what is called ' tanglin' the
witness.'

" ' Mr. Wyatt,' said the attorney, ' a man that you
can't believe about nothin' is the worst man you can
find, ain't he?'

" ' He's a purty bad kind of man,' said Wyatt.

" ' He's worse than a thief, ain't he? You can

121

lock up ag'in' a thief, but you can't lock up ag'in' a liar.'

"The argument seemed sound and Wyatt replied in the affirmative.

"'An' if he's worse than a thief he's about the meanest kind of man you could find, ain't he?'

"'I reckon he is,' said Wyatt.

"'An' if there's such a man as that in this town he ought to be run out of it, oughtn't he?'

"'But there's no such man in this town,' said Wyatt.

"'I ain't sayin' there *is,*' replied the attorney. 'I'm sayin' s'pose there *was.*'

"'Well,' said Wyatt, 'if there was a man in this town that you couldn't believe about nothin' I reckon the people would be justified in runnin' him out.'

"'All right,' said the attorney.

"'Now, Mr. Wyatt, a thing can happen only one way; ain't that so?'

"'I reckon that's so,' said Wyatt; 'a thing can only happen one way.'

"'An' if a man's there an' sees it happen he knows the way it is, don't he?'

"'I reckon he'd know,' said Wyatt, 'if he was on the ground and saw it happen.'

"'An' if a thing can only happen one way, an' a

man was there on the ground an' saw it happen that way, he couldn't be mistaken about the way it happened, could he?'

"Wyatt hesitated; the nature of these questions began to disturb him. He did not understand toward what end they moved, but he felt that they led up to some sinister *dénouement*. He endeavored to escape a direct answer.

"'He wouldn't be apt to be mistaken.'

"'An' he wouldn't be mistaken, would he?'

"'It ain't likely.'

"'Answer yes or no,' said the attorney.

"There seemed no escape, and Wyatt answered, 'No.'

"'All right,' said the attorney.

"'Now, Mr. Wyatt, if a thing can only happen one way, an' a man was on the ground and saw it happen, an' he couldn't be mistaken about the way it happened, an' yet he went out an' told people that it happened two or three different ways, what would you call him?'

"Wyatt hesitated. His attorney observed the hesitation and objected to the question. Before the judge could pass on the objection Sheets stepped out into the floor before the witness chair, drew himself up very straight on his heels, raised his right arm, extended the index finger and brought it down like a cocked pistol before Wyatt's face.

"'If your lawyer's afraid for you to answer that question,' he shouted, 'I'll answer it for you. You'd call him a *liar*!'

"The word seemed, in the silence of the court-room, to explode like a projectile. The attorney waited for a moment with his finger pointed toward the witness, then he returned to his table, put his hands into his pockets, planted his feet wide apart, and resumed his ordinary tone.

"'Now, Mr. Wyatt,' he said, 'if you catch a man lyin' about one thing you can't believe him about nothin', can you?'

"Wyatt was now alarmed and afraid to reply. He began to tap on the floor with the toe of his boot. Finally, he resorted to a subterfuge.

"'I don't just understand that question,' he said.

"The pettifogger had a stock checkmate for this move of a witness.

"'Very well, Mr. Wyatt,' he said, 'just state to the jury what it is about the question that you don't understand. It seems plain enough.'

"There was nothing about the question that Wyatt did not understand, and he did not know what to say. While he hesitated, the attorney leaned over the table and spoke to him in a low, confidential tone:

"'There ain't nothin' that you're tryin' to conceal, Mr. Wyatt, is there?'

"Wyatt saw how his silence could be thus made to reflect upon him, and he sat up in the chair.

"'No, sir,' he said.

"'Then answer the question,' said the lawyer.

"'Just say it over again, Mr. Sheets,' said Wyatt.

"The attorney repeated the question, making a gesture after every word:

"'If you catch a man lyin' about one thing, you can't believe him about nothin', can you?'

"'Well,' said Wyatt, 'if I caught a man lyin' to me about one thing I wouldn't like to believe him again.'

"'An' you wouldn't believe him ag'in about nothin', would you?'

"'I wouldn't like to.'

"'An' you wouldn't?'

"'No, sir.'

"'All right,' said the attorney.

"Sheets paused, smoothed his hair with the tips of his fingers, buttoned up his coat, and stepped around in front of his table.

"'Now, Mr. Wyatt,' he said, 'let's apply these

sound, general principles to this case. This thing could only happen one way, an' you was there an' saw it happen that way, an' you couldn't be mistaken about the way it was, an' yet you went out an' told the blacksmith that you hit the infant plaintiff for fun; an' then you went an' told the justice of the peace that it was accidental, an' that you didn't go to hit him; an' then you went an' told the clerk of this court that you hit him to make him go home so he wouldn't fall into the run an' be drowned. Ain't that so?'

"Wyatt's mouth became suddenly dry. His fingers began to wander over the buttons of his waistcoat. He moved his feet up under the chair, and crossed one over the other.

"The attorney turned around toward the spectators in the court-room.

"'There sets the blacksmith,' he said, 'an' there sets the justice of the peace, an' there sets the clerk.'

"He indicated each of these persons with a sweeping gesture, his hand open and extended, the thumb pressed against the forefinger.

"'Do you *dee*ny it?'

"Wyatt did not reply. He took a clean, cotton handkerchief out of his pocket, unfolded it and wiped his face. The courthouse was as still as death. For fully two minutes the attorney waited, his arms folded across his chest, his head thrown back, his eyes fixed on a remote corner of the courthouse ceiling, then he spoke:

" ' That's all, Mr. Wyatt; you can stand aside.'

" Wyatt went slowly out of the courthouse and up to the bank. There he sat down in his splint-bottom chair before the door, and began idly to tap the hitching-post with his cane. The afternoon sun was warm. Swarms of yellow butterflies moved in the road. Thirty minutes later a small boy appeared, running from the direction of the courthouse. He stopped, panting, before the bank.

" ' Mr. Wyatt,' he said, catching his breath after each word, ' the jury brung in a verdict fur the nigger fur one cent damage.'

" The victory did not seem to impress Wyatt. He remained seated in his chair, his mouth open, his head fallen a little to one side, the cane moving in his hand. Finally, he got up and spoke to the cashier through the window.

" ' I guess we'll close the bank,' he said; ' you can put up the shutters.'

.   .   .   .   .   .   .   .

" On the first day of October the Southern drummer for the Baltimore Drug Company made his annual visit to the village. As he entered the local drug-store he passed an old man coming out. The drummer stopped and looked after the man.

" ' Ain't that old Dolph Wyatt? ' he said.

" ' Yes,' said the druggist.

" ' Um,' said the drummer, ' he used to be your leadin' citizen; what done it? '

" ' Same old things,' said the druggist: ' liquor an' dope.' "

The doctor concluded. He struck a match and relighted his cigarette.

" Now, gentlemen," he said, " what becomes of your very pretty theories? Here is a man, innocent of any crime, crushed under circumstances that were set going by the slightest incident. Very like an innocent traveler on the road who is buried under an avalanche started by a loose pebble. But here is your impulse, inherent in events, my dear Flint, pursuing an innocent person like a hound on a false trail. Or, Father Jerome," the doctor indicated the priest with a gesture, " here is your Providence of God hard at work after the wrong man."

" Dr. Lennard," said the priest, " your story is not complete. You have given us the history of this man's acts, but not the history of his conscience. It is not necessary that men should accomplish overt acts of injustice in order to be visited by punishment.

If that were true, only those who possessed a certain courage would be the subject of retributive justice. A man will not escape because he lacks this physical courage if he have, in fact, within him the intent of wrong doing. Here was a man, utterly selfish, whose life was narrow and hard, set upon a single object — his individual welfare. It is quite certain that this dominating idea would have led him far afield had it not been for his fear of the law and public opinion. We have seen how willing he was to falsify facts in order to protect himself. In the scheme of things, such a personality is not useful to God's work, and it is to be expected that in the end such a person would be destroyed and removed."

"Father Jerome," said the judge, "I think you touch there upon a profound truth. You interpret it, however, upon a wrong hypothesis. This impulse or tendency in nature may have a far larger object than merely to overtake and punish the criminal agent. Renan said, 'Believe me, the universe labors at some great work.' We shall, perhaps never understand the ultimate object of this labor, but we can see some methods, and one of the clearest of these methods is a tendency on the part of nature to remove the things which hinder it, or are harmful to it, and to preserve and protect the things that are beneficial, or that assist it. This tendency has been called the Survival of the Fittest, but the term is not always understood. It means the survival of those fittest to carry out or advance the work at which the universe labors. Let me illustrate what I mean. Imagine a scene like this:

"The night was advancing. The rain pattered on the canals of mud that trailed off through the hills, on the great squares of rusted pipe piled along the railroad track, on the heaps of frayed cable, on the jam of wagons behind the freight shed.

"The shanties on the edge of the hideous raw town were all dark, except a single one built on piles and opening with a decayed porch directly into the mud road. This was the office of the doctor — a single room, filled with shelves and bottles, a table, a chair or two, and a bed screened off with a calico curtain. Within, on the table, a new tallow candle burned in a tin candlestick. Hot tallow in a white pulpy mass was pushed up around the base of the candle, showing that a new one had just replaced one already burned out.

"The doctor was walking backward and forward through this room. Sometimes he stopped before the window, dingy with smoke and dirt; but the night

was like ink and he could see nothing. He was a
young man with what had once been a delicate
physique, but he was now bronzed and toughened.
Sometimes, as he walked, the man paused as though
to listen, but there were no noises save those of the
rain.

" An hour passed. Then, from the canal of mud
running off westward into the hills, there arose a
sound as though a lake of batter were being thrashed
with a gigantic flail. At the sound the doctor's anxiety ceased; he came over to the table, thrust the
candle more firmly into the candlestick and sat down.
The gigantic thrashing sound increased and a moment later the door opened and a man entered hurriedly.

" The man was covered with soft yellow mud; it
trickled in thick, viscous rivulets over his big Saxon
face. He was no usual person — tall and muscular,
with a thin, bony, hawk-bill nose, a head that was
perfectly bald, and a wide, straight mouth. And,
in spite of the evidence of his bald head, he was in
the very prime of life. He looked around at the
shelves of little bottles, the stove, the table covered
with medical journals, old letters and scraps of paper,
the saddle-pockets in the corner, the calico curtain
screening the bed, and the nails in the wall that did
service for a wardrobe.

" ' True to life, Charlie,' he said.

" ' Why not?' replied the doctor, rising. ' It is life.'

" Then he went over to a shelf, took down a glass jar half full of some amber-colored liquid and set it on the table. There was a stone pitcher with a broken mouth on an inverted nail keg by the window, and a cloudy glass. He rinsed out the glass and placed it beside the jar.

" In the meantime, the big man got out of his rubber coat. He threw it with his hat on the floor and he wiped the rivulets of mud from his face with a handkerchief; then he noticed what the doctor was doing.

" ' Not for me,' he said, ' I've cut out the booze, Charlie; but if you have any tobacco in this joint, let me have it.'

" The doctor put a box of stogies on the table. They were strong, black and bitter from the green tobacco out of which they were rolled, but the big man seized upon them as though they were a sort of treasure, bit off the end of one and lighted it from the doctor's candle. Then he sat down and began to draw the smoke into his mouth and slowly release it, as though it were a soothing and delicious incense.

" ' This is a fine place you roost in, Charlie,' he

said; 'I came from that flag station through a mud river.'

" ' They've been hauling pipe,' replied the doctor, ' and with the rains the roads are batter.' Then he added: ' I could not be sure that you would come, but you are the only one whom I could trust.'

" ' You might not have been sure that you could trust me,' said the big man, ' but I think you could have been sure that I would come. You came once when I sent the word. I'm a good Indian, Charlie.'

" ' Well,' continued the doctor, ' I said to myself: " Arkman's the man; he will come and he will stand up." '

" ' You're half right, Charlie, anyway; I'm on the ground.' Then he looked about him.

" ' How long have you been doing this sort of thing? '

" ' Well,' replied the doctor, ' I've been here two years. I located this for the place when the oil company got its big well out on Rock Creek. This town sprang up in a night; money has been pouring in here like water through a sluice. I knew that in such a place everything would be a sort of temporary makeshift — buildings half put up, everything cheap and flimsy, everybody taking a chance, and any sort of old stuff run in and made to do until the oil blew out and the boom collapsed. And, Arkman, I was right — you never saw so much money floating around. All kinds of birds have picked fortunes out of this mud hole — saloons, dance halls, faro joints. The corner drug-store offered me a thousand dollars a month to stand in its back room and write prescriptions for liquor. . . . And all the time I've been practicing medicine.'

" ' And straight . . . with your little old saddle-pockets?' said the big man.

" ' Arkman!' replied the doctor. ' I'm the only man in this whole country that is straight. I'm the best citizen in it. The oil companies plunder this region as though it were a captured province, and the place is full of sharks, pirates and grafters. Arkman, I'm the only man that any one of them will either believe or trust. The farmers ask me about their leases; and the crooks come to me when they get in trouble. I'm full of the trusts and confidences of sick men and dead men. I've got the reputation that I wanted to get. I've been square! What I say is the truth and what I do is on the level. I'm the doctor, the lawyer, and the priest for this whole corner of hell!'

" The doctor moved his chair nearer to the table beside which his companion sat. He caught his under lip between his thumb and finger. His eyes looked beyond the wall.

" ' It's been a hard life,' he said. ' You can't imagine it. I haven't shirked the part! I've gone at every call, in rain and snow and mud up to the horse's belly. I've eaten food that would kill a dog; and I've slept on the floor, and in the saddle, and in beds so full of vermin that I had to burn my clothes to get rid of them. And I haven't selected out the good patients. By Jove, the part I was playing made that easy! The poor devils down on their luck have had the first call. It wasn't their fees I was after.

" ' Two years of that — four years, counting the nights! And all the time, Arkman, do you know what I've been thinking about? I've been thinking about a cabin on an ocean liner, and the smell of the sea, and the dock at Cherbourg, and the ride through the wheat fields and the red poppies, and Paris! And I've been thinking about the restaurants over there! And I've been thinking about a touring car and the great roads; and the feel of clothes that fit you; and the smell of a good cigar; and the taste of champagne; and the good things of life!

" ' That before your mind — And before your eyes the mud road, and a woman coughing herself to death with tuberculosis, and a child choking with diphtheria, and dirt and poverty and squalor. And half-cooked pork swimming in lard, to eat, and yellow biscuit, and coffee that would poison a cat! '

" 'How about it being good to be good — nothing in it?'

" 'Nothing in it!' replied the doctor; then he hesitated —'Oh, well, darn it, yes! — you're glad to help the poor devils. But that's not the point.'

" Again he stopped and remained for a moment silent.

" 'Well, what's the result? One is, that from being about the poorest excuse for a doctor that ever straddled a horse, I've got to be a good one.' He moved the medical pamphlets on the table.

" 'I take all their truck,' he said, 'and I know who's guessing and who's seen the sick man sweating in his bed — that's result number one. Result number two is that I haven't five hundred dollars, while every Tom, Dick and Harry has made his pile and skipped. But I've got the thing I was going after. I'm above suspicion! There isn't a man, woman or child that could be convinced by an angel of God that the doctor could do anything wrong. They wouldn't believe it. You couldn't convince them. They'd laugh in your face; or they'd curse you till a fly wouldn't light on you.'

" 'You haven't done it by halves, Charlie.'

" 'Not I,' said the doctor; 'I planned to do one big job, and only one, and I took my time. I guess you didn't believe me. Well, that night in Chicago, when I turned the box upside down on the faro table and got up out of the dealer's chair, I meant what I said. No more little skin games for me! I took a turn through a fake college in Cincinnati and struck up here — playing my part and keeping my eye on the main chance. And now the job's ripe.'

" ' What's in it? ' said Arkman.

" ' Six hundred thousand dollars,' replied the doctor. ' A hundred thousand for you — five hundred thousand to yours truly. That may look like giving you the short end. But figure it up. You put in an hour. I put in two years — besides, I've kicked out the rabbit.'

" The big man whistled low and softly.

" ' Good Heavens! Man,' he said, ' are you cracking a subtreasury? '

" ' The independent oil company has sold all of its producing wells to the central company, and the money's in the bank to close the deal,' replied the doctor —' came in to-day.'

" ' Got that straight? ' said Arkman.

" ' Straight! ' echoed the doctor; ' I'm a director.'

" Again the big man whistled.

" ' What's the safe like? Can I drill it with a steel bit? '

" ' You won't have to drill it,' replied the doctor. ' I told you that everything was a temporary makeshift in this place — that's what I counted on — the safe is one of those big, old-fashioned junk boxes. All there is to do is to putty up the cracks of the door, leaving little holes at the top and the bottom, put an air pump on the bottom hole, a paper funnel full of pulverized powder on the top one, and suck the powder in with your pump, cover the door with a wet blanket and puff it off.'

" The big man took the half-smoked stogy from between his teeth.

" ' Charlie,' he said, ' people are sure not leaving their money in an old carpet-sack like that. There must be somebody watching it with a gun.'

" ' There is,' said the doctor.

" ' What's he like — a farmer?'

" ' Not by a long sight,' said the doctor. ' That watchman makes up for anything that the safe lacks. He sleeps in a cot set up against the safe door and he has an arsenal of shooting irons laid out all around him — and they're not there for looks either. He's no toy desperado, that man; he's the real thing. The bankers know that — that's the reason they trust the old iron box. With that man on the job, the money would be safe in a paper vault. They'd have to kill him; and, believe me, they'd have a mighty hard time doing it.'

" ' Got him fixed?' said Arkman.

" ' I have,' said the doctor.

" ' What's the figger? '

" ' Arkman,' said the doctor, ' do you suppose I'm organizing a syndicate?  What do you imagine I've been playing the part in this God-forsaken mud-hole for?  To end up with the same old game?  Not I! I propose to remain above the suspicion of any man in this county.  Don't you see what I've been after. I don't want to be hunted when this job's over. Listen!  I'm going to bring the money up here and put it in my old saddle-pockets there in the corner. After a while the doctor's health will begin to fail; he will bear up as long as he can, then he'll take his old saddle-pockets and go down East to the experts.  Word will come back that the doctor's all in.  The experts will send him to Germany.  And in its good time the word will come that the doctor is no more.  And do you know what they will do here in this place?  They'll build a monument to the doctor.'

" ' But how about this Johnny with the guns? Got him lured away? ' asked Arkman.

" ' Lured! ' said the doctor.

" ' Eats out of your hand, then? '

" ' Arkman,' said the doctor, ' you didn't use to be a fool.'

" The big man blew out a cloud of smoke.

" ' Charlie,' he said, ' ain't this thing got a joker in it?  You didn't mention this gentleman with the fortifications.  You sent me a wax impression of the door key and you said the safe was rotten — but no word of this other little difficulty.'

" ' There is no other difficulty,' replied the doctor; ' the watchman will be asleep.  You will take hold of one end of him and I the other and we will lift him around out of the way; that's all there is to it.'

" The big man suddenly laughed without disturbing a muscle of his face.

" ' Your friend must be a mighty sound sleeper.'

" ' He'll sleep to-night,' replied the doctor.

" The doctor rose and held the candle up to a little glass jar on the shelf.  He turned the jar so the label could be read.

" ' With three of those morphine tablets in you, Arkman, you'd never wake up.  That watchman's got four in him.  He will wake up because he's got an iron heart, but it will be to-morrow afternoon, and it will take me four hours to do it.'

" For amazement and for admiration, the big man had one method of expression — the low whistle on a single note — and he gave it now.

" The doctor sat down.

" ' It was all in the plan.  I've worked up the

140

case. The man has a little muscular rheumatism and I'm giving him soda.'

" Arkman chewed the end of his stogy, then he threw it away, got another out of the box and lighted it at the candle. For some time he was silent, then he spoke as though he pronounced a reflection.

" 'Now, that's what I call genius,' he said. 'Well, I'm glad the job's easy, because I'm going to chuck this sort of business.'

" ' What's the matter with you anyway? ' said the doctor anxiously.

" The big man took the stogy out of his mouth and looked the doctor calmly in the face.

" ' I'm afraid! ' he said.

" The doctor's chair scraped on the floor as he thrust himself back with his extended legs.

" ' Afraid! ' he said; ' I thought there wasn't a living thing in the world that you were afraid of.'

" ' There isn't,' said Arkman.

" ' You're not afraid of the dead? ' exclaimed the doctor.

" ' Nor the dead,' said Arkman.

" ' What is it, then, that you're afraid of? '

" ' Charlie,' said the big man, ' I don't know.'

" The doctor looked at his companion as though he were a patient with some deadly obscure disease.

" ' Afraid of something and you don't know what it is ! ' he replied.

" ' No,' replied the big man; ' I don't know what it is. Nobody knows what it is.'

" ' Hasn't it got a name ? ' said the doctor.

" ' Yes,' said the man; ' it's got a lot of names — none of them any good. You'd call it chance.'

" ' Chance ! ' and the doctor laughed. ' Why, Arkman, that's a word men invented to cover up their incompetency. Chance ! That's a word that means lack of foresight. When you say you're afraid of chance, you simply say that you are afraid of yourself.'

" ' There,' said Arkman, ' I told you the names were no good. Sure they're not worth anything — any of them. To give a thing a name, you've got to know what it is; but nobody knows what this thing is; so all the names you give it mean something else. Then when you get to going on one of these names, you're not talking about the thing — you're talking about what the name means. Try them all: There's Providence ! You don't believe there's anything that fits that name, now, do you ? '

" ' I do not,' replied the doctor. ' The term implies that an authority, which has got the universe going according to a fixed set of laws, capriciously interrupts these laws at its pleasure.'

" ' Sure,' said Arkman, ' the name's no good. But the racetrack name's no better, now, is it? When you say " luck," you begin to talk about something else right away.'

" ' You begin to talk about something that's rot,' said the doctor. ' You are assuming that there is an influence external to yourself that impels events to assist you or to destroy you.'

" ' There you are! ' said the big man; ' you can't name it, but it's on the job, Charlie. And when it starts out to land you, all your precautions are not worth a whoop. There will be some little unforeseen accident that will put you to the bad.'

" The doctor made a gesture of disgust.

" ' Rot! ' he said.

" The big man chewed the end of his stogy.

" ' All right, Charlie — look where the boys are; look where they all end up; Sing Sing's full of them; Joliet's full of them; and look what they say.'

" ' A man will say anything when he's soft,' said the doctor.

" ' Was Vronsky soft? ' replied the big man. ' Was that old cockney Ponsford soft? I was with Vronsky the night he was hanged. He kicked the preacher out of the cell; and he sat there smoking a cigar, just as I am doing. And do you know what he said? " The thing's crooked, Arkman; you

143

can't beat it." And Ponsford said the same thing
—" 'T"int sife." '

" 'Nonsense!' said the doctor. 'The thing is
probably only a per cent of accidents.'

" 'But why is that per cent of accidents always
against us?' replied Arkman; 'that's what I want to
know. I've thought about it often.'

" 'Any preacher will tell you,' replied the doctor;
'step into a church.'

" 'I did step into a church,' said Arkman, 'but it
wasn't a preacher who told me. I was standing in
the door one night downtown, in New York. It
was raining, and a man who was waiting for a car
came in and stood beside me. He didn't belong in
the crowd; you could tell that by everything about
him. He listened a moment and then he said to me:

" ' " That's all folderol. Nature is laboring at
some great work; those men who are useful to her
purpose, who assist her, who aid her, she endeavors
to preserve; and those who are useless or harmful,
she endeavors to destroy — it's a law." And he
went out.

" 'Wait a minute, Charlie — isn't that about the
size of it? We're on the wrong side; we're not help-
ing anything along; we're against it; we're not useful
to the thing; we're in its way. And it's a-trying to
get rid of us! Now that's what Vronsky meant

144

when he said the thing was crooked; he meant that our side wasn't getting a fair deal — that there was something working against us. He didn't understand what it was; but he was a Slav with a head full of brains and he could see the thing at work. I've been watching it, Charlie, and I know it's picking us off! That's what makes me afraid. And there's another thing Vronsky said —" You can't beat it," and you *can't*. Try to think of anybody that it didn't finally land. They've all got theirs, sooner or later. Count them on your fingers!

" ' Say! Charlie, anybody can see results. Even old Ponsford saw results —" 'T'int sife!" Sure it's not safe! I saw that just as well as Vronsky, just as well as Ponsford, but I didn't understand why until that stranger told me.

" ' Charlie, what the deuce do you think we've been trying to do? We've been going up against the Thing that runs the whole universe — and we've been trying to beat it at its own game. See! It's playing all the time — all the time, day and night, morning and evening — to advance, advance, and to keep everybody and everything that helps it, and to get rid of everybody and everything that hinders it. And it knows everything, and it sees everything, and it understands everything. And us bucking a layout like that! The nerve of it! '

" At this moment the latch of the door clicked.

" The doctor arose and threw the door open. An old negro stood there. The doctor was angry.

" ' Didn't I tell you to clear out? ' he said. ' What's wrong with you — what are you hanging around for? '

" The negro was frightened and he stammered.

" ' Yes, Doc,' he said, ' I'm goin', Doc, yes, sah; ' and he shuffled away through the mud.

" The doctor closed the door.

" ' Who was it? ' said Arkman.

" ' A worthless nigger who sweeps out the office,' replied the doctor. ' He's a nuisance. He's always breaking something and he's always in the way, but somebody has to keep him.'

" The doctor stopped by Arkman and took hold of his wrist. The man's skin was cool and his pulse was deep and placid.

" The big man smiled. ' Did you think I was losing my nerve, eh, Charlie? ' he said.

" ' Judging from the gait you were hitting up that rotten line of talk, I did,' replied the doctor.

" ' The talk's all right, Charlie, believe me.'

" The doctor laughed.

" ' Then your mysterious influence ought to be on my side,' he said; ' I've been doing its work for a couple of years.'

" The big man took the stogy out of his mouth.

" ' Sure, Charlie,' he said, ' I hadn't thought of that.'

" The doctor continued to smile. ' Well,' he said, ' we shall see if it is.'

" ' And if it is, you stay on the job ? '

" The doctor sat down; his face lengthened into an ironical smile; he put out his legs and thrust his hands into his pockets.

" ' I'm willing to back my own intelligence,' he said; ' I've worked the thing out. I've considered everything and provided for every contingency — I'm not taking any chance. If your mysterious influence can trip me O. K.; I'll stay on the job.' Then he jerked himself up.

" ' What drivel ! ' he said. ' An incompetent jackass makes a rotten plan, and when it goes to pieces he says some supernatural agency threw him down; or some lotos-eater blows a big shiny bubble, and when it collides with the sharp edge of a fact he says that Heaven's against him ! Or some old stiff forgets the part he's playing.

" ' Look at the men you've been talking about: Take Vronsky. He planned to kill Gates. He found out that the old man worked in his library with the window open. It was summer, and the library looked into the garden. Vronsky reasoned that he

147

could go into that garden on a dark night, shoot Gates, and that under cover of the darkness no one would know who it was that had done it.

" ' Vronsky was right about several things: He knew that he could get away. He knew that no one would suspect him unless he was seen, because he was believed to be in Australia; and with his skill with a gun he knew that he would not miss. Moreover, he knew that, he being in the dark and Gates in the light, Gates could not see his assassin even if he were not instantly killed.

" ' Now that was all sound. Everything that Vronsky thought about, he figured out right — but there was one thing that Vronsky didn't think about. Well, he pulled it off the way he planned — and what happened? Gates saw Vronsky's face by the flash of the pistol and shouted his name as he fell. Now, what had Heaven to do with that?

" ' Take Ponsford: What did he do? He'd cracked the Empire Bank and the whole country was looking for him. He was hiding over on the East Side, and he was safe; but he got lonesome one night, put into his pocket the small tool with which a burglar forces a window, and went down on Long Island to rob a house. The village police picked him up. When he saw them coming he threw his tool into the gutter. The police asked him what it was he threw away and he said it was a stogy.

"'That was all right. The police believed him. They took him to the station-house, looked him over and told him he could go. Well, what did the old fool do? He sat round and got chummy with the police, and finally, when one of them offered him a cigar, he said he didn't smoke!

"'Was that Providence, or luck, or chance? Nonsense! The thing is to make your plan exclude these contingencies.'

"'Man,' said Arkman, 'you've got to take a chance.'

"'No, you haven't,' replied the doctor; 'there's where your brains come in.'

"'Why, Charlie,' said Arkman, 'you're taking a chance right here. Suppose your watchman doesn't swallow his dope; there are a dozen things that might keep a man from taking a dose of medicine.'

"'There's nothing that will keep that man from taking his,' said the doctor.

"'Why?' said Arkman.

"'Because he has already taken it,' replied the doctor. 'Damn it, man, do you think I'm a fool! I planned his medicine to run out to-day, and when he came here at nine o'clock for some more I gave him the tablets myself. I had to be sure of him; he'd shoot you to death before you got the key in the lock.'

" Again the big man whistled low and softly. He turned around in his chair; he put his hands together on the table. He looked at the doctor with a quiet smile.

" ' Charlie,' he said, ' you're a wonder! '

" The doctor took out his watch. ' It's about time we were getting the traps together,' he said, and he rose. He started to go behind the calico curtains, when a sound reached him and he stopped."

# CHAPTER IX: *The Sport of Fortune*

IT was the sound of horses plunging in that canal of batter, and a minute later a voice called. The doctor went to the door. The night was black as ink and the rain pattered on the soft mud. A man riding a horse and leading another was there in the road.

" 'Is that you, Doc?' he said.

" 'Yes,' replied the doctor.

" 'Then git in this saddle quick. A scantlin' fell at the Jones No. I and cut the driller's head open. The blood's spurtin' like a gusher.'

" 'Damn it!' cried the doctor, ' was there no one to put his finger on the artery?'

" 'Yes,' said the man; ' Hinkle's got his thumb on it, but he can't hold it there all night. Hurry, for Heaven's sake!'

" The doctor sprang for his saddle-pockets.

" Arkman got up. ' Charlie,' he said, ' you're not going, are you?'

" The doctor did not seem to hear him. He was jamming his arms into the sleeves of his greatcoat; the muscles of his face were stern and rigid.

"Arkman went up close to him. 'Come, Charlie,' he said, 'you're sure not going to throw the job?'

"The doctor replied with an oath — and he was gone. The door banged behind him and the horses galloped in the flying mud.

"The man went over to the little dingy window and looked out into the vat of ink. He stood there for a long time with his hands behind him. Finally he sat down, fingered the box of stogies, at last took one out, carefully cut the end of it and lighted it at the candle. The end of the cigar glowed and he sat motionless. Two hours passed. The man's face seemed to have lengthened and grown old.

"Then the door opened and the doctor entered. Arkman looked up. The doctor flung his soaked coat into a corner, wiped the mud from his face with a dirty towel, jerked the calico curtain aside, and began to empty the contents of his saddle-pockets out onto the bed.

"'Get up, Arkman,' he said, 'we've got to hurry.'

"The big man did not move.

"'Hurry for what?' he said.

"The doctor turned sharply.

"'Are you asleep?'

"'No, I'm not asleep,' he said; 'but you're not going to risk the job after that, are you?'

"'After what?' said the doctor.

" ' After that — that — warning.'

" The doctor looked at the man a moment in astonishment, then he began to curse.

" ' Warning! Are you that big a fool? Don't things happen all the time; don't men come for the doctor at all hours of the night? Don't be an idiot.'

" ' But, Charlie,' replied the man, ' you said —'

" The doctor interrupted him with an oath.

" ' Are you still harking on that drivel?' Then he turned savagely. ' If you're going with me, come on.'

" ' And if I don't go?' said the man.

" ' Then,' cried the doctor, ' I'll do it myself!' And he caught hold of the door. When his fingers touched the latch the door swung, and the old negro fell into the room. The doctor caught him by the collar and jerked him to his feet.

" ' You back here again!' he cried.

" ' Don't, Doc,' the negro whined; ' I want to tell you somethin'.'

" ' Then why didn't you tell it when you were here before?' said the doctor.

" ' I . . . I . . . was 'fraid to,' the negro stuttered.

" The doctor shook him.

" ' Out with it; what is it?'

" ' This mornin', Doc, . . . when I was sweepin'

. . . I spilled all the stuff out of one of them little bottles into the water bucket, an' I filled it up out of one of them cans.'

" 'What can?' cried the doctor. 'You'll kill somebody, you fool!'

" 'That can,' replied the negro.

"The doctor seized it. His face changed.

" 'That wouldn't hurt anybody,' he said, 'that's soda — now what bottle did you knock over?'

"And the negro pointed to the bottle of morphine."

The doctor laughed.

"That is an illustration of my theory, Flint," he said. "A pure accident saves a couple of crooks from a punishment which they doubtless well deserved. It is a body blow at Father Jerome. Luck, not conscience, saves these persons, or else Providence has again, somehow, got over on the wrong side."

There was a pathetic note in the priest's voice, as though he were endlessly weary of endeavoring to make these men see farther than the mere form and physical reality of things.

"The case is very clear," he said; " Providence interposed to save two men. One of them had seen the error of his way and was ready to reform. The other was a person who was useful to God. He

" ' Out with it ; what is it ? ' "

had cared for the poor, the distressed, and the unfortunate. He would not have done that if he had been altogether vicious. Moreover, he had promised to be guided by a sign. God gave him that sign."

"But, Father Jerome," said the doctor, "this man did not believe in God."

"Not before he was rescued from death, perhaps, but afterward — how can you say what he came to believe?"

"What one believes," said the judge, "is only important as it may come to influence what one does. It is what one does, I think, that effects the work at which the universe labors. If it be true that nature has some definite object, then it is permissible to believe that the persons who assist in realizing that object, will be taken care of by nature in the scheme of things, and that those who hinder that object, will, in like manner, be removed. This is a method to be observed everywhere in nature.

"The organ in a plant or animal which is useful or beneficial to it, nature develops and perfects; while the organ which is useless or harmful, it eliminates. It is not a violent conclusion to assume that the same method of preservation or elimination is applied to the individual. That the criminal should be overtaken and destroyed by these forces, may mean only that he is a useless or deterrent agent in the scheme of things, and nothing more than that."

"Your hypothesis is ingenuous, and it might be sound," said Dr. Lennard, "if it were not for the fact that the forces of nature seem wholly unable to discriminate when they come to deal with men. These so-called forces destroy the upright and the just, no less quickly than the vicious and the abandoned.

"I have given you one illustration which ought to have been conclusive. Let me give you another."

The doctor flung his cigarette into the fireplace, and assumed the pose and manner of a story teller.

"Most of the congregation had gone when David Talbott came out of the church. There had been a little business to transact on this Wednesday afternoon, and he had remained to speak with the class-leader. He got on his horse and began to descend the country road winding through a wood into the valley below. It was a day of early autumn. The sun lay warm on the many-colored foliage. There was silence. Nature seemed gently sinking into slumber.

"Talbott was sixty-five years old. About him was every physical evidence of a never-ceasing, rigorous conflict with the soil; his shoulders were stooped, his joints big, his hands flattened and covered with a callous like bony plates. The man bore also the aspect of a rigid economy — the economy that cannot permit the tiniest detritus.

" Everything about him spoke to the very slightest expenditure of money. His clothes were of jeans — that material which is country woven and wears like a skin. His boots were of cowhide, and hand-made by the village shoemaker. His shirt had been purchased at the country store, and was of that tough material called in the South ' hickory.' Usually he wore these shirts without a collar, but to-day, out of respect for the religious service, he had added a paper one, fastened with a detachable button, the head of which was some bright-colored composition enclosed in a brass band.

" This man represented life maintained against a mean soil that would hardly support it. But industry, a painful economy, and an exact, accurate knowledge of conditions had enabled him to advance. He owned a little farm of some fifty acres, and he was out of debt. His habit of purchasing only those things which he actually required, and paying for them in cash, and his extreme care in contracting about what he would do, had in the end established his reputation for integrity.

" When a man advances against difficulties that

beset him, in whatever avenue of life, he takes on a certain feeling of security. In him, in spite of the humility engendered by religion, there develops a deep and abiding belief that the human mind is master over the mysterious and unknown agencies with which it is forced to contend. And in his aspect the man will come to carry this egotism. Talbott rode with his legs thrust out, his chin depressed, and his face in repose. Those things which he had wrung from the soil, and the esteem in which he was held by his neighbors, had endowed him with a feeling of security.

" When Talbott turned out of the wood at the foot of the hill, he saw a man standing in the road, and beside him, drawn up on the sod, was a horse and wagon. The wagon was covered with a tarpaulin drawn over wooden bows, and within sat a woman, wrapped in a bed-quilt. Talbott knew these persons for gipsies. It was their custom in the autumn to follow this road over the mountains into the South, and to return North upon it when the winter had passed.

" Talbott nodded as he approached. The gipsy stopped him.

" ' I would trade horses, mister,' he said; ' it is a good colt, but I travel, and I require an old horse.'

" Talbott glanced over the horse which the gipsy

indicated. It was a big, iron-gray gelding; evidently young, compactly built, with short, flat, bony legs, and a deep chest. Talbott's horse was nearly fifteen years old. He saw the possibilities of this young animal, and he got down out of his saddle.

" ' I'll look at your horse,' he said.

" He went over to the wagon and began that careful examination which those who cannot afford to be mistaken are accustomed to make — that examination which scrutinizes everything, and by its sheer care eliminates the element of chance. Without the knowledge of anatomy taught in veterinary schools, this man was a judge of a horse. By long experience and by the closest observation he knew every point of the animal.

" Talbott was profoundly puzzled. The horse appeared to be sound. And yet there must be some reason why this man wished to exchange a young animal for an old one. And he began again to apply those tests upon which he was accustomed to rely. Finally he discovered the trouble; the horse was ' graveled '— that is, a tiny pebble had entered the hoof under the shoe. This was not a serious thing, but it would cause the horse to go lame until it gradually worked out through the top of the hoof.

" Talbott rose and turned to the gipsy.

" ' Your horse is lame,' he said.

"The gipsy began profuse explanations. He ran to the horse and pointed out the small hole in the hoof which Talbott had already discovered. It was nothing; the gravel would presently work out; the horse required only to be turned to pasture for a week. But for him that was impossible; he must go on; therefore he would trade — he would trade at a sacrifice — this young horse for an old one. A certain thing pressed him; he could not stop.

"What the gipsy said of the horse, Talbott knew to be true, and he would have willingly exchanged his old horse for the young one. But the evident anxiety of the man moved him to ask a bonus. And after the manner of those among whom he was accustomed to barter, he named a sum very greatly in excess of what he could hope to receive.

" 'I'll take twenty dollars to boot,' he said.

"To his astonishment, the gipsy seemed to consider this absurd demand. He began to talk, to gesticulate, to complain of the hard terms, and the situation in which he was placed, and as he talked, in his excitement he began to speak in Romany. He pointed to the woman. Talbott did not understand, but he saw that the gipsy was exceedingly anxious for this trade, and he remained firm. The man went over to the woman, they talked in Romany, excitedly and with gesticulations. Finally they got a twenty-dollar bill out of a greasy wallet; the woman held it in her hand and spoke for some time in a low voice, then the man came out into the road and handed the money to Talbott.

"Talbott took his saddle on his arm, and, leading the young horse, returned to his home.

"His little farm, with its thin, inhospitable soil, lay beside the river. Here in the early autumn there was some pasture, and he turned the horse into the field. That night, before the fire, alone in his house, he began to review the incidents of the trade. Why had the gipsy been so willing to give him this twenty-dollar bonus? These men were proverbially excellent judges of a horse; this one must have known that the young animal was superior to the older one for which he had exchanged it. And he became fearful lest this horse had some obscure defect which he had not discovered.

"He was uneasy. And very early in the morning he caught the horse and began again with that thorough, painstaking examination that excludes error. It was the eye of which he was especially fearful. And with care and with patience he made every test, and created every condition in which a hidden defect would appear, but discovered nothing. Nevertheless, he was not wholly convinced, and throughout the day, as some further experiment occurred to him, he would return, and again verify the examination which he had made. But no defect appeared. And in spite of the abiding conviction that some potent reason must exist for this extraordinary trade, he was at last convinced that the horse was sound.

" By one accustomed closely to consider the trivialities of life, no problem is abandoned. Such a one does not dismiss a puzzle that touches him at any point. His margin of gain is so slight that he dare not be involved with a thing which he does not understand, and the habit is established to remain before the enigma until its meaning appears.

" Talbott continued to consider this extraordinary trade. All day in the field, about his labors, he subjected it to a certain method of exclusion after the manner in which he had examined the horse for a defect. And one by one he dismissed those theories which seemed the less likely to contain the truth. By virtue of this proceeding he finally arrived before the suggestion that probably the twenty-dollar bill which the gipsy had so easily paid over was not good money.

" He stopped before this possibility, and certain evidences advanced to support it. Counterfeit money was associated, in this country, with the stranger, the circus, the traveling salesman, the gipsy. Moreover, the man and his wife had discussed this bill, and they had easily paid it over. Having reached this point in his consideration, Talbott's mind remained there.

"That evening when he went in from the field he got the bill from his leather wallet and scrutinized it carefully before the candle. It appeared not precisely the proper color. He laid it aside until morning, and examined it in the daylight. It seemed faded. He replaced it in the wallet, which he kept concealed in the mattress of his bed, and sat down to consider what he should do. He did not permit himself to decide upon the validity of this bill. He had the right to the security of the doubt. He had received it in the course of trade for valid money, and he had the right to so dispose of it. Moreover, the discoloration was slight, and had he not been seeking for the gipsy's motive he knew that he should not have marked it.

"The storekeeper in the neighboring village had been urging him to purchase a certain fertilizer for his field. He had refused because he had not the money and could not afford the debt. He determined now to make this purchase, and he went in the afternoon to the village. The storekeeper was pleased to agree to Talbott's proposition. He would purchase twenty dollars' worth of the fertilizer, provided the storekeeper would undertake to sell at the

store those extra bags which Talbott would not require for his field.

" ' When will you be goin' into town? '

" ' I'm expecting to go Saturday,' replied the
storekeeper.

" And Talbott promised to bring him the money
before that day.

" On Friday evening Talbott went with the twenty-
dollar bill to the village. The evenings were a bit
chill, and there was a crowd about the stove when
he entered the store. It was baiting the storekeeper.
The topic of conversation was a traveling circus, advertised to visit the village, and someone was saying:

" ' You've got to look out for that set, Andy;
they always leave their plugged half-dollars with the
country storekeeper.'

" The crowd laughed.

" ' They won't leave any with me,' replied the
storekeeper. ' I always examine silver when I take
it in.'

" ' S'pose it's a greenback? ' someone said; ' you
can't always tell about a greenback.'

" ' I can't,' replied the storekeeper, ' but the bank
can. The cashier always examines your money when
you deposit it, an' if you had a bad bill he'd stamp
it " counterfeit." Now, I always remember who I
get a bill from, an' if a man give me a bad one, I'd

go after him an' I'd make him fork over good money for it.'

" Talbott stopped. He remained a moment in the door, then he spoke to the storekeeper.

" ' I guess I won't buy that fertilizer, Andy.'

" The storekeeper was surprised and annoyed. He received a good commission on this article.

" ' You've already bought it,' he said; ' I've ordered it.'

" Talbott was now alarmed.

" ' Well,' he said, ' I've been thinkin' it over, an' I find that I ain't just exactly in a position to take it.'

" The storekeeper was insistent.

" ' You said you'd take it.'

" ' Yes,' Talbott replied, ' I thought I could manage, but things have turned out a little different from what I expected.'

" ' You mean you haven't the money? '

" Talbott hesitated. ' Well, yes, . . . that's about it.'

" The storekeeper did not continue. He went around the counter to his desk and began to write a note countermanding his order. He knew that if Talbott had not the money, it was useless to insist; such a man could not be persuaded to incur a debt. But he was angry, and when Talbott was gone out he said:

" ' Now, who'd a-thought that ol' Talbott would back out of a trade?'

" And he began to relate the incident, and to explain how definitely the transaction had been concluded. The crowd about the store, with the exception of the blacksmith, were inclined to take the side of the storekeeper. The blacksmith said:

" ' A man's sometimes disappointed about layin' his hands on money to pay for a thing, an' that's excusable. If he's got the money an' he won't stand up to his bargain, that's different. Now, I'd say that, if Talbott had the money on him, he'd be no man to back out.'

" This sound comment silenced the crowd. But the chagrin of the storekeeper over the loss of his commission remained. And that night he related the story to his wife. She said:

" ' If there's a yellow streak in a man, it'll come out when he gets old.'

" Talbott returned to his home. He was annoyed over this incident. In order to extricate himself from a purchase which he now feared to make he had in a manner repudiated his word, and he had drawn perilously near to a statement that, from one point of view, was not precisely the truth. He had not the money for this purchase unless the bill was valid.

And the certain test indicated by the storekeeper had alarmed him. In that moment in the door he had seen the danger. If the bank stamped this bill, he would have to find other money in its stead. And on the instant, without reflection, he had been forced to withdraw from the difficulty in the best way that he could manage.

" That night he reflected. He had done no wrong. He had received this money innocently and in the course of trade. He had taken it in good faith, and he was entitled to the benefit of any doubt. But deliberately to make a test such as the storekeeper indicated was neither prudent nor necessary. And it seemed to him that if the bill quietly entered the avenues of trade, other than through the doors of a bank, no one would suspect it and no one would suffer loss.

" On Monday, at work in his field, he saw a young man approaching along the road. When he drew nearer, Talbott recognized him for one who had come into the community and established a summer subscription school. This man was from a distant State; his school had closed, and Talbott was curious to know why he remained. He went down to the fence and engaged the school-teacher in conversation. He learned that the man was going about to collect certain subscriptions that were due him; when these were secured, he would set out for his home. The man complained that the persons in his debt were able to pay, and in the end would do so, but they required him to await their pleasure.

"Talbott had an inspiration. 'How much do the people owe you?' he said.

"'About twenty-five dollars,' replied the school-teacher.

"Talbott appeared to reflect. 'I might be able to help you out a little,' he said.

"And he explained that to accommodate the school-teacher he would advance him twenty dollars and take an assignment of these subscriptions.

"The school-teacher was pleased; this arrangement would enable him to set out on his journey without further delay.

"'If you have the idle money, Mr. Talbott,' he said, 'and if it won't inconvenience you, I would be very much obliged.'

"Talbott assured him that he had the money in cash; that for the present he had no use for it, and that it would gratify him to do this favor. And it was arranged that on Friday the school-teacher should come with an assignment of the subscriptions and receive the money.

"In a small country community everything is known. A few days later, when Talbott entered the village on his way to the post-office, the storekeeper stopped him.

" ' I thought you was short of money,' he said.

" Talbott, who divined some reference to the fertilizer, sought refuge in an ambiguity.

" ' Well, yes,' he said, ' I've been a little hard up this fall.'

" The storekeeper nodded his head. ' I knew it wasn't so,' he said.

" Talbott saw that the man referred to some other incident. ' What wasn't so? '

" ' That you was goin' to advance the school-teacher twenty dollars.'

" Then Talbott realized the position into which he had unwittingly entered. He made some equivocal reply and went on to the post-office. He was greatly disturbed. He saw no way out of this dilemma except to say that he found himself unable to carry out his suggestion. And, obtaining a sheet of paper and a stamped envelope from the postmaster, he wrote a letter to the school-teacher.

" There is this disadvantage in a life of integrity, that an indiscretion is all the more conspicuously marked. One does not observe a stain upon that which is already stained; it is the white background that proclaims it.

" A few days later the school-teacher came into the

village with the letter which he had received; he was disappointed, and he went about showing the letter, and explaining that Talbott had agreed to advance him the money, and had then repudiated that agreement. He had made his arrangements to depart, depending on what Talbott had said, and he complained.

"When the gossip came to the storekeeper's wife, she said, 'I always knew that ol' Talbott was crooked.'

"These two contracts from which Talbott had withdrawn after his word had been given, his conflicting statements about the possession of money, and his disingenuous excuses were discussed. Such conduct in one hitherto beyond reproach aggravated the obliquity of it, and public opinion began to reform itself upon this data.

"Without hearing it directly, Talbott became aware of this change. Such a thing is intangible, like the air, but, like the air, perceptible. He felt it moving around him, extending itself, gaining with every day.

"This change in public opinion presently became indicated in certain acts which Talbott understood, but could not resent. When, in the course of his petty trades, an element was his promise to do certain things on his part, it was suggested that the agreement be reduced to writing. And when an element was his promise to pay money, he was asked for an earnest upon the bargain. He recognized these requests as the ones which he himself had been accustomed to exact when dealing with persons not entirely to be trusted. And he recognized the excuses with which they were suggested as the very ones which he had made to the tricky and unreliable — namely, the uncertainty of life and the custom and usage of trade.

" Deeply smitten by this evident distrust, he strove to discover in what esteem he was held; and he endeavored in every way that he could to surprise this secret out of those with whom he conversed and with whom he associated. But in this he never succeeded.

" In such old, isolated communities, public opinion insinuates itself behind the amenities of life. By the word and by the manner of his neighbors one cannot learn that he has fallen. The liar will be no longer believed, and the thief no longer trusted, but he will not hear it from his neighbor's mouth. In the multitude of excuses, and in the safeguards with which his neighbor hedges himself about, it will sufficiently appear. Nevertheless, like one ill of some desperate malady, who suspects the physician of having warned his family while offering to himself consoling words, Talbott, in his manner and by the subtleties of speech, probed for the truth. But it was by accident that he found it.

"One evening in the village he passed some children at play; they spoke to him pleasantly, but when he had gone by he heard the storekeeper's little girl remark to a companion, 'You'd think ol' Talbott would be ashamed to show his face after my pap caught him in a lie.'

"Talbott went on, but the truth was now naked before him. He walked past the blacksmith's shop, out to the little house by the roadside where the shoemaker kept the village post-office. There he stopped and reflected; this matter must be somehow cleared up. It was unjust that he should be so regarded. But how could he clear it up? How could he explain? What could he say? The incidents going to establish this conclusion were all incontrovertible. And yet this opinion of him was unjust. He had been caught in a certain conjunction of events and carried forward, whither he had not willed. His theory of life had been very simple — that one received here what his acts deserved. Virtue had its reward, and its negation its reward. And over the affairs of men a Judge presided who dealt according to this rule of thumb. One controlled events. One's agency was free. What one did and what one did not were wholly matters of one's own selection. Or how else could the scheme of things be just? He had depended on this theory, and now, somehow, it had failed him.

" That night alone in his house, he sat for a long time before the fire. He was perplexed. He was like a litigant who has got an unjust decision from a judge whose integrity he cannot doubt. Such a one reviews each detail in his case with painful recurrence, seeking that aspect of it which could have influenced the court against him. And Talbott, like that litigant, believed himself the victim of some error. Certain injustices were, in this case, too clearly indicated. His conscience was not against him; he had intended no injury to any man, and he had, in fact, done no man an injury; and yet as a result of certain trivial events he would be ruined.

" And after he had gone to bed he lay a long time staring at the whitewashed ceiling. How could it happen that one questionable thing outweighed all those blameless acts that heretofore had made up the sum total of his life? He had told the truth innumerable times; he had dealt fairly innumerable times; and yet the force and virtue of this mass yielded before a single disingenuous incident, and that incident of the most trifling moment. How did it happen that such a hideous virility lay in those events that are hostile to us?

"He could not sleep, and he got up and went out onto the porch of his house. A fog was rising from the river and creeping across the field slowly toward him, and he thought how this heavy mist symbolized that sinister influence which had been let loose against him, and which he could neither seize nor resist. And the oldest explanation in the world to account for the evil potentiality of incidents otherwise slight and trifling occurred to him — that by virtue of supernal powers, and through the agency of vicious persons, petty things were sometimes charged with an influence that compelled one to an evil destiny. And he recalled all the housewives' tales and all the scraps of legend that in every community lie incrusted on this ancient belief.

"The hard common sense of the man dismissed this testimony. But that vague fear which lay at the root of this belief he could not dismiss. And, in spite of the sane conclusions of his reason, he began to associate his ill fortune with the possession of this twenty-dollar bill. Here were incidents of the family of those tales: the thing was a piece of money, and he had got it from a gipsy.

"He returned to his bed, but he did not sleep.

The suggestion remained, and he continued to regard it. The man's austere religion, rooted in the Hebrew Scriptures, accepted certain ancient legends that comprehended this idea. The ruin of men, innocent of wrong, of women, of children, of whole tribes and cities, had followed the possession of articles in themselves harmless, but charged with an evil influence. And here a suggestion presented itself, namely, that of some expiatory act. And vaguely, through the half-sleep into which he presently entered, this idea moved with the problem that disturbed him.

" The following day this suggestion took on the habiliments of fancy and withdrew. Talbott went about his labors. The health of the sun and of the air encouraged him, and he endeavored to believe that the change in public opinion had not been so great or of so wide an influence. But an event of the afternoon eviscerated this hope.

" When he came in from the field he saw a man sitting on his porch and a horse tied at the gate. The man was the Superintendent of Free Schools, and, as Talbott was a member of the district board, this call did not disturb him. The man remained during the entire afternoon. He talked with Talbott on every conceivable subject except that one which had moved him to this visit. As the hours passed, and the man's

conversation remained general, Talbott became uneasy. He knew what this subterfuge portended;
when one had a disagreeable thing to say he remained
for a long time, and always approached it after an
interminable discussion of subjects in no way related
to it. Talbott's anxiety was presently justified.

"When the Superintendent of Schools had finished
his visit and gone out to his horse, he finally said the
word:

" ' By-the-way, Mr. Talbott, the people think that
the school board ought to be made up of men who
have children to educate — naturally, a man with a
family could afford to give more of his time to school
matters; so, if you have no objection, the people
would like to have Henry Lightwood on the board.'

" Talbott was forced to express himself as satisfied
with this successor, and the Superintendent of Schools
rode away.

" Talbott was not deceived by these excuses. And
that night the idea of some sinister influence attached
to the piece of money assailed and possessed him.
The reputation which during a lifetime he had laboriously established seemed now to be attacked by a
deadly and insidious erosion. He was like one forced
to observe a bronze which he cherished, eaten by some
invisible agencies lying in the very odors of his garden. And on every occasion and at every hour he

could see the metal that once had been so hard and bright scaling from the figure, and he could see this figure, that once had been a thing of beauty, changing perceptibly into something formless.

" And the suggestion of an expiatory act returned to him with a greater force. Those visited by misfortune have in all ages believed that the authority moving events could be appeased. One brought an offering to the temple, or cast a gift into the sea. And, under forms and subterfuges, the custom remains. This man, possessed by fear, and prepared by the precedents abounding in the sacred books of his religion, moved toward this idea."

CHAPTER X: *No Defense*

THE following Sunday an itinerant minister preached at the church. This man was a sort of celebrity, who, on occasion, traveled through the country. The unrestraint of his speech and his violent and erratic manner assured him an audience. On this day the grove before the church was filled with horses; every seat in the church was occupied, and persons stood along the wall. Talbott sat on the first bench before the pulpit. He had made up his mind about what he intended to do, and when the man called upon him to take up the collection, he put the twenty-dollar bill into his hat.

" The minister rose and began to speak to the congregation while the collection went forward. In order to prick this man to some intemperate speech, it had been the custom of certain mischievous persons to put mutilated coins, tokens, and the like into his collection, and it was against this habit that he now uttered his invective. He threatened such offenders with the law. Such acts were comprehended by the criminal statutes against counterfeit money; they were felonies, punishable by imprisonment in the penitentiary. He had consulted with the authorities.

He would put up with it no longer. And with gestures and with violence he presented the terrors and the severities of the law.

"The dense crowd forced Talbott to move slowly, and as the minister spoke he was seized with terror. He had not thought of the law, and the fear of it chilled him. If this bill were counterfeit, he was on the point of committing a crime. This man would denounce him, and he would be wholly and inextricably ruined. And as the minister continued, and as he went forward with the collection, the thing which he was about to do seemed to be the very refinement of madness. Finally, appalled by the danger, as he turned the collection out on to the table he slipped the bill into his hand, and, returning to his seat, got it into his pocket. He was cold and his body was sprayed with sweat. He sat on the bench breathing deeply, like one who, with his foot extended, is plucked backward from an abyss.

"When the minister announced the result of the collection, some eighteen dollars, there was a whispering about the congregation, and when the service was concluded some persons went forward to speak with the minister. This was usual, and without giving it any attention Talbott went out with the crowd. He had got his horse, when someone came to the door and called him; when he entered there was a little crowd in discussion before the pulpit. The minister came forward.

"'Brother Talbott,' he said, 'I wish you'd look under the band of your hat; some of the congregation thought they saw a twenty-dollar bill in the collection.' And he began to explain how, when the hat was turned over, money sometimes slipped under the band and remained there.

"Talbott was appalled. He presented his hat and began to turn up the band. But nothing appeared.

"The persons standing around the minister made no comment while Talbott remained. But when he had gone out somebody said:

"'An' he's a thief, too!'

"On an afternoon of early March, Talbott rode again down the wooded hill from the country church. Beyond him the great road ran over the mountains into the South. He was on his way into some new country. He had sold his little farm, and about him, on the horse, he carried all that he possessed. At the turn of the wood he saw several covered wagons moving along the great road from the direction of the mountains. He continued to observe them now and then through the openings of the trees. Finally, at the foot of the hill, he met these wagons. As he approached, in the last team he saw his old horse that he had traded to the gipsy. He stopped. The man walking beside the wagon ran over, and, lifting the foot of Talbott's horse, began to examine it.

" ' He's got well,' he said, ' the young horse. I have sorrow to trade him.' Then he rose. ' But a child was to be born and I must get to my own people then.'

" He drew back a corner of the tarpaulin and revealed a woman holding a baby in her arms.

" Talbott was not listening to this speech; he had been getting out his wallet.

" ' I want you to take back this counterfeit money,' he said.

" The gipsy looked puzzled.

" ' What is that you say, mister?'

" Talbott presented the twenty-dollar bill.

" ' I want you to take back this counterfeit money that you gave me.'

" The gipsy came over to Talbott; he looked at the faded bill, then his face brightened with comprehension.

" ' That money, mister, it have been wet with water, but bad! no, it is good. I will give you gold.'

" And he handed Talbott two eagles.

" Now, Flint," the doctor concluded, " I should be happier if your tendency in nature had a little more discriminating intelligence. Old Talbott was not a bad citizen. Why should he have been so desperately pursued?"

"That he was pursued, Lennard," replied Flint, "is evidence of the impulse, nothing more. For my part, I think the explanation lies in the preceding illustration. The man was somehow useless to the scheme of things. My theory will bear the weight of your heel, but I am afraid your indictment is a true bill against Father Jerome's Providence."

"We do not always understand the ways of Providence," replied the priest. "There are cases which finite reason cannot follow, and we must accept their wisdom by analogy from the cases that we can follow. This, however, is not one of the obscure cases. In the first place, I do not agree with Mr. Flint, that what one does, alone, is important — what one determines to do, or what one in his heart would do if he could, is of precisely the same value. Here was a man who began by taking an unfair advantage in a trade, and who after that became fearful that he would sustain a loss; he, therefore, endeavored to tranfer that loss to another. Now, these were all contemplated wrongs, accepted by the man's conscience. In his conscience the man had surrendered to temptation, hence the Providence of God visited him with his reward."

"You have interpreted the evidence, Father Jerome," said the attorney, "with the skill of an appellate court determined to uphold a statute. I am willing to admit, with Goethe, that we are all hopelessly anthropomorphic, but not all of us to the extent which you suggest. There can hardly be an agent of an overruling authority that goes about rewarding the good, and punishing the evil. The thing is something inherent in the very order of events themselves. What that thing is, I admit that we can hardly understand. What, for instance, is the thing imprisoned in the shell of an acorn that causes it to develop into a tree. Nature is full of these tendencies, these impulses — or any name you like. Let me illustrate exactly what I mean. Get this scene before your eye:

"There was no sun. The city sat like a ghost in a shroud of dirty, yellow fog. This fog entered the court-room. The gas jets were lighted. The air, heated by these jets, was tainted with the stench of the janitor's mop. It was early in the morning. The judge, a number of prisoners who had been brought over the arched bridge from the jail, the officials of the court and a little group of young attorneys, awaiting assignments to defend those without counsel, were alone in the court-room.

" There was an atmosphere of silence. The whispering of the attorneys, the scratching of the clerk's pen, the words of the judge, the responses of the prisoners, their breathing, the moving of their feet, the creaking of their chairs as they arose and as they reseated themselves, were all sounds detached and audible in this silence. There was here no one of those things that warm and color life. The heat of passion, moving men to violence; the love of adventure; the lust of gain; the lights, the sounds, the words, the gestures — the infinite stimuli that had urged these men against the law — were absent. There was here only the presence of penalty.

" When the clerk called the State *versus* Johnson a young man arose from the line of seated prisoners. Judging by his dress, the man might have been a bank clerk. He got up slowly and stood with his chin lifted, looking at the judge. There was no interest in his face. There was in its stead a profound unconcern. His white, nimble hands, always moving, fingered his coat-pockets. It was a habit rather than a nervous gesture. The resignation in the man's face, in the lift of his head, in the pose of his figure, precluded anxiety. He knew exactly what was going to happen.

" The judge did not look up. He inquired whether the prisoner was represented by counsel, and being told that he was not appointed one of the attorneys to defend him. He continued, addressing the attorney:

" 'If you wish to talk with the prisoner you can take him into the vacant jury room; I will have a page call you before I adjourn; be ready to plead to the indictment.'

" The attorney beckoned to the prisoner and the two of them went into the jury room. The attorney sat down and indicated a neighboring chair with his hand.

" 'Well,' he said, 'what is it — not guilty?'

" The prisoner did not at once reply; he went over to the window and stood a moment, looking idly through the dirty window-panes. Then he answered.

" 'I don't care,' he said.

" The attorney was astonished. ' Do you want to go to the penitentiary?'

" The man turned sharply on his heel.

" 'No,' he said, ' I don't want to go; nobody wants to go. . . . Do you know what it's like down there? . . . It's hell down there.'

" 'Then we have got to get busy.'

" The prisoner shrugged his shoulders. The flash of energy, moving him when he spoke of the penitentiary, was past; he was again listless.

" 'Come,' said the attorney, 'we must tell the judge something.'

" 'You can tell him the truth if you want to,' replied the prisoner.

" 'Well,' said the attorney, 'cut along with the story. If there's anything in it that will do any good I'll put it up to the judge.'

" The prisoner again shrugged his shoulders indifferently.

" 'It's no use,' he said.

" The attorney was beginning to be annoyed.

" 'How do you know it's no use?'

" The prisoner sat down in a chair; he put his nervous white hands firmly on his knees. He looked the attorney in the face; a bitter resolution entered his voice.

" 'I know it very well,' he said; 'when you hear the story you'll know it, too. Listen: I'm what the police call a " dip "— that is, a pickpocket; and I'm a good one — the cops never pick me up on a job. I know my business.' He suddenly flashed his white, nimble hands. ' I can go into a jam at a railroad station and get a pocketbook whenever I want to, or I can go into a crowd any time and get a watch. There's no fly cop that can pinch me at it; they have all had a try. I pass them all up. Of course the police know I do it. You can't keep them from knowing that. But they never caught me at a job; they never could catch me.'

" ' They seem to have caught you this time,' said the attorney.

" ' They — the police! ' The prisoner made a contemptuous gesture. ' It was something bigger than the police. Did you ever hear of Scott, the man who invented the method of sawing through an iron bar with silk thread and emery dust? No? Well, when it came to brains he had us all trimmed. Scott understood it. He used to say: " Boys, it's not the police. You always have a chance against the police, but when that other Thing gets in the game you haven't got a ghost of a chance." '

" The attorney was puzzled.

" ' I don't understand,' he said.

" ' Never mind,' replied the prisoner; ' you'll understand in a minute.'

" He stopped and sat a moment with the muscles of his mouth drawn, his teeth together; then he continued:

" ' I thought Scott was dopey; I thought he was talking rot. I laughed. " All right, young man," he said; " you're too little yet for the Thing to notice you; but just you wait until you attract its attention! That Thing's on some big job; it has no time for you until you begin to annoy it. Then look out! Mind, it won't land you with a clean upper cut. That's not its method; its way is to do you with a lot of little, trivial, picayune tricks that you will mistake for a run of hard luck. It's like this: it's like an ant crawling over a man's hand when he's busy; for a good while he doesn't notice it, but when he does he knocks it off into the fire. . . . Only there's this difference; a man, when he finally did notice it, would brush that ant off into the fire at once; but this Thing takes its finger and heads the ant off here, and it heads it off there, and it steers it and turns it until it drops off into the fire itself; and every one of those turns and twists and head-offs that ant thinks is an accident." '

" He paused a moment, his slender fingers tightening on his knees.

" ' I thought Scott was giving me a line of hot air, "Everybody has luck," I said. "Sure they do," said Scott, " but this Thing's not luck — it's intention. Luck's a thing that comes by chance, but there's no chance about this Thing. Luck's an accident here and an accident there, without any connection; but this Thing's a system." '

" ' What has all this got to do with your case?' asked the attorney.

" ' I'm coming to that,' replied the prisoner. ' Listen: It was in the afternoon; the sun had brought everybody out. The snow was melting and the gutters were running full of dirty slush, but the side-walks were dry and warm. I was coming along the street. I wasn't out for business. I wasn't looking for anything. Finally I hit a crowd on the corner. A faker had a piece of black carpet laid along the sidewalk, and he was selling a mechanical toy — two little dummy figures. He'd make a speech about the wonders of science, then he'd put his mechanical toy down on this carpet, and the two little figures would begin to dance, and they'd keep on dancing — they'd dance forever. The crowd was wild. The faker was selling this toy for twenty-five cents, put up in a neat box with instructions, and they were going like gold dollars.

" ' It took me a minute to get on to his game. There was a tiny black thread stretched along this carpet, and out at the other end — on the edge of the crowd — a hobo with his hands in his pockets was working the thread. The faker just hooked his toy on to this thread, and of course it would dance until the hobo's elbow wore out.

" ' I was standing there watching this bunch of suckers take the hook when, out in the crowd, I noticed a big man with his hat on the back of his head, a cigar in his mouth, a diamond in his shirtfront, and a gold watch chain, as thick as your little finger, stretched across his waistcoat. The thing was like an invitation. I didn't have a pair of nippers on me, so I didn't go after the diamond, but I moved out into the crowd and lifted the watch. I dropped it into my pocket, edged out of the crowd and sauntered on up the street toward home. The big man never missed the watch; he was standing there spread out, with the cigar in his mouth, when I passed out of sight.

" ' I went on. As I turned into the street on which I live I met a policeman. I knew him; he was a friend of mine.

" ' " Hello, Johnson," he said, " I was looking for you."

" ' " What do you want with me? " I said.

" ' " Well," he said, " I guess I've got to take you along to the station house."

" ' I was astonished, but I kept my nerve.

" ' " Now, look here, Scally," I said, " you haven't got any charge against me."

" ' " I know it," he said.

" ' I was more astonished now.

" ' " Then what kind of a bluff are you running? " I said.

" ' " I'm not running a bluff," he said; " the chief has just issued an order for us to round-up all the old suspects and bring them down to the station house."

" ' I understood it then. Whenever a new chief

has nothing else to do he takes the census. I tried to get off.

" ' " Now, look here, Scally," I said, " what's the use of taking me down there?"

" ' " No use," he said.

" ' " Then pass me up, old man."

" ' " Can't do it, Johnson," he said; " you're on my list and I've got to account for you. If you didn't show up they'd say I tipped you off."

" ' Then he tried to smooth it over.

" ' " They've got nothing against you; they'll turn you loose in an hour."

" ' " I know that," I said, " but I'm tired of the same old questions, and the same old Bertillon measurements, and all that rot — ain't there some way round?"

" ' He shook his head.

" ' " Not this time; you're located in my district. I've got to produce you."

" ' I saw it was no use, so I tried to get him to permit me to go into my house before we started — so I could get rid of the watch in my pocket. It was only a few doors farther on. I gave him a good excuse and he would have done it, but just then a mounted sergeant came along. He knew us, and we had to start for the station house.

" ' We went out to the corner and turned down

the street that I had just come up.   We walked along until we approached the faker and his bunch of suckers.   Then, just as we were coming up to them, that big man out in the crowd suddenly missed his watch, grabbed the man who was standing next to him and began to holler.   There was a general mix-up, and someone turned in the patrol alarm.   The wagon came in a hurry.   They hustled the big fellow and the man he had nailed into it just as we came up. And Scally said to me:

" ' " It's a mile to the station house; let's ride." ' "

" The prisoner stopped.   He got up and went over to the window.   The fog lying on the city had deepened.   The million lights struggling in it seemed about to be extinguished.

" There was a knocking on the door.

" The attorney replied.

" ' All right,' he said; ' in a minute.'

" Then he turned toward the prisoner leaning on the sill, looking out over the submerged city.

" ' Well,' he said.

" The prisoner continued:

" ' We got in. . . . There's not much more. . . . I had to get rid of that watch.   The dirty slush was running deep in the gutters.   I determined on a plan. As I got out of the wagon I would make a misstep, put my right foot into the slush and let the watch slip down the leg of my trousers. I worked the watch out of my pocket into my hand, and when we stopped I stepped down, stumbled, lost my balance; my right foot went down into the slush, I caught the rail with my left hand, leaned back and let go of the watch.

" ' The next minute I knew that I was all in. In catching the band of my trousers between my thumb and finger I caught also the band of my undergarment, and the watch was in my shoe! ' "

The doctor smiled. " I quote De Goncourt," he said, " ' Fatality, which on the marble of ancient tragedies bears the name of a god, and on the tattooed brow of the galleys is called no luck.'

" Thus, when the human mind is made to entrap itself by its own careless lack of foresight, it straightway believes itself to have been pursued and overcome by some vast inevitable fate. I admit, Flint, that your explanation is more advanced than that of Father Jerome, but Father Jerome's is more comfortable and human. What advance have we made in human knowledge if we are to accept your theory in preference to that of Father Jerome? Father Jerome believes that there is a sort of cosmic constable who claps us on the shoulder and hurries us off to the lockup, when we violate the village ordinance.

But you believe that the village ordinances, in some no less mysterious manner, enforce themselves.

"Well, perhaps, in order to get rid of the impulse, the tendency, the intention, we must first get rid of the constable. Perhaps it is easier for us to put an impulse or tendency out of the window, than it would be a human officer of justice, and, if so, I am glad of your advance. But they must both go out of the window for all that. The physical universe does not take the human family or its little morals into account. If your so-called justice goes with the turn of the wheel, well and good; if not, well and good.

"Man used to believe that the universe was made for him. He now sees that it is simply the manifestation of a certain order with which nothing interferes, and if he is to exist in it, he must conform to it, since it, in no sense, conforms to him. There is truth in such words as luck and fortune. They mean that happily by inadvertence, the individual has been able to conform to the inevitable workings of this great physical machine. Taine, commenting on the philosophy of Mill said, 'Chance is at the end of all our knowledge, as it is at the beginning of all our postulates.' He meant, and the idea broadly means, that where we have not understood how we happened to adapt ourselves to the workings of nature, and, yet, without intention, we have, in fact, so adapted ourselves, we have called that luck or fortune. There is no quarrel with the terms; they are as good as any we could get, and we shall continue to make use of them until we shall have learned how to adapt ourselves precisely to nature at all points, and then we shall no longer have any use for them."

"Your idea is monstrous," said the priest. "You would have us caught in a great physical fatalism, out of which we cannot escape — a fatalism, concrete and hideous, from which honor, justice, benevolence, and every high and noble emotion of the human soul, is excluded." He arose. "It is late, and I must visit a man who is dying."

The other two men got up.

"You will take my carriage," said Dr. Lennard; "it is at the door, and you must dine with us tomorrow night. Mr. Flint will remain. He wishes to visit Druce's house, and to see the room in which the man was killed. We may have some further light on this profound mystery. You will not refuse?"

"I shall be glad to come," said the priest. "I wish to think about this unexpected legacy and why it should have been devised to me. The whole thing is a profound mystery. This man lived in fear, he died in fear, and now, he leaves his estate to God."

## CHAPTER XI: *The Pressure*

IT was Father Jerome who opened the conversation. The three men were dining alone. The priest had been late, and he supplemented his apology with a bit of explanation.

"When I left this house last night," he said, "I was surprised to find that the dying man who had sent for me, was Druce's butler. He had contracted pneumonia from his exposure on the night of Druce's death. He died at daybreak; but, before he died, in the solemnity of death, he told me that his story was all substantially true. He repeated that the cement walk before the library windows was covered with wet tracks, that there were a great many of these tracks, that the whole walk was wet. He believed that these tracks were made in blood, but he did not know this. He was running and in terror, and he could not be absolutely certain, but from the shooting, and the circumstances attending Druce's death, it is a fair inference." The priest paused, "I myself believe it to be a fair inference. The man was dying, and he certainly believed his story to be true."

"Poor devil!" said the doctor. "He did not,

after all, escape. As to his story, I have no doubt that he believed it true, but we must remember that he was drunk on that night, and hardly in a condition to distinguish between realities and allusions.

"To-day, when Flint and I were examining the room in which Druce was killed, I made a slight observation which had before escaped me. This trivial event, however, suggested an experiment. I caused this experiment to be undertaken by a local chemist, in whom I have a good deal of confidence, and I am promised his report to-night. Now, to prevent our going off at a tangent on some fanciful theory, I would prefer to wait until I have the promised report, and then put the whole matter before you."

"I am glad you make that suggestion, Lennard," said the judge. "I have obtained a good deal of data from my inquiries, which put together, ought to give us this man Druce's history. I lack the confirmation of my conclusions, which I am promised at some time this evening. A reply to my telegram ought to arrive at any hour. I gather from Dr. Lennard's suggestion, that his experiment will likely throw some light upon the manner in which Druce met his death."

"I think," replied the doctor, "that my experiment will clear up that part of the mystery, but I cannot be certain, and I do not want to go into the subject until I have the result of the experiment. However, I venture to assert that the ultimate agency behind Druce's death is the very thing that we were discussing last night."

"You mean," said Father Jerome, "that his death was brought about by the Providence of God?"

Dr. Lennard smiled. "You are pleased to call it the Providence of God," he said. "Mr. Flint has another name for it, while I venture to call it by still a third name. There seems, in fact, to be no adequate name for it. Of course, when I say that we do not agree upon a name for this thing which visits the criminal with punishment, I do not mean to assert that we, in any sense, differ about the innumerable and varied agencies by which this result is accomplished. The jeopardy of the criminal agent does not lie exclusively in the fact that he overlooks or fails to foresee some relation of events. Often the greatest jeopardy to the criminal lies in the peculiarities, the tendencies, and the delusions of his own mind."

"Now, there," said Father Jerome, "you come strongly to my aid. I have said that the Providence of God has to do with the conscience of man, and it is through the medium of the criminal's mind, that the Providence of God, perhaps oftenest brings him to punishment. I was afraid last night that I had not made this point clear, and I have been anxious to support it with a further illustration."

They went from the table into the library, and over the coffee, the priest began his story.

" As the days passed after the tragedy, the thing that impressed the man was the ease with which he had escaped all those jeopardies which are supposed to attach themselves to a criminal agent. His story had been accepted for the truth; the evidences which he had hastily manufactured has sustained it, and public imagination, always responsive to suggestion, had supplied the gaps.

" In the first hideous realization of his act his impulse had been to hide himself and escape. He now recalled that impulse with a shudder. Had he acted upon it, he would now be a fugitive, hunted by the law, and sentenced to a life of disguises. But he had had time for reflection.

" The little farmhouse stood back from the country road. The two men lived alone in it. No one had observed the tragedy. Carpenter's plan was the oldest and commonest subterfuge — what is known in criminal trials as the ' straw man ' or the ' mysterious stranger ' defense. The evidences, which he had hastily arranged, were slight — some tracks made

14          199

with an old boot and the like — but public imagination had come forward to their support. A woman of the neighborhood had seen a stranger crossing the fields, and as a discussion of the tragedy proceeded, her fancy supplied what her memory lacked. Children had also reported fresh tracks in the dust of the road.

" What the woman had seen was Smith Hinkle on his way to the country store in a direction entirely opposite. And the tracks in the dust were those of the Widow Dix's negro, Mose, driving a cow. But they were enough to corroborate Carpenter's evidences. Moreover, thus stimulated, other persons fancied that they had seen the assassin, or nearly seen him, and little thefts, depredations and the like became violences which this mysterious stranger had committed on the way.

" If there had been a suspicion of Carpenter he had silenced it by his zeal in the search for the assassin and the one hundred dollars, which he had deposited with the prosecuting attorney, as a reward for any information that would lead to the arrest of the murderer.

" Another thing about which Carpenter had had a good deal of apprehension, proved to contain no substantial danger for him. The teachings of the common religion and old wives' tales pictured the murderer as tortured by conscience and harassed by obscure and mysterious agencies set on plucking his secret out of him. But nothing of this sort appeared in his experience. The only terror that he had felt was at the time of the tragedy when he realized the danger of his position, and his anxiety of conscience was always inseparably allied to some fear of discovery. When events fortunately shaped themselves to remove that fear, they removed also this anxiety.

"The evidences of this torture, so vividly set forth by the preacher and the housewife, such as sleepless nights and the like, were also merely the attributes of this particular fear, and did not exist apart from it.

"All the other properties of these tales were sheer, lurid imaginings. He was glad to make this discovery, for while one might believe these dangers to be mere creatures of the fancy, one could not be certain until one actually entered the country in which they were said to exist.

"There is a certain profound sense of comfort following the day in which one has escaped out of deadly peril. It is like the pleasurable languor of convalescence — one is at peace in a certain large and generous fashion. It was in this peace, with its sense of security, that Carpenter smoked a pipe on the little porch before his house. It was an evening of early autumn. A thin sun lay on the brown fields. The sky was almost without a cloud. And there was silence.

" In this intense stillness Carpenter heard the creak of a wheel on the road. It was a long distance away, hidden by the wood through which the lane entered to his little farm. In the first days after the tragedy the sound of a horse, the rumble of a wheel, had filled Carpenter with apprehension. But now he was not disturbed by this creak. He was like one who has passed a night in a haunted room, and has about him the security of daylight. But before that, the creak of this wheel, heralding the approach of someone whom he could not see, and charged perhaps with a jeopardy that he could not divine, would have been a thing ominous and sinister, like the sound of footsteps moving about one in that haunted room.

" The sound approached and presently a one-horse buggy turned in from the wood and stopped before the house. A little old woman got down, tied the horse to the paling fence with one of the lines, and came up the path. She wore a black alpaca dress and a black sunbonnet tied under her chin, and although she was nearly seventy, she stepped along with vigor and decision. She had a beady, hazel eye and that curious expression which cannot be translated, but which is to be observed on the faces of persons of fanatical energy, and the violently insane.

"Carpenter prepared to meet his sister the moment the horse appeared. He knew that she came with some dominating idea that no one could turn her aside from, and his plan now, as always, was to conciliate and get rid of her.

"She began to talk before she reached the house.

"'Dan'el,' she said, 'I want you to get right on your horse and go to town.'

"'What for?' he replied.

"'There's a man there who can find out who killed Adam.'

"'Who's the man?' said Carpenter.

"She stopped in the path and drew down her chin.

"'Professor Leon Surey, that's his name. He's stoppin' at the Valley House.'

"Carpenter recognized the name. He took the county newspaper and he had seen the advertisement of this traveling clairvoyant.

"He went into the house and brought out a chair. The woman sat down and pushed back the sunbonnet.

"Carpenter was relieved. He feared for a moment that the prosecuting attorney might have sent to the city for one of those mysterious persons called a detective, of whom he had sometimes read in his newspaper. He was not afraid of this clairvoyant, who came now and then to the county seat, like the traveling dentist. The sane common sense of the man rejected a belief in supernatural powers.

" ' How's he goin' to find out? ' he said.

" ' Well,' replied the woman, ' ain't he got second sight, an' don't he get messages from the spirits? Can't he ask Adam who done it? '

" Carpenter answered, indicating some doubt. And the old woman began a recital, in detail, of all those persons who had visited the clairvoyant and received messages from the departed. These messages were vague and Delphic — the sort of formula that any disaster or fortune would fit into. But when that disaster or that fortune arose the person remembered the message and believed himself to have received intelligence of it through the medium of this clairvoyant.

" As the old woman talked her voice took a higher key and the curious expression on her face became more pronounced. It appeared that she had gone about the country to visit these persons, and that she had discussed her plan with everybody in the neighborhood. When she had finished her recital of these instances, she imperiously swung back to her first command.

" ' Now then, I want you to get right on your horse an' go to town.'

" Carpenter began to make some excuses. He wasn't certain there was any good in it. He would go another day or the like.

" The old woman entered upon a violent tirade. What was the matter with Carpenter? Why did he want to delay? Was it possible that he did not wish to learn who had killed Adam? What was back of his objections and excuses? Well! She would find out! If he did not go, the people would know the reason why. Everybody said he ought to go. It would be mighty strange if he did not. The people would talk. They would say that he was afraid to go, and so forth, with violence and with gesticulation.

" Carpenter saw the danger in this. It was evident that his sister had already talked the matter over with the whole community, and that she would continue to talk. He knew how ridden she became with any idea that possessed her, and in her eye and face he saw the exaggeration of that insane violence that had stained his own hands with the blood of his fellow.

" He knew that no consideration or common sense would prevail over the dominion of this idea that she had got into her head. Moreover, he saw to what end suspicion might lead if she should start it on its way. It was clear that she did not realize the import of the words which she had uttered, but in her zeal, she would repeat them, and the suspicion which he had evaded, might double back on him.

" He saw this while the old woman lashed about in her monomania, and he hastened to reassure her. He could not reach the county seat that night; it was already late, but he would go the following day. And he began to speak of the hope of learning something about the mysterious assassin, and how anxious he was to bring this man to justice and the like. And out of his experience, and by various indirections, he was finally able to conciliate the woman, and so get rid of her. But he knew only too well that she would adhere to her idea and that his visit to the clairvoyant was inevitable.

" Carpenter had no difficulty finding the clairvoyant. There was a square piece of white oilcloth painted with black and red letters, hanging before one of the windows of the hotel. This sign, which Professor Surey could fold and carry about with him, repeated in flamboyant language exactly what was set out in his printed advertisement, with the addition of certain signs and pictures, which were intended to indicate some mysterious association of astronomy and the human hand.

"Carpenter tied his horse to the hitching-rack before the hotel door and went in. The clairvoyant received him in a room somewhat darkened by having the blinds drawn down. He was a little fat man, with a great shock of gray hair that curled on his shoulders, and protruding myopic eyes. He seemed to know the story of the tragedy as current in the community, and he began to discuss it, walking up and down the room, but stopping at intervals to thrust out his short neck and fix Carpenter with his protruding eyes.

"His profession had made him a judge of human nature, and the essentially delicate requirements of it had educated him to question his visitors with great skill and finesse. He drew out of Carpenter all the details of the tragedy, and he seemed to put these details into a certain order, and to weigh them upon certain theories, as an occasional question touching upon some obscure point indicated. He managed this with a fine evasion, so that his visitor seemed to take little or no part in the conversation. His questions were never direct, and the replies of the visitor seemed to be a sort of gratuitous comment: the very base of his profession rested upon his ability thus to arrive at the obscure moving impulses of his visitor, since it was upon his skill here that he depended for the material for his Delphic utterances. He interlarded this talk with a discourse on the persistence of human identity after death. He said there was no doubt about this as the Scriptures and innumerable evidences proved it. But he said that the medium in which one found himself after death was certainly unlike our present physical environment, and, consequently, it was only with difficulty and at certain favorable moments, that such an one could get into communication with the living.

"This was another arm of his profession upon which his bread hung, and he managed it with the nicest judgment. He avoided extravagancies. He examined doubts fairly. He joined the visitor in his own beliefs. He drew his persuasive cases from the life which the visitor knew, and from the things which he had faith in, and in his manner he was conciliatory and convincing. His whole object was to make the subject feel that he had found a powerful friend who intended to do all that he could to help him, and nothing more than that.

"Carpenter was very much surprised. He had expected to find a blatant fortune-teller, and here was a reasonable man, who seemed to be honestly concerned with a certain kind of experiment. Carpenter did not believe in the experiment, but he was not so sure as he had been, and if he could have managed he would have avoided a test. But the clairvoyant had already made his preparation for it.   He had gone behind a curtain that divided the room, and came out with a small, thick slate.

"He wiped the face of this slate with a little moistened sponge, that was attached to the frame by a string.   Then he sat down in a chair and put the slate between his knees.   He explained that he had experimented with the various devices used for communicating with those in the spirit world, and had found the slate to give the best results.   He asked Carpenter to be silent and to concentrate his mind on the dead man.

"For some time there was absolute quiet.   Then, in the intense stillness, Carpenter heard a faint scratching as of a pencil on a slate.   It continued for a moment and then ceased.   The clairvoyant, without looking at the slate, handed it to Carpenter and told him to take it to the window and see what was written on it.   Carpenter drew back the corner of a blind and examined the slate.   There were five faint wavy lines that seemed to form words, and below them a hieroglyphic.   As Carpenter turned the slate about, the clairvoyant spoke.

" ' Can't you make it out? '

"Carpenter replied that the writing was too indistinct to be read.   The clairvoyant explained that this was not unusual at the first effort, and they must try again. He told Carpenter to wipe the slate with the little sponge, and return it to him. Carpenter sponged the slate clean and took it back to the clairvoyant.

" In the silence that followed, the scratching sound as of a pencil was more distinct, and when Carpenter took the slate to the window the fine faint lines seemed to have come out into words, and the hieroglyphic to have arranged itself into a letter. He could now read the message:

" ' You are in great danger.— A.'

" Carpenter looked quickly around, but the clairvoyant sat with his head down and his arms hanging like a man exhausted. Carpenter hesitated, then he wiped the slate with the sponge.

" ' It's just the same,' he said.

" The clairvoyant got up. He said that this sort of experiment was very hard on the medium, and that he was too tired to make another effort this day, but that if Carpenter would come back he would try again. He said that Carpenter was not to consider this result as a failure. It indicated that the dead man was making an effort to communicate with him. He thought that the trouble was that Carpenter had not himself settled upon any one clear, distinct inquiry; that if he would now determine upon a single question, and think about that question alone, and continue to think about it, he would be very apt to get a reply at the next sitting. He explained that no one understood why this mental effort of the living helped the spirit to get the message through, but it evidently did help, as though it somehow wore a thin spot in the invisible partition that divided the two worlds.

"All the way home and that night alone in his house, Carpenter continued to think of this extraordinary message. He was profoundly disturbed. The thing was against nature, against his judgment, and against his common sense; and yet, there it was. He had seen it. And, moreover, he alone had seen it. The clairvoyant believed the experiment to be a failure. But he knew better. And he began to consider the stupendous fact. He recalled what his sister had said, and he began to review all the cases which she had brought forward. Why, after all, did we consider this communion so impossible? The whole world believed that the spirits of men persisted after death. And these dead men, wherever they might be, would they not strive endlessly to communicate with the living?

"The idea overpowered him and he went out of his house and stood looking up at the stars. The night was clear and the vast spectacle impressed Carpenter as it has impressed all men since the beginning.

What mysteries lay among the stars! He had been told that each one of them was a world like our own. There were millions, then, of vast turning worlds, swimming in that infinite ocean of space. On which one of them were these innumerable dead men? And he wondered how much that is hidden from us, these dead men knew. And if they labored to reach the living, might they not, in their larger wisdom, find a way? And he was oppressed and disturbed by this idea.

" But more than anything else he was shaken by the substance of this message. At the very hour when security was assured, when there was no danger, when suspicion had gone by him, this warning had arrived. There was terror in that. What was it that the dead man saw creeping upon him? He could not sleep, and through the night and the day that followed, he never ceased to consider it. And he never ceased to review all the incidents of the tragedy, and every event that followed, in the hope that he might come upon a clew to this danger, but in this he never succeeded. The idea that this peril was a thing which the dead man alone could see seized and appalled him, and he began to feel like one who is being trailed by an invisible enemy — like a traveler in the night, who is followed by a beast of prey. And he thought how the dead man saw him in his fancied security, and this peril on its way, as he had seen some little animal at sport in the sun, while the hunter dog crept upon it.

" All this moved the man to a conclusion. If he would know what this peril was, he must inquire of the one who had warned him. The one who had sent the message alone could interpret it. The clairvoyant had asked him to return, and there appeared no danger in so doing. He need not disclose his inquiry. And if there was a message he could again erase it.

" Nevertheless, he did not go at once to the county seat. The natural caution of the man and his strong, practical instincts held him back. But a secret fear is a thing difficult to resist; it waxes and wanes, but it never ceases, and in the end one flees, or confesses, or accomplishes some bizarre act under its pressure. In the night Carpenter would go, and in the day he would not. But the fear that every hour, night and day, this peril approached and increased, overcame him and he returned to the clairvoyant.

" He came to this second experiment prepared as the man had directed. A single precise inquiry possessed him, had consumed and occupied him unceasingly. What was this danger? If there was a gain to be got from that mental state, surely now he would receive it. He had followed the clairvoyant's direction, in this behalf, more desperately than the man could dream of. He had burned his soul with this query, and the result of that labor presently appeared. When he carried the slate to the window the writing upon it was now clearly legible.

" ' It will be found; hide it again to-night.'

" This time Carpenter was prepared to act his part. He turned the slate about, peered at it, held it a little closer to the light, and accomplished the acts and manner of one who puzzles over a cipher.

" Finally he announced that the writing was illegible, wiped the slate clean, and returned it to the clairvoyant. A second and a third experiment produced only formless lines. These Carpenter showed to the clairvoyant. The man seemed discouraged, and Carpenter presently departed."

## CHAPTER XII: *The Thief*

HE knew what the message meant. The only thing that he had hidden was the old boot with which he had so fortunately made the tracks in the soft earth near the spring-house. The other things, the implements with which the deed had been accomplished, he had left beside the body. This message touched, then, upon the vital evidence. These tracks had turned suspicion from him. The discovery, now, of that old, unused, mildewed boot would falsify this evidence and destroy him.

"He smoked his pipe by the fire and waited for the night to deepen. He felt a sort of nervous dread. To touch anything relating to the tragedy was like going back into it. He put out the pipe and stood for some time before the fire. The bright moon outside and the noises of the night disturbed him. He listened and moved about on tip-toe. Finally he went out, got a spade, removed the boot from the hollow tree in which he had concealed it, crossed to the wood which circled the house at some hundred feet, and there buried the boot in the earth.

"Then he hurried fearful to the house. His grotesque, changing shadow seemed to pursue him, and he was afraid to look behind him, as a child apprehensive of ghosts is afraid. But once inside his house he felt secure, like one who has summoned courage to go down in the night and lock an open door against a robber. And he slept.

" The following day the timeliness of his act was strikingly verified. When he came in from the field at noon, he saw a man walking about the premises, and a horse tied at the gate. He stopped, and his heart raced as he recognized the sheriff of the county. The dead man had known what was on the way. Here was the one who would have found the hidden article. How narrowly he had escaped! By a night only! And with a sort of awe he thought of the strange and varied events that had moved together to save him. How they had forced — driven him, and how he had yielded only in the scantiest time!

" His apprehension was at once allayed by the sheriff's explanation. He had come out to collect some delinquent taxes, and the prosecuting attorney had said to him:

" ' If you happen to run across Dan'el Carpenter, tell him to ride in with you. I want to see him.'

" The casual and contingent nature of this direction restored Carpenter to composure. The prosecuting attorney doubtless wished to return to him the one hundred dollars which he had deposited as a reward for the assassin.

"He got his horse and returned with the sheriff to the county seat. The prosecuting attorney's office was in the courthouse, and Carpenter attached no significance to the fact that the sheriff went in with him. The outer office of the prosecuting attorney was empty, but someone who contended was speaking in the private office.

"'Well! Didn't I earn the hundred dollars? . . . I thought there was something fishy about the ol' man's story, an' I took a chance pop at him. . . . When he rubbed out my fake message an' lied about it, I knew he was the man. Then I came to you. You said the tracks bothered you, an' I said he might have made them himself, an' hid the boot. . . . Well! I took another crack at him on that theory. . . . Easy money! . . . What! Didn't I sit out there in the woods all night?'

"Carpenter lifted himself up stiffly on his toes; then he turned like an animal in terror. But there was a sharp click and a hand-cuff snapped on his wrist.

"Now, here," said the priest, "is a conclusive illustration of how God's Providence forced a criminal to confession through the medium of his own mind."

" The word forced," said the lawyer, " is well used. The man was ' pressed,' but not, I think, merely through the medium of his mind. He was pressed from every side by a perfect sequence of events. There could be no clearer illustration of the fact that there is abroad in the universe, an impelling intent in all human events to accomplish and establish justice, and these events press upon the criminal from all sides, invisible like the air."

" On the contrary," said Dr. Lennard, " the case merely illustrates what I have just said. That the jeopardy to the criminal agent lies in no slight degree in the structure and tendencies of his own mind. In spite of all that we can discover, the human mind remains profoundly mysterious. All men have delusions of some sort, and often pronounced delusions along certain lines. It seems also to be a fact, that if the criminal continues to consider a secret crime, the effect will be, that in the end, he will accomplish some bizarre act that will lead to his ruin. The mind is often unbalanced and destroyed by the constant consideration of some dominating idea. If this idea is attended by fear, the mind may finally become possessed of the most extraordinary delusions. Various forms of insanity are developed, all of which have been classified and studied by alienists. Criminals come to believe themselves pursued. They believe themselves to see their victims. Delusions of persecution arise and all forms of extraordinary mania.

" But I do not see in all of this proof that the forces of the universe's moving events are, in any sense, moral.  On the contrary, it often happens that through chance, accident, or the like, a rogue is injured, when there is no intent apparently, on the part of anybody to injure him.  A college mate of mine when he was a young doctor in Paris, had an experience that illustrates this point.  I give it to you in his own amusing words.

" I had to get out of Paris.  There was no train that would set me down at the coast by five o'clock of the morning.  But Monsieur Delcasse, the pleasantest buccaneer in France, who maintained Le Garage Continental, solved the problem for me.

" ' With a racing car, M. le Docteur, and Jacques le Rouge to drive it, one could be in Paradise by morning; that is to say, if the road was open, and there was petrol to be had along it.'

" And he rubbed his hands and smiled as I think Kidd used to smile on the Spanish main.

" ' But can a man drive this car all night ? ' I said. ' It is a long journey, and I shall travel fast.'

" ' A man ! ' echoed Monsieur Delcasse, ' perhaps

a man could not, but Jacques le Rouge is not a man, M. le Docteur, he is a *thing.*'

"And the proprietor of Le Garage Continental shrugged his shoulders and looked up at the sky. If he could have seen them, I would have believed that monsieur was counting up the stars. But it was not the stars that Kidd's successor was counting up.

"'M. le Docteur will need a great coat — I have it here; and goggles — I have the very best in Paris. See, monsieur, the fur keeps the dust out, and the mesh lets the air go in so they do not cloud.'

"I knew upon what Monsieur Delcasse reckoned, he must be careful. How he would sorrow this night in his bed, if now, by inadvertence, he should overlook a thing that I might be charged for.

"Then, when he had got the items grouped together, I put the question which Monsieur Delcasse had been buttressing himself about to meet.

"I thought he would weep upon my shoulder when the words were out. Things were going to the devil in his trade. There was a time when one could live, but now Americans brought their own cars with them as one brings his luggage. Who was there to hire a great racing car like this one? And he stroked the hood lovingly and ran his fingers over the bulging eyeglass of the lamp, every piece like the jewel in a watch, and all as smooth as the inside of an artery.

But it could not sit idle in his shop, and he could not die of hunger — a thousand francs!

"I told him plainly that I would not pay it.

"The Theâtre Française has not seen a thing to equal what followed after that. I would be the death of him. I would drive him this very night into the Seine. He had little children, they would be orphaned. And he plucked his hair as though he would root it out. Had M. le Docteur ever heard little children cry? Well, one could not coin one's blood to feed them — eight hundred francs then!

"And what could I do? When one is a poor devil of a doctor, and his richest patient — to whom dollars are as the sands on the seashore for multitude — telegraphs him to meet his yacht at daylight, shall one yield to the perversities and evil circumstance of a continental railroad, or shall he gird himself about with resource and triumph over them? And shall the one who obeys, count the cost too closely when the one who commands does not at all count it?

"In the twilight we slipped out of Paris, the lean gray car sobbing like a mastiff choked down with leashes. We glided through the maze of cabmen in their black shiny hats, around the trucks, and the great Norman horses. And so escaped out of that city of good-natured and pleasant sin. I turned about in Monsieur Delcasse's goggles, and looked back. Beware of Paris! One feels there, like Mr. Nash in the 'Tragic Muse,' that he ought now to be bad in some larger and more gracious fashion.

"We crossed the Seine, and took the great road to the sea. I do not know this road, nor any road that we followed on this night. Monsieur Delcasse had traced it out among his maps, and I left it to him as one leaves the high roads of the ocean to a pilot. Jacques le Rouge wagged his red head above the maps and put down his greasy finger now and then upon a line, and grinned, and I had stood twiddling my thumbs like a helpless soul by Charon.

"Paris dwindled into a nest of lights. Jacques le Rouge shifted his levers and the great car thundered out upon its journey, a red glow under its hood, the exhaust cracking like musketry, and the engine humming like a million bees. Cottages, farmyards and forests flashed by. The solid earth and the realities thereof, departed out of life. We entered, upon this monster, into a land of wonders. The road was the pale wake of some fleeing star, and in cloud and haze and darkness, we followed hard upon it. Not alone, for like demons swarmed upon this phantom highway. We stole upon them and flitted on, and they bore down upon us with their great lidless eyeballs glowing like a furnace,

222

and crashed by. . . . Forms and images and fig-
ments from the world I knew, traveled on this road.
They appeared, and they were not. I could not tell
you where they went to. We seemed to cut away the
air beside them, and they seemed to fall behind us
into some abyss. Sometimes the demon that we
rode on screamed, and strained backward on its
haunches, or shot out into the darkness or tilted
on some ghostly curve. And I remembered how
Monsieur Delcasse had said that with Jacques le
Rouge to drive, we could reach Paradise by morning. Morning! Somewhat earlier, I thought a
thousand times upon this journey. Why, the miscal-
culation of an inch, the delay of a millionth second,
would have sent us crashing into that Blessed City.
But Jacques le Rouge never failed of that inch or
that millionth second; his hands moved and they were
timed like the explosions in the cylinders. Monsieur
Delcasse was right, he was a *thing*!

" We stopped for petrol. I don't know where it
was, but I think it was somewhere in one of A.
Lang's colored fairy books, for there came an obsequious goblin to the door. Petrol! One would
have thought that he distilled it out of orchids. He
had not a liter. He had sold the very stains and
odors. . . . But stay! There was a car housed
there for the night; the tank was full; he would

steal the petrol out of it. Alas, how crude the Saxon is when he would gain a little upon a bargain!

"We waited for this felony to be accomplished. Wherefore is it that the upright and the just so cheerfully enter into any criminal commerce when they would avoid the customs or the asperities of travel? I had sat in the churches, from my youth upward, with the righteous. I knew the decalogue, and before me was the example of the saints. And yet if this roadside goblin had bid me wait until he killed a man and bled the petrol out of him, I should have put back Monsieur Delcasse's goggles and got out my wallet.

"We went on then, whipping death around the homing peasant and his cart, and through the empty villages and across the provinces of France, a Nibelungenlied demon that leaped out of the darkness, yelled, and vanished.

"But it is not my object to describe this journey. There is an adventure in this tale and I must get along to it.

"It was an hour of midnight by the clock when we entered some little city. I counted the strokes tolled out in the darkness. And upon the interval between them I could have reckoned up our speed. I hardly heard the first stroke, it was so far away, and the last boomed from a tower above our heads.

.We had not been over-considerate of any burgo-master's road rules, and I thought we would have shot through this nest of spectral gables somewhat like Monsieur Verne's celestial cartridge. But not so. Jacques le Rouge pulled up, made a turn or two about the cobbled streets and stopped before an inn.

" 'M. le Docteur,' he said, 'there is oil on the magneto, I shall have to take it off and clean it. We shall be here two hours.'

" ' Two hours!' I gasped, ' and the coast to make by five!'

" The reply of Jacques le Rouge was like the pronouncement of some fate.

" 'M. le Docteur shall be there by five,' and then he added, ' M. le Docteur dies of hunger. He shall be served the best dinner to be had in France.'

"Was the secret out in that final sentence, or had this steel beast, in fact, some trouble with his viscera? I could not know that! I have no knowledge of such creatures, and the anatomy of man would hardly guide me. In the meantime, since I needs must sit here two hours, it were foolish to go hungry. I had got only a crust in Paris, and I could have eaten St. Peter's sheet full of unclean beasts.

" I got down. I shall not describe that inn, it is to be found in any romance of the Louis', but it is also to be found in France if one travels toward the coast on a night with Jacques le Rouge. The inn was empty, but the host spread me a white cloth and sat me down before it, and I sipped a glass of liqueur while the dinner cooked.

"I was stretching my legs, when a stranger bowed to me in the doorway. He was tall and lean, his clothes were shabby, and I have not seen so villainous a face. It was webbed with little purple veins, the jaws were gaunt, the mouth was slack and the hollows below the eyes were puffy. There was a thin wiry beard trimmed into a point, with a long blue scar lying beneath it along the jaw. But the man was neat and clean, and he had the manner of a Brummel. He carried a little volume under his arm, very carefully and with evident concern, as though it were a sort of treasure.

"'I trust that I do not intrude upon Monsieur,' he said, 'but we are two gentlemen, and it is dull to dine alone.'

"I was taken with a certain fancy. The creature was so evidently upon the very curbstone of the gutter, and yet he carried that estate with so suave an air that one must admire him. I got upon my feet, made the best bow I could, and invited him to share my dinner.

"He put out his hands with a gracious gesture.

"'Ah, monsieur,' he said, 'the courtesy of your

nation is so direct. You have forestalled me. I was about to ask that very condescension of monsieur. This is my country, I would be the host.' And he bowed again.

"I could have laughed. There were not the evidences of a sou about him, and he had determined that I should provide his dinner, and yet, for all that, he drew me into a contest upon the point, and forced me to insistence, and finally gave way to me like one who condescended, with a gentle fillip of the fingers, and:

"'I cannot struggle with monsieur!'

"He dropped into the chair before my table, and put down his little volume on the cloth. He touched the leather cover lovingly.

"'We have it from Homer,' he said, 'that life is a struggle and a hell.' He sighed. 'And is it not so, monsieur? You see before you a poor gentleman, the Viscount de Champderien, fallen somewhat upon evil days, but of the oldest stock in France.' Then an idea struck him and he interrupted the confession. 'I can do monsieur a trifling service out of a special knowledge of what these inns afford.'

"He called the host to him, inquired what I had ordered, and revised it like one accustomed to dine upon the best. The host took this direction with a certain care for he saw my purse behind it, but without that vision, I think he would have thrown the viscount through the window.

"'Monsieur travels out of Paris!' he added. Then he paused, 'Paris!' and lifted his face as before an idol, 'thou art beautiful!'

"He remained a moment in this ecstasy.

"'Pardon, monsieur, these are the words of the thirteen who cast themselves down into the City of Brass, that wondrous city which the Emeer Moosa found in the mountains of Arabia by following the directions written in the Book of Hidden Treasure. But not the Emeer Moosa alone has visited this enchanted city . . . you and I have been there. It is Paris!'

"He clasped his hands together on the cloth.

"'The parallel, monsieur, is no subtle riddle. Who can open a gate of Paris from without? And who can see that the maidens "like moons" are illusions until he is as old as the Sheik Abd-Es-Samad. And then, monsieur, believe me, he can only do it by "repeating the praises of God, and reciting the Verses of Safety"!'

"He laughed, and beckoned the innkeeper to set on the wine. It was a wine with little globules of sunlight in it, and there was fungus on the cork.

"'I have ordered a bottle of the best,' he said, with a courteous inclination of the chin and a movement of his extended fingers.   'Monsieur, I think, is accustomed to no other.'

"The thing could not have been done like that in any land but France, and what vagabond but a Latin could have thus neatly forced me to purchase a king's wine for his gullet.   I took it with the best face.

" 'The oldest is yet too new,' I said, ' for the entertainment of the Viscount de Champderien.'

"He bowed, raised his glass, tasted the golden liqueur and put it down.

" 'Monsieur does me too much honor,' he murmured, ' and yet I am glad that the Viscount de Champderien is to go out of the world, as he came into it, with something of the best about him.'

" 'To go out of the world!' I echoed.

"He sighed.

" 'Yes, monsieur, and not to be found again, in the pasture land of horses, as Homer says it, or upon the back of the wine-red sea. . . . Ah, monsieur,' and he caressed the little volume, ' there has been no poet in the world but Homer.'

" 'When does the viscount make this exit?' I said.

" 'Why, monsieur,' he answered, ' upon this very night, and, like Elpenor whom Odysseus left dead in the hall of Circe, unwept and unburied.'

"I was curious to know what the creature meant.

Nothing was beyond him. I think he had not eaten this day, his clothes were about to fall to pieces, and from every corner and aspect of the man he had not the resources of a beggar. Life for him, as he had quoted from Homer, was clearly a struggle, and one that he was hardly in condition to continue. Some bizarre plan to end it was not unlikely. This ornate speech was not indigenous to me, and the ugly suggestion shocked me into the crudities of my native tongue.

" ' You would kill yourself? ' I said.

" One would have thought that I had touched him with a whip-lash. He shrugged his shoulders and wrinkled up his face.

" ' Ah, monsieur,' he answered, ' *la langue anglaise!* It is so abrupt. It is the language of violence, those who despised the courtesies and the tendernesses of life have made that language, and they have named things with outrageous names. . . . Monsieur has doubtless marked this difference between the speech of the Saxon and that of the Latin peoples. When an act is to be described, the former makes one see the ugly realities of it, while the latter makes one feel its soul. . . . I have thought to write a thesis upon this, monsieur,' he added, ' but I have been much occupied with lighter matters.'

" The viscount was interrupted by the innkeeper with his platters. But he went on while the plates were laid.

" ' Monsieur's remark does nearly comprehend the idea in a certain fashion, but not quite. The Viscount de Champderien is to depart this evening out of life, but not gibbering to the fields of asphodel, as Homer says it. . . . And the exit is to be effected by my hand, but not in blood, nor by Artemis with a visitation of her gentle shafts. *Tiens!* I shall this night assassinate the Viscount de Champderien, but I shall not die with him. *Comprenez-vous?* '

" I understood then, the scoundrel was about to change his name, and I laughed.

" ' But why,' I said, ' should the viscount be thus foully murdered. He is of the oldest stock in France?'

" He stroked his beard.

" ' I will tell you, monsieur, the viscount is too unlucky. I cannot afford to have him with me any longer. I struggle, I labor, I make a little entry into fortune, and by some ridiculous faux-pas he ejects me out of it. He is a child of Saturn, this Viscount de Champderien. His destiny is evil. . . .'

" ' Does monsieur believe in destiny? . . . He does not. Well, Homer did. " A man shall endure," he said, " such things as the stern spinning women drew off the spindles for him at his birth, when his mother bare him. . . ." And Herodotus believed it. "Amasis," he wrote, "having read the letter that came from Polycrates, felt persuaded that man could not rescue man from the fate that awaited him." And Cambyses said: " It belongs not to human nature to avert what is destined to happen."

" ' Monsieur, this was the wisdom of the ancients. And it is out of this wisdom that I shall take the viscount's life. I have labored with him as Amasis labored with Polycrates. But he is fated to those seizures of ridiculous misfortune, and he must perish.'

" He sat back to permit the innkeeper to put on the dinner.

" ' Now, monsieur, I am about to hazard my last venture at fortune, I shall have no other. It is *le dernier essai,* and I cannot go upon it with this ill-starred viscount.'

" He paused and sniffed the dinner.

" ' Besides, monsieur,' he added, ' there is a further reason for his death.'

" The cat was out in that final sentence. I was sure the vagabond had now come to the real reason. Was now, after all his pedantic vaporing, about to touch upon the truth.

" ' And what is that? ' I said.

" He indicated the smoking dinner with a gesture.

" ' My poor affairs shall not make monsieur go hungry.'

" The dinner was excellent. Jacques le Rouge was right. I have not dined better in the whole of France. I ate like a man who has been shipwrecked, and against my prowess, the Viscount de Champderien held his own with some advantage. How could the creature be so empty!

" It was with the last bottle, and over my Havana that the viscount took up his discourse.

" ' I was born in Dijon.' He made an irrelevant gesture. ' I pass over that. And my life? . . .' He shrugged his shoulders. ' I will not tire monsieur. I have had exigencies of fortune. Let them pass! . . . But, monsieur, I have got ashore from the shipwreck of my life with a certain respectable vocation.' He bowed with dignity. ' I am a professor of elegant letters. It is true that at present I am not in the pay of a university. But what would you have! These things go by favor and I am a poor gentleman. Besides, monsieur, I am somewhat old-fashioned, holding a nice courtesy to be of a greater benefit than Euclid.'

" He paused.

" ' I hoped to found a school in Paris. Ah, monsieur, what a dream that was; to draw about me the best youth in France, and upon the bald stem of this commercial age, to engraft the culture of the Louis' — a suave and gracious manner, a jeweled and elegant speech, *mon Dieu!* '

" He caught his thin beard between his fingers.

" ' It was not to be! ' And he bent his gaze upon me. ' Monsieur, there is only one country remaining to a professor of elegant letters, and that is Russia. Russia would put on the culture that France is putting off. It is not in Paris that one will hear the purest French, or observe the nicest manner, it is in Moscow and in Petersburg, about the Tzar. Instead of Paris, I should have traveled into Russia.'

" He emptied his glass and refilled it from the bottle.

" ' Meanwhile, even a master of polite letters must have a bed and a dinner now and then. There is no manna in Paris, and the ravens there do not take a guest. The Viscount de Champderien entered service. Whose service, monsieur? Bah! There is only one master to be served in Paris, and believe me, he is not so black as he is painted. He has some good points; he pays upon the spot, and while one is alive to bite the coin. And his Majesty is very capable of allowing a poor gentleman a little something beyond the letter of the contract. There are perquisites!'

"He held his glass before the candle and studied it with a discriminating eye.

"'The Viscount de Champderien does not complain, he came into his duties with little preparation, and I fear served his Majesty indifferently well, but he did it, I may say, monsieur, with a willing heart, and with what skill he could. . . .

"'But monsieur, the unskilled servant, in whatever trade, is always subject to a certain peril that the skilled servant escapes. And nowhere is this truth less academic than in the service of *Le Roi de L'enfer*. Persons of the first order in society and commerce and through a knowledge of custom and the law accomplish his Majesty's designs without entering into jeopardy. But beginners, like the Viscount de Champderien, take a certain chance. One cannot blame his Majesty for this. . . . It is an admirable system, monsieur, and encourages a man of spirit to get on. Look at it closely. The danger is upon the ignorant, the crude and the unskilled, and it diminishes in a certain established ratio as one advances in the service.

"'And so, monsieur, it is no fault of his Majesty that the Viscount de Champderien is just now *persona non grata* in Paris. He was, as I have said, without a special training, and he made some errors. And this fact, monsieur, taken with the creature's incomparable ill luck, decides me on his disappearance.'

" And so the truth got finally to the surface; the police were looking for the scoundrel, and he was about to take an alias. He drank off the wine and emptied the dregs of the bottle into his glass. His face took on a certain resolution, and his speech became direct.

" ' After monsieur's conspicuous courtesy,' he began, ' I am desolated to ask a favor. But monsieur is a gentleman and can appreciate. I have saved up a little money, and I am on my way to Russia. I will need this little fund there. I have got thus far without laying a finger on it. From the coast I can reach Odessa in a tramp ship. But from here to the coast is yet some distance. Would monsieur advance a poor gentleman twenty francs upon his word?'

" I could have laughed in the black-leg's face. It was the very oldest trick in all the Republic of Vagabondia. The trick of the drunken sailor who needs just one coin more to pay his way back to his ship, the trick of the young man in the railway station who wishes to go and bury his father, but lacks a dollar on his ticket. I told him, no!

"Then I called the innkeeper, and got out my wallet. I took from it what I thought was two twenty-franc notes, but I was mistaken, one was a fifty and the other a hundred. I put the fifty on the innkeeper's plate and thrust the other into my waist-coat pocket. As I was taking up my change from the table a five-franc piece fell to the floor. As I stooped to pick it up I felt a hand touch my waist-coat, and glancing up I saw my hundred-franc note slipped between the leaves of the viscount's Homer.

"I got up, the viscount also arose, bowed, put the copy of Homer into the outside pocket of his coat, and bade me adieu. A plan occurred to me. I went out beside him, and as we passed through the door, I put my hand into his pocket, took out the copy of Homer and dropped it into my own.

"We said adieu in the street before the inn. His high spirits had returned, and we parted in genial fashion.

"I went on to the coast with Jacques le Rouge. We were there by five. That night on the sea, when I went to my cabin to dress for dinner, I got the copy of Homer out of my pocket, held it by the covers and shook it so my hundred-franc note would fall out. It did fall out, but there fell also a shower of other notes, old, new, crisp and faded, from between the leaves of the book.   I gathered them up and counted them in astonishment.   They aggregated eighteen hundred francs."

"And so," said Father Jerome, "you imagine this rogue to have lost his ill-gotten gains by chance. I cannot understand that.   This man had undertaken the devil's work.   His facetious speech does not even disguise that fact.   He was in the devil's service; he received the devil's pay.   Who could expect that he would ever have any ultimate benefit from that? The thing is the clearest work of Providence.   The man's ill-gotten gains were taken from him and were given to another, who, doubtless, put them to some useful purpose."

The judge had not been listening to this story. He now spoke.

"I have been thinking, Lennard," he said, "about the part played by the criminal's own mind in this universal scheme of justice.   There can be no doubt that you are right about the fact of a great jeopardy lying here to the criminal agent.   It would sometimes seem as though this impulse, inherent in events or moving them, took a sort of sardonic pleasure in causing the criminal to entrap himself without the interposition of any agency exterior to his own acts, as though this impulse in events were also at work in the criminal's mind, and used the man's mind as an implement against him.

"I happened to be at one time very closely associated with a case turning upon this very point. It related to the affairs of the Commonwealth Life Insurance Company of America. As I had something to do with the case, permit me to give it to you in a detached manner."

The judge got a cigar, lighted it, and began to speak.

"The president of the Commonwealth Life Insurance Company of America [1] arrived at the little southern county-seat after a long journey from New York. He had been summoned by an urgent telegram from the general counsel, who had gone there to contest a case that the company believed to be a fraud. When he got down from the Pullman at the dilapidated station the general counsel met him; and, instead of taking the ancient hack that carried passengers over the half mile to the little town, the two men determined to walk. It was the hour of sunset. A path ran through the hills. The autumn evening was clear and bright.

"For a time the two men walked along with no conversation other than a casual comment on this old,

[1] Names of persons and institutions are fictitious.

239

indolent, raw land, where the crude civilization carried by the pioneer into the foothills of the Alleghanies remained. Finally, however, the elder man touched the vital issue.

"'So it is your opinion, Graham,' he said, 'that we would better compromise this case after all?'

"The attorney was a man in middle life. There was minted into him the distinguishing characteristics of a metropolitan city. It was the only life he knew and he was accustomed to judge all life by its standards. He believed this swiftly moving civilization to be the highest type; and, as he came a product of it, he cherished that superiority with which it had endowed him. He was impatient of crude men, of crude methods.

"'That is my opinion,' he said, 'but I wished you to confirm it before I acted.'

"'I thought,' continued the president, 'that you believed this whole case to be a deliberate scheme to defraud the company.'

"'I do believe it,' replied the attorney. 'I am certain of it. But what is one to do? The jury will find a verdict against us. That verdict will be wholly the determination of certain questions of fact and the supreme court of this state, following the old Virginia rule, will not disturb the verdict of a jury on questions of fact. That means that in the end we shall have to pay the full face of the policy and the costs.  To-night, before the case goes to the jury, we can compromise it for one-half of the face value of the policy, or twenty-five thousand dollars in cash. That is why I sent for you.'

" The older man prodded the path with his walking stick.

" ' I hate to compromise with a fraud,' he said. ' When one does that one encourages the next swindler; but, as you say, what is one to do?  We have to consider the stockholders' money.'

" ' That is it,' replied the attorney.  He walked on.  Then he added: ' I don't believe this man is dead.  I am convinced that he manufactured the evidence of his robbery and murder.  I believe he is a crook.  I believe his wife, who is now suing on this policy, is a crook.  But my opinions, my beliefs, my suspicions, are not evidence.'

" They had now reached the top of the little hill across which the path trailed.  Below them lay the county-seat, an ancient village with an unpaved clay road for its main thoroughfare.  There were great trees along this road, indicating how old the village was.  Midway of the village stood the courthouse, with its plaster pillars, its long windows, its white dome surmounted by a huge wooden image of George Washington.  Before the courthouse was a square fenced in by hitching-posts. Behind the village a mountain range abruptly rose; and beyond this smoke ascended.

"The topography of the country was unique. East of the county-seat it was a farming country of little hills; west it was a rugged alpine country of broken mountain ranges, through which a river fought its way with a sort of berserk fury. The thin-soiled farming land remained as the pioneer had left it, but the wild region, which he had rejected as worthless, had been found rich in coal measures. Its deep gorges were pots of smoke where, with her hideous surgery, Industry was beginning to disembowel the mountains.

"The attorney extended his arm toward these mountains.

"'The plan of these two adventurers,' he said, 'is plain enough to me. They are a pair of competent, practical crooks. Scott and this woman came here with a well-defined idea of what they intended to do. They went to live in that coal region over there. Scott obtained an interest in a coal company, presently became its superintendent, and through this relation he secured the insurance with us on his life. Then, when the opportune moment arrives, he disappears, leaving behind him the evidences of his robbery and murder; and his wife sues for this life insurance.'

" ' But how does she prove that Scott is dead?'
said the president. ' I understand that no human
body has been produced for identification. Is not
the burden of proof on the plaintiff to show that the
insured is in fact dead before she has any standing
in court?'

" ' That is the law,' replied the attorney; ' but the
death of the insured may be shown in other ways
than by the identification of his body. If there is
sufficient evidence of violence, and that violence is
shown to have been exerted in such a manner as to
account for the disappearance of the body, the question of the insured's death becomes one for the jury
to determine.'

" ' And with a jury,' said the president, ' any woman
has an advantage, unless one can bring out her history on cross-examination. What did this Mrs. Scott
say?'

" ' Nothing,' replied the attorney.

" ' Nothing!'

" ' Not one word. If she had gone on the stand
I would have gouged her history out of her. She
knew that.'

" ' Could you not have put her on the stand yourself?'

" ' And make her my own witness? And be bound
by what she said! Certainly not. If she had testi-

fied in her own behalf I could have cross-examined her without being compelled to accept her answers as the truth, but I could not make her a witness for us.'

" ' What evidence did she produce, then?'

" ' Ah!' said the attorney, ' that is where the shrewdness of these adventurers presents itself. They did not intend that anyone who knew their design should be questioned. Their cunning plan was that physical facts should speak for them. Events! Mark this distinction: An event speaks only to a certain action. It does not disclose the motive behind that action. One cannot cross-examine an event. One cannot make it hesitate, stammer, contradict itself. It is the safe witness. . . . Writers on evidence have said facts cannot lie. It is true. The one who constructed the facts may be the very prince of liars; but if he does not appear, if he only sets up his chain of physical events and leaves them to testify for themselves, how can one show that they have been manufactured to a design? Look at this case:

" ' On the first day of November, as he was accustomed to do on the first day of every month, Scott left the office of this coal company of which he was superintendent. He carried in a leather bag the money with which to pay the workmen at the mine. It was early in the morning. There was considerable fog. His way lay across the river, which was spanned by a high footbridge. . . . He did not arrive at the mine. Some workmen, crossing about an hour later, found the bag on this bridge, cut open with a knife, its contents gone. There was evidence of a struggle and the railing of the bridge on one side was broken. The bridge at this point is a hundred feet above the water; the water below is deep and swift. These are the direct facts. They are certain. They are indisputable.

" ' There are also certain collateral facts, quite as indisputable: that Scott was known to be the superintendent of the mine; that his custom was to carry the money over this bridge from the office to the mine on the first day of every month; that the murder and robbery of a mine superintendent, under like circumstances, have sometimes occurred. . . . It is also certain that one cast from the bridge into the river below, if he were not already dead, would be killed by the fall; and it appears that the bodies of persons known to have been drowned in this river have not always been recovered.

" ' Now the plaintiff in this case presents these facts to the jury. Let us not delude ourselves! The jury will conclude that which these facts obviously indicate: that Scott on this morning was waylaid on this bridge, robbed, murdered and his body cast into the river. . . . We cannot dispute a single one of the certain incidents from which this conclusion is drawn. How, then, can we dispute the conclusion itself?'

"The attorney extended his hands like one who takes hold of a concrete physical thing.

"'How does it avail us that this chain of concatenated incidents is also consistent with our theory of a design to present the appearance of a robbery and murder unless we can make that design appear? . . . We cannot make it appear. The woman does not take the stand. Every witness who does take it is telling the truth; and these physical incidents, as I have said, cannot be examined upon the motive that called them into being.'

"He turned his hands, like one who turns about an object in his fingers; then he thrust them suddenly forward, like one who casts that object away when he is wearied with the useless puzzle of it.

"The two men began to descend the little hill into the village. The elder one walked with his head down, his hands thrust into the pockets of his coat. Presently he asked: 'Have we local counsel in this case?'

"The lawyer smiled. 'Well, yes,' he said; 'I suppose one could call him that.'

"'What is his opinion about this compromise?'

"'I have not asked his opinion,' replied the attorney. 'These chimney-corner lawyers are a nuisance in a trial. I made it plain to him that I needed his assistance only in striking the jury — and no further. It is just as well to have these things clearly understood in the beginning. I have had no trouble with him. He knew every man of the jury panel. He gave me the detailed personal history of each one; and after the jury was struck he quite understood that his services were no longer required.'

" ' He withdrew from the case, then?'

" 'Well, no; not exactly that. He remained in his chair by the defendant's table.'

" ' But he did nothing?'

" The attorney smiled. 'Well, yes; he did two things constantly. He kept his eyes open and his mouth closed.'

" The president of the Commonwealth Life Insurance Company lifted his head; the muscles of his jaws tightened. He walked for some time thus, his shoulders thrown loosely forward; then he spoke.

" ' Let us go and see this man,' he said.

" They stopped and entered a gate before an old brick manor house, standing half hidden in a grove of oak trees. Within this gate, near the street, stood a little one-story building, also of ancient brick. Two stone steps led up to the door. The men knocked. A voice bade them ' Come in!' and they entered.

"The room into which they went was a kind of office. There were a few law books on open shelves — no modern ones: the Grattan Reports, the Code, Mayo's Guide, Chitty, and the like. There were a few chairs, an ancient mahogany desk with a cabinet top inclosed by doors having diagonal glass windows set in strips of veneer. The top of the desk was covered with a heap of court papers inclosed in blue wrappers and tied up with bits of faded tape.

" At this table sat a figure out of some antebellum story: a tall old man, with a shock of white hair. He wore a black frock coat, a white handkerchief folded about his neck and fastened with a long, curiously shaped garnet pin. He was writing on a sheet of foolscap; his hand trembled a little and he wrote slowly. Beside him sat a country farmer, his trousers inside his cowhide boots, his hat beside him on the floor, his body leaning forward in his chair.

" The old man looked up over the rim of his spectacles when the two entered.

" ' Have a chair,' he said. ' I shall presently be at leisure.' Then he went forward with the sentence upon which he was engaged.

" The president of the Commonwealth Life Insurance Company was astonished. No member of the legal profession, when he called upon him, had ever said, ' Have a chair ' and gone on with what he was

248

writing. Urban attorneys were accustomed to spring up when he entered, to come forward with a gracious salutation and, dismissing the thing with which they were engaged, to await his pleasure. The New York attorney was likewise unaccustomed to wait when he entered a law office and he was accustomed to require the attention that his prominence demanded.

" 'Mr. Page,' he said in his big, impressive manner, ' this is Mr. Curtis Beech, president of the Commonwealth Life Insurance Company of America.'

" The old man merely nodded. 'In a moment, gentlemen,' he said; and he went on writing slowly on the sheet of foolscap.

" Finally he finished it, pointed out with his finger where the countryman was to sign and, when the paper was folded, went with the farmer to the door.

" 'Good-by, Benny,' he said. 'If the bank crowds you come to me; I won't see you robbed.'

" Then he turned about and extended his hand to Mr. Beech. After that he returned to his chair.

" The president of this insurance company was a man whose advance in life had resulted from his excellent judgment of men. Something about this strange old man moved him to a sudden resolution.

" 'Mr. Page,' he said, 'Mr. Graham here, our chief counsel, is of the opinion that we would better compromise this case. What is your opinion?'

" The old man removed his spectacles, folded the frame and placed them in a tin case; then he turned about in his chair.

" ' My employment in this case, I believe, was for the purpose of assisting in striking the jury — and for no other purpose. It is not my custom to intrude my services where they are not requested.'

" ' But I am now requesting your opinion,' said the president.

" ' Sir,' said the old man, ' when a client puts his case into the hands of an attorney it is the ethics of our profession to regard that attorney as the directing authority until he is formally removed.'

" This nice courtesy pleased the New York lawyer.

" ' Ah, yes, Mr. Page,' he said in his exalted manner, ' I should be glad to know if you do not agree with my opinion.'

" The answer of the old man reached Mr. Graham like a projectile.

" ' I do not,' he said.

" The blood flashed into the attorney's face.

" ' Do you criticise the manner in which this case has been conducted?' he said.

" ' No,' replied the old man; ' the case has been excellently conducted.'

" The tribute restored the attorney to equanimity.

" ' I think we have done all we could,' he said,

using the pronoun of kings; 'but if this case should go to the jury to-night upon the evidence a verdict would certainly be returned against us. Do you doubt that conclusion?'

" ' I do not doubt it,' replied the old man. ' If the jury should take the case to-night on the evidence it would surely find for the plaintiff.'

" ' Then you are advised of some further evidence that we ought to introduce?'

" ' No.'

" ' You think there is a chance that the trial judge might set aside the verdict?'

" ' No.'

" ' Then your hope is with the supreme court?'

" ' No.'

" The attorney was annoyed.

" ' Well, Mr. Page,' he said, ' you advance, doubtless, some excellent sentimental reason when you say he case ought not to be compromised; as, for instance, that fraud ought to be resisted, even to the extent of permitting it ultimately to triumph — and incidentally to mulct our stockholders of fifty thousand dollars instead of twenty-five.'

" ' Sir,' said the old man, ' I entertain no such reason, although, since you mention it, I may reply that in my opinion fraud never can ultimately triumph if it be courageously and intelligently resisted.'

" Mr. Beech made a decisive gesture.

" ' What is it exactly that you advise, Mr. Page?' he said.

" ' That the case should proceed,' replied the old man.

" ' But the case is closed,' said the attorney; ' there remains but to argue it.'

" ' Argue it, then,' said the old man.

" The attorney again made that peculiar gesture with his extended fingers, as though he held there for examination some concrete material object. When he spoke his voice was ironical and hard.

" ' You have a greater faith in the potency of human eloquence than I have, Mr. Page,' he said, ' if you believe that mere words are going to win this case for us. What would you say if you were to argue it to-morrow?'

" ' It does not matter what I, who am not to argue it, would say,' replied the old man. ' The important thing is what you, who are to argue it, will say.'

" ' Very well, sir,' said the attorney. ' I will enumerate the only points in the case upon which the defendant company can base an argument and I shall be glad if you will indicate as I proceed, the one of these arguments upon which we could depend to secure a verdict.'

" He turned his hands with their extended fingers

as though he were passing concrete material before him.

" ' There are only two features of the case that it can possibly benefit us to discuss: one is the doubt of the insured's death; the other is the element of design. Now, as to the first, the body of Scott has not been found. Do you consider that fact sufficient to turn the case? '

" ' No,' said the old man; ' the jury will remember that a peddler was drowned in this river and his body never recovered; that two workmen were observed to fall from a bucket into the water and one of them was never again seen. The jury will bear in mind that this river has a sinister reputation for not giving up its dead.'

" ' Then,' continued the attorney, ' there remains only to argue that the whole case is a cunning plan to defraud. And to do that one must attack this woman as an adventuress; one must comment on her silence; one must file her painted face as an exhibit; one must pin her to the wall, lash her, grill her on the fire.'

" The old man's back straightened in his chair, his fingers moved, his keen brown eyes grew bright in his head. When he spoke his voice was like a bell.

" ' In this country,' he said, ' we do not vilify a woman.'

" ' But I am not of this country,' said the attorney;

' I am of a country that believes no sentimentality should protect a criminal, be that criminal male or female. This woman must be flayed.'

" The old man raised his long index finger. ' You must not utter one word against her ! If you do your case is ruined. If you abuse this woman every man on the jury will despise you, though she be as designing as Esther; though she be as painted as Jezebel ! '

" ' Then why do you say I ought to argue this case to the jury ? '

" ' I have not said that.'

" ' Ah ! ' said the attorney, his voice lengthening into a sarcastic drawl. ' You would do it better ! '

" ' I would do it differently,' said the old man.

" The attorney turned to his companion. His ironical manner remained.

" ' It seems unfortunate,' he said, ' that Mr. Page is not conducting this case.'

" The president of the Commonwealth Life Insurance Company had now one of those inspirations that had made him.

" ' I think it is,' he said. ' I put the case into his hands ! ' "

## CHAPTER XIII: *The Locked Bag*

THE court-room was crowded. In the South, remote from cities, the court-room has to the citizen the interest of a theater. He postpones his visit to the county-seat until the court convenes; then he comes in and sits all day long on the uncomfortable benches. He follows the examination of the jury panel, the charge of the judge, the trial of a cause, with the absorption of one before the footlights. Moreover, under his eye the forensic contests take on the sharp interest of the stadium. He knows with an intimate and personal knowledge every actor out there beyond the railing, and he constitutes a second tribunal that considers and disposes of every case. It is a custom not to be despised. It is the people watching over their administration of justice; but it transforms the attorney into an actor and it makes for extravagances of passion.

" The counsel for the plaintiff had presented his opening argument. One could have heard him from any doorstep. He had thundered his invective. Here one who was dead had paid over the wages of his life to a great institution in order that the woman of his hearthstone might be cared for when God took him. And now, having got that wage, this perfidious institution turned its back! Nay, more! It resisted with every trick and every artifice. Observe the deeps of infamy to which it had descended! It would foul the dead man with its innuendoes. . . . And under this tornado the plaintiff wept — to the jeopardy of her painted face.

"When, instead of the city attorney, Mr. Page arose there was evident disappointment. The jury had supposed that the defendant would have brought a great orator to address it. The members of the second tribunal had the keener disappointment. They had hoped for high declamation — and here, to speak for the defendant, was only a plain man like themselves.

"On the plaintiff's table, before the jury, was the bag that had been introduced in evidence. It was a big, heavy, alligator-skin bag, closed. Two small straps were buckled across the top better to secure it, and a great ragged slit traversed the side of it where it had been cut open. Through this opening its contents had been removed. The bag had been set there by the plaintiff's counsel before the jury's eye. It was a witness, he said, that proclaimed murder with a thousand tongues.

"The old man remained for some moments standing motionless behind his table, his tall body erect, his heavy white hair brushed back from his forehead, his features composed with an impressive dignity. Finally he spoke.

" ' After the experiences of life,' he said, ' and after long reflection, I am of the opinion that human ingenuity cannot successfully imitate the Providence of God. . . . Every natural event is so dovetailed into other events that precede and follow — it is so delicately fitted into the intricate machinery of human affairs — that only an infinite intelligence could make that exquisite adjustment. Over and over again every variety of human intelligence has endeavored to create an arbitrary consistency of events; and over and over again it has failed.'

" The old man paused. He moved a little closer to the table.

" ' If you will carefully examine any natural event in its delicate adjustment you will presently realize that if an intelligence placed it there, then that intelligence must have known everything that preceded and everything that followed this event with an infinite sweep of comprehension. . . . But if you examine an event arbitrarily created by a human agent you will presently realize a certain limitation; you will see that there were certain things that the author of this event knew and certain other things that he did not know.   And if you press that inquiry you will discover that this particular, certain thing could have been known or not known only to a particular, certain person. . . . Let me illustrate this profound truth.'

" He looked up at the judge.

" ' Your Honor will recall the case of The State vs. Van Baker.   In that case Van Baker, after killing the inmates of his own house, undertook to give the house the aspect of a robbery in order to divert suspicion from himself.   He was an intelligent person and he manufactured his evidence with skill.   But among the drawers of a bureau rummaged by the supposed robbers there remained one that had not been opened.   Instantly the query arose, Why should an assassin unfamiliar with the house, seeking loot, pillage every drawer of the bureau but this particular one? . . . The drawer was opened.   It was found to contain the clothes of a little child long dead.'

" The speaker paused.   He stood for a moment silent: then he added:

" ' A thing that, of all living persons, Van Baker alone knew! '

" The audience on the benches moved with a sudden dramatic impulse.

" The old man came out from behind his table. He stood now before the jury.

" ' There is here a vital query,' he continued. ' Have the physical evidences of murder in this case been created by a human agency? If so the defendant must prevail; if not so the plaintiff must prevail. It is the one fact upon which this case turns as on a hinge.

" ' Let us not abandon ourselves to conjecture. Let us apply the test that I have indicated and be certain. If William Scott created these events in order falsely to present the aspect of his murder, they will bear somewhere within them the distinguishing mark of their paternity — some certain, particular thing that he alone definitely knew.'

" The second tribunal and the first advanced now to that tense mental status where one hazards his fortune on some decisive test as upon the turning of a die.

" The old man took up the bag from the plaintiff's table and presented it to the jury. Again, and with careful scrutiny, the jury examined it; they observed the heavy alligator leather of which it was composed; the two small straps buckled tightly across the top; the great ragged slit cut through the side. Although the bag had been on the table for two days, there was now a seizure of consuming interest. Every man in the court-room examined it with the jury. There was silence. The moving of a foot, the creaking of a bench, were sounds sharply audible.

"When the bag was again in his hands the old man continued.

"'Gentlemen of the jury,' he said, 'you will observe that the great cut in the side of this bag is ragged. Henry Dillworth, your foreman is a saddler. He will tell you that this ragged aspect of the cut shows that it was made with a dull knife.'

"It was not in the etiquette of jurors to reply to counsel; but they might indicate their approval by a sign. The foreman nodded.

"'He will tell you another significant thing — namely, that as the leather of this bag is hard and thick it was a considerable labor thus to cut it open with a dull knife.'

"Again the foreman indicated his approval with a sign.

"The old man raised the bag in his hands; he held it so the two small straps buckled across the top could be seen. He swung around toward the plaintiff's counsel. His voice expanded in volume.

"'Why was it,' he said, 'that the one who sought the contents of this bag thus laboriously cut it open when, with a single slash of the knife, he could have severed these two small straps that hold the jaws of this bag together?'

" ' Gentlemen of the jury,' he said."

" The attorney for the plaintiff was on his feet in a moment.

" ' I will tell you why,' he shouted. ' Because the bag was locked! '

" The old man raised his extended arm, closed his fingers and brought his clenched hand slowly down with an abrupt gesture that emphasized each word.

" ' Not because it was locked,' he said; ' but because the one who cut that bag open — that specific, definite person — alone knew that it was locked! '

" Then he sat down.

" Behind him, on the benches, the audience packed into the court-room moved with a common, decisive impulse.

" The New York attorney flung himself across the corner of the table.

" ' Good God, man! ' he said, ' why didn't you go on? Why didn't you say that assassins would have been in desperate haste? — that to cut that bag open with a dull knife would take time? — that no sane person would take the time to do that slow cutting until he knew that he could get into the bag in no other way? Why didn't you say that assassins could not have known that the bag was locked until the straps were cut? And, if they had cut the straps and found the bag locked, why didn't you say they never would have dared to stop on that public thoroughfare to slowly cut that long ragged slit in the hard alligator leather?  Persons were apt to come over that bridge at any moment.   It was too perilous a place to remain in.  Why didn't you say that assassins would have carried the bag to some safe place to thus laboriously hack it open?  Why didn't you say that the thing was a slip of Scott's mind?  Why didn't you name the crook?  Why didn't you drive in the conclusions that are inevitable?'

"The old man looked him in the face.

" ' The jury will do that for me,' he said.

" And they did."

The priest had been listening with the deepest interest.

" Ah!" he said, " the old attorney was right. No human ingenuity can successfully imitate the Providence of God.  It is only an infinite intelligence that can understand the complete relation of one event to another.  Only God can make a thing happen so that it is consistent with all other things. When a man, in his egotism, undertakes to do a work which can only be accomplished by the Providence of God, he always fails to his ruin."

The doctor was smiling.

" Flint," he said, " I was not expecting you to furnish evidence to prove my case.  I have said that the thing which ruins the criminal agent is his own contributory negligence, and you have now brought forward evidence to sustain me. I have asserted that neither Providence nor an intent in nature threatens the criminal with discovery — that his discovery and punishment always results from his inability to realize how one event is related to another, and, therefore, his inability to create a false consistency of events. And, further, he must always leave about his work some indication of his own personality. I think if every case were carefully and intelligently examined, it would be found that the criminal signs his crime as the artist signs his picture. Now, do not get an incorrect impression from what I say. I do not mean that the criminal is punished from his lack of foresight or prudence any more pointedly than other men. Nature is like Buddha: 'I have the same feeling for the high as for the low, for the moral as for the immoral, for the depraved as for the virtuous, for those holding sectarian views and false opinions as for those whose beliefs are good and true.'

" I say to you, gentlemen, that I have seen a man who was not a criminal, and who had committed no crime, as desperately punished for his indiscretions as any murderer who ever went to the electric chair. I can see the man.

" He had been in a little Southern town so long that his story was covered up with moss like a fallen gravestone. I had a lot of trouble to unearth it. But the physician, the lawyer, and the priest have easy access to the under side of life. He maintained the pretense of a bookshop, but he had only a few old books, selected for their curious bindings or their ancient prints. No one wanted this rubbish, and he would have starved but for the newspapers and magazines which he had added. He never spoke to anyone who came in. The price was marked on everything he had, and if you wanted it you put down the money and carried it away. He always sat in the farther end of his shop by the dirty window, poring over some old volume with a little glass. He was very thin and white, and his clothes were miserably poor. But his poverty was not the thing that gripped you. It was his face that did not change, like that of a life convict upon his bench, until one spoke to him, and then it seemed to awaken. And a sense of the dull, hopeless, inexorable monotony of life seized and possessed it. So we came to go in on tiptoe, and go out without a word, as where one lies for burial. In the evening a woman came and took him away. I often saw her. She carried the little long basket of a laundress. Her hands were red and rough; her face was not unpleasant, but it was stamped over with the cares and anxieties of life. She was much younger.

. . . . . . . .

"Mrs. Hudson had undertaken to establish a feudal relation between her country house and the village lying in the valley below it. The little town acquiesced because Mrs. Hudson paid for the distinction. It suffered her to clean its streets, to roll and sod its vacant lots, and to indicate the places where its telephone poles should be put up. In return, it went to Mrs. Hudson for a cheque whenever a house was burned, a workman killed, a baby born in poverty, or a leak discovered in a church roof.

"The village disliked Mrs. Hudson. A thing that particularly annoyed it was her custom of attending every public function that the town got up. It could hardly bear this big, blonde, domineering woman, forever present as a sort of overlord. Nevertheless, it always met her with a certain obsequious manner because of the cheques.

"Mrs. Hudson got no pleasure out of attending these functions. They always bored her, frequently interrupted her plans and often caused her no end of trouble. But she had learned in England that 'one must take an interest in one's village.'

"When the town wished to levy an unusual tribute on Mrs. Hudson, it made use of her custom under some subterfuge. Thus, when it wished to purchase an addition to the poor farm, it wrote Mrs. Hudson, explaining that a thousand dollars must be had from some source, and that it had determined to give a charity ball under her patronage. This meant that whatever sum under a thousand dollars the ball failed to realize, Mrs. Hudson would be expected to contribute. Experience had demonstrated that such affairs never return more than two hundred dollars, and, shorn of its diplomacy, the thing was merely a levy of eight hundred dollars. Mrs. Hudson was not in the least deceived by this subterfuge; but having assumed the obligations of a feudal relation, she met them at any cost.

" The town had indicated a date in April. This was a month earlier than Mrs. Hudson was accustomed to return. Nevertheless, she brought down her servants, opened her country home and invited some guests. As the weather was still a bit sharp, the guests sent regrets. There was one guest, however, who regarded Mrs. Hudson's invitation as in the nature of a command. This was her brother. Mr. Henry Livingreen Taylor. He was a person of the greatest use to Mrs. Hudson. He went everywhere; he knew every convention exactly; he played all games with skill. He was a little better dressed than anyone else. Having no vocation, he affected polo and miniature painting. Mrs. Hudson said that 'Henri' was the most accomplished gentleman in America. Mr. Hudson said that 'Henery' knew more things, out of which not a dollar could be made, than any man he ever saw.

"In the carriage, on the way to the village, Mrs. Hudson occupied the time in giving her brother an exact list of those to whom she wished him to pay certain attentions. With great diplomacy Mr. Taylor endeavored to reduce this list to the fewest possible persons. He pointed out that one might give a personal attention to a beggar, but not to a shopkeeper; to a person under one's authority in a certain relation, but not to an independent bourgeois. He excluded all the young girls in the village by a single objection, namely, that his attentions were those of his sister, and could not go to one without going to all.

"The discussion continued down the long drive through the forest, across the village to the town hall. When the carriage stopped Mr. Taylor had pruned the list to the mayor's wife, the rector's old maid daughter, the local doctor's wife, the secretary of the Village Improvement Society and Mrs. Hobbs. Mrs. Hobbs was a useful person. She could be depended on to do exactly anything that Mrs. Hudson wished, and she was satisfied with a quasi-social recognition — invitations to tea when there were no guests, and so forth.

"The town hall was decorated with branches of holly tacked over the entire wall. Among this holly were innumerable red paper flowers, so placed as to give the idea of a monstrous, tropical, crimson vine, interlaced through a Northern thicket by some mischievous god, who had no regard for climate. Across the ceiling hung loops of bunting. Near the door was a bowl of very sweet, purple-colored punch.

"As Mr. Taylor was dancing with the doctor's wife, he noticed a young girl whom he had never before seen in the village. She was one of those exquisite creatures, sometimes born in a cabin, that for a brief period in their youth, seem almost to accomplish the romantic ideal of an Ariadne, a Nicolette or a Chloe. Slender, delicate and fresh, with that indescribable sheen of things newly created — as, for instance, the first blossoms of the wild brier that fall to pieces under the human hand.

"She wore a simple blue frock that seemed to be as much a part of her as wings are a part of a butterfly. Mr. Taylor followed the young girl through the dance. Then he went and stood beside his sister, but he continued to regard the young girl, his arms folded and his lips compressed, precisely as he was accustomed to regard a miniature, offered for his comment.

" Finally he spoke to his sister.

" 'Hermione,' he said, 'who is that exquisite child?'

" Mrs. Hudson inquired of the mayor's wife.

" The mayor's wife said, 'That's Susie Mills from the country. She's stayin' with Mrs. Hobbs. Ain't she a pretty little thing?'

" 'She's perfect,' replied Mr. Taylor. Then he went to find Mrs. Hobbs.

" 'Mrs. Hobbs,' he said, 'I have divined your secret. You are a fairy godmother.'

" Mrs. Hobbs did not understand.

" 'Oh, Mr. Taylor,' she said, 'how you do make fun of everybody.'

" Mr. Taylor indicated the young girl with a gesture.

" 'Confess,' he said, 'that you brought this Cinderella here in a pumpkin coach.'

" Mrs. Hobbs was enlightened.

" 'That's Susie Mills,' she said, 'from down the country. May I introduce her to you?'

" 'I shall be honored,' said Mr. Taylor, 'only she is not Susie Mills, and she does not live down the country.'

" Mrs. Hobbs was alarmed.

" ' Why, Mr. Taylor,' she protested, ' indeed she is Susie Mills, and indeed —'

" Mr. Taylor interrupted, ' Impossible,' he said, ' you got that fairy child out of an oak tree, but I promise not to tell. Now, present me.'

" Mrs. Hobbs beckoned the young girl with her fan, and when she came presented her to Mr. Taylor.

" Mr. Taylor made a weavy ' T ' with two strokes of his pencil in several places on Miss Mills' card, and carried her away in the next dance. She was light and supple, and she danced as though every motion were the expression of a moving delight, which she was unable to restrain. Mr. Taylor, who did all things well, observed this with an increasing interest. He observed also how absolutely faultless her neck was just where the little vagrant strands of hair curled at the base of her head; how her abundant hair had nothing of that dead look, which women's hair begins early to take on; how blue her eyes were, and how her skin, in its delicate texture, resembled some of his miniatures.

" He continued to dance with her. Finally he came and stood beside his sister.

" ' Hermione,' he said, ' I must paint a miniature of that young girl.'

" Mrs. Hudson regarded Miss Mills through her lorgnette.

" ' She is dainty and pretty. But it is the daintiness and prettiness of the young animal. There is absolutely nothing in her face.'

" ' You are quite right,' replied Mr. Taylor, ' but if one could put something into her face, how superb she would be. If, for instance, one could put there the consciousness that she is what she looks to be — a dryad from some sacred grove.'

" ' If one could do that,' replied Mrs. Hudson, ' she would be exquisite. But one never could do it. These girls of the country are impossible.'

" ' I am not so certain, Hermione,' said Mr. Taylor, ' a young girl at sixteen is as sensitive to a suggestion as a photographic plate. If one should continue to say to her, " You are not Susie Mills. You are not from the country. You are not a farmer's daughter. You are the fairy sister of King Arthur, coming from your enchanted palace, under Land's End," she would believe it in a week, and when she believed it, why, there it would be in her face.'

" This speech touched on the latest metaphysical fad, and for nearly two minutes Mrs. Hudson discussed the subconscious mind, suggestion, telepathy and the like. She repeated the current rhapsodies. She did not believe what she said, neither did she disbelieve it. She had, in fact, never taken the trouble to think on the subject."

## CHAPTER XIV: *The Penalty*

MR. TAYLOR did not follow these platitudes. He stood watching the young girl with a discriminating eye. He was a very good-looking man, under forty and rather tall. His abundant gray hair somehow gave his face a youthful appearance. His sister had taught him to thus come and stand beside her. She thought he lent her a certain distinguished background. He continued to study the young girl.

" Presently he said: ' By Jove, I'll do it! '

" There was something in her brother's voice that caused Mrs. Hudson to at once descend from metaphysical heavens to the earth.

" ' What, exactly, is it that you intend to do, Henri? ' she said.

" ' I am going to paint a miniature,' he said, ' that will not be subject to Lady Landendale's criticism, that all American subjects look as though they were trying to be somebody else. I am going to paint a fairy woman, who believes that she is a fairy woman — a dryad that not only has the physical aspect of a dryad, but is a dryad. I am going to put the appropriate consciousness into that child's exquisite face and then transplant it to ivory.'

" The practical note remained in Mrs. Hudson's voice.

" ' And how, exactly, Henri, do you propose to go about this psychological experiment?'

" ' Quite in the simplest way,' replied Mr. Taylor. ' I shall treat this young person precisely as I should treat the fairy daughter of Abu Jaffer, if she were to arrive at this village on her magic carpet, and I, alone, were in the secret.'

" ' And then, what?' said Mrs. Hudson.

" ' Why, then,' replied Mr. Taylor, ' in a fortnight she will believe it.'

" ' And what becomes of Susie Mills?' said Mrs. Hudson.

" Mr. Taylor was annoyed.

" ' My dear Hermione,' he said, ' what becomes of all such young girls in the country? The period during which they have the exquisite proportions of a hamadryad arrives early and does not remain beyond three years. Then they become what is called buxom, marry a young farmer, present him with a great many children, and die at an advanced age. They rarely have a look over the wall.'

" ' But is a look over the wall good for them?' said Mrs. Hudson.

273

" ' It is knowledge,' said Mr. Taylor.

" ' But is knowledge always good for us?' said Mrs. Hudson.

" ' We must believe it,' replied Mr. Taylor, ' since Eve was permitted to have her fling.'

" Mr. Taylor crossed the room to Mrs. Hobbs.

" ' Mrs. Hobbs,' he said, ' how long does your guest remain with you?'

" Mrs. Hobbs did not know what to reply. She had asked Susie Mills to the village for the dance, and that meant only a day or two. But she had marked Mr. Taylor's interest, and this inquiry might mean that Mrs. Hudson had something in view to which the girl would be asked if she were available, and, of course, Mrs. Hobbs with her. Mrs. Hobbs gave herself an elastic measure.

" ' A week or two,' she said.

" ' Good,' said Mr. Taylor. ' Does she ride?'

" Mrs. Hobbs wondered if Mr. Taylor was driving at a hunt breakfast. To her, one of those extreme functions, full of elegance and mystery, of which she had observed the horses, the red coats, the hounds, with the emotions of a small boy, who watches the paraphernalia of a circus entering the big tent, to which he has not a ticket. A great joy possessed her. She did not know whether Susie Mills could ride or not, but she said yes. Then she remembered that all country girls could ride a horse. However, she added the precaution: 'But she has no riding habit here.'

" ' My sister has a guest box full of riding things,' said Mr. Taylor. ' There ought to be something that would fit Miss Mills.'

" ' She's easy to fit,' said Mrs. Hobbs.

" ' To-morrow morning, then,' said Mr. Taylor, and he went back to Mrs. Hudson.

" Miss Mills could ride as all country girls ride. That is, she could sit squarely on the horse, adapt herself to its motions and keep her seat at any gait. But she knew absolutely nothing about the art as taught by a riding master. The smart habit, the boots, the English saddle, were strange devices to her. In them she was a bit stiff and awkward, but it was not a stiffness or an awkwardness that was unattractive. It had rather a certain charm, a piquancy, as of a pretty danseuse attempting to do her steps in a grenadier's uniform. The way in which the girl endeavored to manage two reins when she was accustomed to only one on a bridle, her manner of holding the crop, as though it were a twig broken from an oak limb, and the constraint which she felt in the snugly-fitting habit, amused and at the same time, charmed Mr. Taylor. This quaint unfamiliarity with things ordinary and conventional, aided the illusion with which Mr. Taylor had determined to amuse himself. By skillful, indirect suggestion he brought this illusion forward, and insinuated the young girl into it. She accepted it, and responded in the manner of a child playing at make-believe.

" To her, Mr. Taylor was a superior mortal, from a world of which she knew nothing, but which she imagined to abound in things wonderful and elegant. The attentions of such a person charmed and intoxicated her. When he pretended that she was the fairy daughter of a Caliph of Bagdad, now and then appearing in the world, and to be recognized only by favored mortals, she entered into the spirit of that pretense. When he called her the Sultana Suzanne she was delighted; and when he told her, with an abundant Oriental imagery, the details of her fabulous history, she entered into the story and lived there as a child does.

" The weather was hard and bright, and these rides every morning in the crisp air, under a sun beginning to coax the grass out of the earth and the buds out of the forest, inspired Mr. Taylor to poetic fancies, and moved him to constantly steep the girl in the illusion which he had brewed.

" The details of these fancies were sometimes anachronistic, they were frequently borrowed, and the edges of one rarely fitted to those of another. But the young girl followed them with that eager interest, that absorption, that complete and utter abandon to make-believe, which enables a child to transform a chair into a bireme or a table into a palace of jade.

" Every evening he bade her an elaborate adieu, since he was not certain that he should ever see her again, and every morning he met her with an extravagant welcome. His manner toward the girl was always that of the nicest courtesy, as though she, in fact, belonged to some royal station above him.

" They continued to ride every day, and Mr. Taylor presently observed in the girl's face what he took to be evidences of that consciousness which he was endeavoring to place there. Other persons also noticed these evidences, but interpreted them upon a different hypothesis.

" Mrs. Hobbs began to come into the girl's room after she had retired. She would sit down on the bed beside her, stroke her hair or fondle her hand, and talk. This talk usually ran on the intrinsic difference which Mrs. Hobbs believed to exist between men in the class of Mr. Taylor and ordinary men, especially in the manifestation of any controlling emotion.

" ' They ain't like our men,' she said. ' They don't try to put their arm around you, nor to hold your hands, an' they don't get mad every time you do anything. They just talk an' insinuate.'

"Then she would sit with her chin in her hand and examine the girl critically.

"'You are pretty, Susie,' she would say, 'there's no gettin' 'round that. You are a lot prettier than the swell girls who come down here to visit Mrs. Hudson. They look peaked to me. I reckon it's the stayin' up nights.' Then she would suddenly swoop down on the girl, give her a tremendous maternal hug, and go out.

"Mrs. Hudson also observed the phenomena, but she contented herself with the assurance that Henri never did anything foolish. A more important matter occupied her attention. At tea one afternoon, in Grosvenor Square, Lady Landendale had presented her to a Russian princess, Madam Povey. Now, she had a note from the Russian, announcing her arrival in New York, and she did not know what to do. Lady Landendale had not indicated who Madam Povey was. Mrs. Hudson was afraid to take her up, and she was equally afraid not to. The fact that Madam Povey had written did not help the matter out. If she were a dear friend, it would be natural for Lady Landendale to direct her to acquaint Mrs. Hudson with her arrival in New York. On the contrary, if she were a mere adventuress, she would be sure to seize upon this introduction as a means of getting on in America. Mrs. Hudson remembered Madam Povey as a woman of thirty, with a quantity of dark chestnut hair, held in place by a great number of very large-headed gold pins, a figure inclined to be a little stout, and a quaint way of saying, ' I d-o-n-'-t know,' as though she believed it to be a naughty expression.

" Mrs. Hudson finally went to Mr. Taylor with the problem. It was after dinner in the library. Mr. Taylor was looking through a recently issued, exquisite edition of Colomba. He sat with a reading glass, examining the water-color illustrations. The Corsican subjects lent themselves to certain vivid effects that pleased him. He examined each picture precisely as a dealer examines a jewel. He would move the reading glass from his eye slowly out to the page, then he would remove it, get the effect with the unaided eye, and replace the glass over the picture. Every now and then he would pause and make a tiny note at the bottom of the page. The reading glass was an exquisite piece of Japanese work. The ivory handle was a mass of carved butterflies, clustering on a cherry limb. The hand holding the lens represented a tiny flight of these butterflies, putting off from either side of the cluster. When Mrs. Hudson began to speak, Mr. Taylor at once gave her his whole attention. He thrust the reading glass between the pages, closed the book and allowed it to remain idly in his hands. His face became grave, perplexed and disturbed.

"'I wish,' he said, 'that one's friends would not leave one to guess such riddles. This Madam Povey may be a Romanoff, or she may be one of those vague persons so common in the salons at Biarritz.'

"'But the title,' said Mrs. Hudson.

"Mr. Taylor's face became more visibly pained.

"'My dear Hermione,' he said, 'it is difficult for one to escape being a princess in Russia. Such titles descend like one's surname. The daughters of a prince in Russia are all princesses and their daughters princesses and so on, as the sons of Jones, and their sons in America, are all Jones'. Do you recall, Hermione, any remark of Lady Landendale, when she presented you to Madam Povey?'

"Mrs. Hudson considered, 'I believe she said, " a Roman acquaintance."'

"Mr. Taylor made an almost imperceptible gesture with his free hand.

"'Unfortunately,' he said, 'Lady Landendale could not have used an expression more Delphic.'

"'But would Lady Landendale know a questionable person?'

"'A questionable person!' said Mr. Taylor.

'No, perhaps not a questionable person. I should not use that word; but an undetermined person, yes, it is quite possible. In England one does not require to be so careful as with us; one's social position is fixed there. One may know anybody. If he proves spurious, one drops him. But in America, one is classified by the people one knows, and one goes down with them.'

" Mr. Taylor put the book and the reading glass on the table, then he arose and began to walk up and down through the library, his hands behind his back, his shoulders a little forward, his lips compressed. Finally he stopped.

" 'Well,' he said, ' one must be on the safe side, Hermione. I will go down to New York and quietly bring Madam Povey out here. There is no one at this time in the country. If she is worth while, you have entertained her; if she is the wrong sort, no one will know.'

" 'But, how can I entertain her here in April, Henri? She would die of it.'

" Mr. Taylor shrugged his shoulders.

" 'She will not die of it, Hermione,' he said. 'Write some obscure acquaintance for a fourth at bridge, and leave Madam Povey to me.'

" 'But your miniature, Henry,' suggested Mrs. Hudson.

" Mr. Taylor elevated his eyebrows.

" ' Oh,' he said, ' that is nothing.'

" When Mrs. Hobbs learned that Mr. Taylor was leaving for New York, she at once sent Susie Mills home.

" ' It's a good plan,' she said, ' to go right away in the middle of things, an' let them think about you.'

" She did not say to whom she referred, but she embraced Susie very tenderly at the railway station and whispered, ' He'll write.'

" When the young girl reached her father's house, every physical thing seemed to present an unfamiliar aspect. The form of nothing had changed, but the essence of everything had changed. She seemed to arrive, awakened in a place which she had heretofore inhabited in a sort of somnambulism. Her first impression was how hard and vivid everything appeared, as though some medium, which used to soften and obscure these things, had been suddenly removed. Her second impression was that these things, which through this medium, had formerly appeared attractive, were now, without it, crude and hideous.

" The very land seemed to have emerged from an illusion. It was now ugly with the waste fodder of the cattle, the plank fences, the clay roads, the unkempt farmhouses, the barns, the mud-daubed vehicles, the shaggy horses. It was now ugly with a real and deadly ugliness — the ugliness of things that do not change. She would stand at the window and look out at it, as one stands at a grating and looks out at a jail yard, until the bones of her face ached as they begin to ache before tears.

" Meanwhile she waited for the letter from Mr. Taylor. At first, as from a certain modesty, she would hurry up to her room and close the door when she saw the postman approaching in his cart, as though she would make no advance — as though Mr. Taylor should, himself, take every step of the way. Then, as by accident, she began to appear near the door when her father brought the mail into the house. Finally she went out, herself, to meet the postman. She made excuses and created pretexts for this. She wrote for samples of things which she saw advertised in the newspapers. And every day she would take a letter out to the postman and buy a stamp for it. She never bought more than one or two stamps at a time. And always she required another stamp or postcard, or she wished to know if the letter into which she had crowded the half sheet of a newspaper, was too heavy for a single stamp.

" The letter from Mr. Taylor did not arrive. She began to fear that it was lost. She recalled how, in the novels which she had read, letters were sometimes lost, and years later discovered in the pockets of old coats in dusty garrets, after the lives of those who had written them were ruined. She was seized with anxiety. She began to inquire of the postman upon this point. Among so many millions of letters, passing through so many hands, curious accidents must happen. The postman knew of a great many instances. Sometimes a mail bag was burned in a train wreck. Sometimes a letter slipped down behind a table or through a crack in the floor, and was never found. But more usually it was mislaid in a country office, or it was left at the wrong house by the postman. He himself had left letters at the wrong house and had never gotten them.

" She was coming to believe that Mr. Taylor's letter had met with one of these accidents, when, one evening, the postman handed her a rather thick envelope in the handwriting of Mrs. Hobbs. The very appearance of this letter alarmed her. It seemed to contain something sinister. She was afraid to open it. She took it to her room, locked the door and examined it minutely. She held it before the window, in the hope of being able to divine the contents. Finally she put it into the bosom of her dress. She was so agitated that, in order to account for the evidences of it, she tied a towel around her head, and explained that her head ached.

"All the evening she accomplished little superstitions which she had heard were lucky. She knocked on wood; she touched various objects; she repeated little rhyming formulas. She even opened the Bible at random in the hope that the first chapter on the page would begin with the words, 'And it came to pass.'

"That night, when the others had gone to bed, she lighted a candle and opened the envelope. In it was a fragment of newspaper, containing a picture of the Princess Povey, and a long paragraph announcing her arrival in America, and her visit to Mrs. Hudson. On the margin Mrs. Hobbs had written in pencil, 'She is riding with Mr. Taylor.'

"She put the picture back into the envelope and sat for a long time, without moving. Then she got up and began to walk about the room. Sometimes she stopped and arranged articles in the room. She did this carefully, as though the position of the article, in a precise spot, were important. Sometimes she stopped abruptly and remained motionless. Finally she went back to the table, took out the clipping and studied the picture. She held it close to the light and peered at it, turning it from one side to the other. She held it with both hands, and strained over the candle flame, in an effort to bring out the blurred features so she could see them. Then suddenly she blew out the candle, undressed swiftly, and went to bed in the dark.

"The next morning she awoke with one of those bizarre resolutions, which sometimes seize on the human mind in its extremity, and which the one acting upon it, can never justify to another. She determined to go and see this woman! She told her father, at breakfast, that the indisposition which she had suffered on yesterday, came from a defective tooth, that the tooth had ached all night, and that she would like to go at once to the dentist. As she was accustomed to driving alone to the neighboring town, he made no objection to this plan.

"The clay roads were heavy, and it was noon when she arrived. She put the horse in a stable, and went at once to the railway station. She waited two hours, then she took a local train to the village over which Mrs. Hudson maintained her feudal tenure. She arrived about three o'clock, crossed the bit of meadow to Mrs. Hudson's park gate, entered it, and walked along the gravel road toward the country house on the summit of the hill.

"The afternoon was bright under an April sun. The buds on the trees were beginning to open; insects moved. The road leisurely ascended, winding among the trees, enclosed on either side with high evenly clipped hedges. At short intervals these hedges were broken, so one could leave the road, and rest on a bench, or take a path through the wood.

" Presently she heard horses on the road beyond her. She stopped with an abrupt jerk of the body. She had been moved by a single dominating purpose, without any consideration of it. She had followed it without thinking what she would do when she arrived, or how she would explain this unexpected visit. Now, like one awakened, she was stricken with terror. She ran through one of the openings, and stood behind the hedge.

" Presently through the green mesh she saw Mr. Taylor riding with a woman. She crowded her body against the thick hedge and peered through it. She saw a woman who sat as straight and clean in the saddle as a figure in a hunting print. She was not pretty and she was not young, but instantly from every motion, from every detail, she knew that this woman belonged to a world above her, to a world that she could never hope to enter, to the world from which Mr. Taylor had descended on the night of the village dance. She looked, and she was overwhelmed with the superiority of this woman. Before her she felt crude, awkward, ordinary — one stripped of her pretensions and sent back to her place.

" They passed close to the hedge without seeing her. Mr. Taylor was talking; he was speaking softly; he was leaning a little toward the woman. The woman was listening, but not as the girl had listened, when she, too, rode with Mr. Taylor. This woman was listening with a whimsical smile, like one who had often heard the very thing that Mr. Taylor was saying. She tapped his arm with her crop, and at the turn of the road, she laughed.

" It seemed to the young girl that it was this laugh that crushed her. She sat down on the bench behind the hedge. She sat awkwardly, her feet drawn up, her head supported by the back of the bench, her hands in her lap. After awhile she arose and started to return. She hurried breathlessly along the road, stopping now and then to listen, but she met no one, and when she reached the station, she hid herself in a corner of the waiting room until the train arrived.

" All the way back she sat by the window, her chin in her hand, looking out. Her features did not change, and she did not move. It was dark when the train arrived at the little town. As she crossed the street a man spoke to her. He was a big, raw-boned, country man of middle life.

" ' Oh, Uncle Calvin! ' she said, and then she burst into tears.

" ' Why, Susie,' he began, ' what in the world —' then he stopped.

" He saw that the girl had given way under some overpowering emotion. He looked around him. He was the clerk of the county court. The courthouse stood opposite the railway station, and it was his custom to look in there at night to see if the windows of his office were closed and the door secure. He was now on his way there. He took the girl's hand firmly in his own big fingers.

" ' Come with me, Susie,' he said.

" They went into the courthouse. The man unlocked the door and they entered his office. He lighted a candle, set it on a table piled with big canvas-covered books, and got a chair.

" The girl sat down. She continued to sob, the tears trickling through her fingers. The man stood beside her and stroked her hair, and he continued to speak to her.

" ' What's wrong, Susie . . . tell me . . . what is it . . .?'

" The words and the sympathy of the man overcame her, and she told him. The story was incoherent, and the man got only detached fragments. He had never married. He did not understand

289

women, and he took such distress to mean only the deepest injury.

"He straightened up to his full height; his hard blue eyes narrowed, and he stood for some time stroking his lean jaw, with its high cheek bones. Then he went around the table, got out a book of forms, carefully filled in certain blank lines with a pen, detached the sheet, folded it, and put it into his pocket. Then he drew out a drawer of the table, got something there, and put that also into his pocket. His manner was now direct, and his face stern and immobile.

"'Come along with me, Susie,' he said.

"They went out of the courthouse and through the town to a public stable. Here the man explained that he wished to drive out to his brother's house in the country and he required a good fresh team. He got a buckboard and two horses, and with the girl in the seat beside him, he left the village."

## CHAPTER XV: *The Goth*

IT was about twelve o'clock. The sitting at
bridge had been long and rather fatiguing to
Mr. Taylor, and he had gone out for a bit of air.
It was a perfect night, hard and clear; a few clouds
were moving, and there was a thin moon. As Mr.
Taylor walked through the garden he saw a pair of
horses and a buckboard standing in the road at the
foot of the park. This was unusual, and he went
down to see what it meant. When he reached the
hedge he stopped. The horses were unattended and
they seemed fatigued. He was puzzled and he remained for some time quite motionless, with his hands
behind him. Then he heard the gravel of the path
grind under a heavy foot, and he turned. A big
uncouth countryman stood beside him.

" ' Is your name Taylor? ' said the man, putting
his hand into the outside pocket of his coat.

" ' That is my name,' replied Mr. Taylor, eleva-
ting his eyebrows. ' Why do you inquire? '

" ' Henry Livin'green Taylor? ' ·

" ' Yes.'

" ' Then, I want you to come with me.'

" Mr. Taylor regarded the man in astonishment.

" ' With you ! ' he said. ' But why ? '

" For answer the man seized Mr. Taylor by the wrist, and jammed the muzzle of a revolver into his ribs.

" ' Never mind why,' he said; ' you come or I'll blow your dirty heart out.'

" Mr. Taylor believed himself in the presence of a mad man, and he offered no resistance.

" The man broke down the beautiful hedge with his heavy cowhide boots, dragged Mr. Taylor through it, and forced him to get into the buckboard, and, driving with his left hand, took the road into the country. The man put his hand holding the weapon into the right pocket of his coat, and Mr. Taylor could feel the steel muzzle jostle against him. Mr. Taylor moved in the seat, and the man turned on him.

" ' I want to say this to you,' he said; ' if I hear a chirrup out of you, or you try to jump, you'll get it good and quick.'

" Mr. Taylor was now convinced that the man was mad. He realized the danger, and he saw that his safety lay in a docile obedience. He did not reply and they went on. In about an hour the man stopped before a little house on the roadside. There was a light in the window. They got out and went up the path to the door. On the step before the door the man again spoke to Mr. Taylor.

" ' You say what I tell you to say, or, by God, I'll snuff you out like that!' and he snapped his fingers.

" They went in. The room was a sort of dirty office. There was a table with a bottle of ink, a rusty pen, and some ill-kept papers. A tallow candle in a foul tin candlestick guttered with the draft from the door.

" A girl sitting in the corner sprang up when they entered; her face was streaked with tears, and her hair disordered. She cried out when she saw Mr. Taylor. She had been told to wait here until her uncle returned. She did not know why she was to wait, and she was astonished.

" ' Mr. Taylor's come for you,' said the man; ' step over here.'

" ' But I don't understand!' cried the girl. ' What do you mean? What are you going to do?'

" The man indicated Mr. Taylor with a nod.

" ' He'll tell you when it's over. We're in a hurry. . . . Stand here.'

" The gesture, the voice, the deadly aspect of the man silenced and compelled her. She crossed the floor trembling violently. The man caught her arm and drew her over beside Mr. Taylor; then he stood behind them. Mr. Taylor's face was as white as

293

plaster, but he did not move, and he did not speak. He felt the steel muzzle of the weapon bruising the flesh against his spine.

"'We're ready, Jake!' said the man. His voice was loud and harsh.

"The door in the opposite end of the room before them opened, and a little old man entered. He carried a folded paper and a candle. He stopped in the middle of the room.

"And with a benevolent smile, and holding the license in his hand, the Justice of the Peace began to repeat the ceremony of marriage."

"I think, Dr. Lennard," said Father Jerome, "that the difficulty with your theory lies in the fact that you have distinguished between wrongs and crimes. Crime is the name which the law gives to those wrongs which it undertakes to punish. These are necessarily limited; but there lies about them a vast zone of wrongs which are equally harmful, but which the law does not undertake to punish. The justice of God deals with wrong, not with crime.

"Here was a man who had committed no crime, as you say, but he had perpetrated a wrong that had inflicted injury upon an innocent person. A man may do an injury to the emotions that will result in as much suffering as any assault with intent to kill.

The law does not undertake to punish these wrongs, but God does. This man was not punished by a chancellor, but by the Judge of all the world."

"Father Jerome is right," said the judge, "in the idea that this power, as Matthew Arnold put it, which makes for righteousness, does not confine itself to criminal statutes. The administration of justice as undertaken by courts of law, is, at best, a kind of makeshift; many of the deepest wrongs the law cannot undertake to deal with. It must leave them to the pressure of public opinion, man's inherent sense of fair dealing, and our ideas of morality. For instance, perfidy and ingratitude may result in as much suffering as murder, but it is obvious that the law could punish neither. But the impulse behind the machinery of the world — call it what you like — will move events to an adjustment of these wrongs, with the same irresistible pressure that it brings to bear upon the highest crime."

"Ah!" said the doctor, "is the universe moral? I have given you Buddha's answer, and I have given you the answer of science, that is to say, man's oldest and his newest knowledge. For the sake of the fairy stories of our childhood I wish it were, but it is not. Let me put my theory into a nutshell. The criminal is always ruined by contributory negligence. Look at the myriad of trivial events which this mass of newspaper clippings gathered by Druce, show to have ruined the criminal. Varieties of little oversights, little negligences, and the like."

" But," said the priest, " these things are but the agencies which Providence uses to accomplish its purpose."

The judge laughed.

" Pardon me, Father Jerome," he said, " when Lennard began to speak of trivialities, the word brought to my mind a most amusing case that occurred in Paris. We may all of us interpret it as we like, but it is upon that very point. 'You both know Paris.

" At four o'clock in the morning M. Duclos entered the Café des Oiseaux in the Rue des Petits Champs. It was an unusual hour for an honest shopkeeper to be out of bed in Paris, but M. Duclos had a sufficient reason.

" Fair dealing albeit somewhat slow of foot, had brought M. Duclos to a substantial shop looking from a cross street into the Rue de la Paix. It was edging him slowly into that fashionable quarter. Already Hugette Rozier, who created hats in the rooms above his shop, had said the word:

" ' Monsieur Duclos, we belong out there! ' — pointing into the Rue de la Paix.

" ' But, madame,' he had said, ' to get on there one must have something in his shop not to be found elsewhere in Paris.'

" ' And that thing you have, monsieur.'

" He had scratched his head then. ' I cannot think of it, madame.'

" ' But I can: it is called honesty, Monsieur Duclos.'

" The creator of hats was very charming and monsieur bowed. Then there came a twinkle into his eyes.

" ' And you, madame? '

" The petite Hugette laughed like a blackbird.

" ' Ah, monsieur, I am perhaps not so fortunate, but for that reason I do not despair.'

" Her hand darted between the buttons of her blouse, a ribbon snapped and she extended her half-closed palm near to the eyes of Monsieur Duclos. He saw there an elegant young man — a miniature studded with diamonds. It was only for a moment that Hugette's rosy palm flashed before the eyes of M. Duclos, but in that moment the shrewd bourgeois dealer in jewels observed a number of things — namely, that the case of the miniature was a genuine antique; that the diamonds were false — the bent tines of the metal proclaiming how recently this paste had been substituted. And the painting on the ivory disk! It had been done yesterday, in the Rue de Rivoli — he could put his finger on the very shop.

"Ah, well, if one were setting up a little modiste in the Rue de la Paix one could not afford to be too honest. There would be expense enough; the baker and the candlestick-maker would not take fairy gold — a bit of deception in this behalf could be forgiven him. If, when he had cast up the cost of the venture, this elegant Lothario had purchased an ancient miniature for a dozen francs, forced the noble face of some subject of a Louis to make way on the ivory disk for his own, set the denuded metal wreath with brilliants and hung it about the charming neck of Hugette under the lace blouse — why, from the viewpoint of an economical bourgeois, he was a prudent young man.

"It was quite as well. Hugette would have no inkling of this prudence until the affair went on the rocks and she came to the pawnshop with the salvage. And then, what did it matter? In loveland all treasures are alike — oak leaves on the morning after!

"The remarks of Hugette had found a lodging with M. Duclos. He was ready for this step into a fashionable quarter of Paris. He would take with him, beyond a doubt, that rare thing which Hugette had named.   But it was not entirely upon this virtue that he would depend out there in the Rue de la Paix.   He had, locked up in the great safe in his shop, thirteen diamonds, that could not be equaled in the whole of France.   He had put in half a lifetime at matching those diamonds.   It was with great acumen that M. Duclos had gone about assembling this treasure.   He had observed that jewels, like the blood, were always moving; and, like that blood, they followed the impulses of the heart.   At least, it was so with diamonds.   If there was a good stone in France it would finally come into the possession of the light-o'-loves that foraged on Paris; and when this flying squadron came to sell its loot M. Duclos could obtain that stone for a fraction of its value.

" It was on account of these diamonds that M. Duclos came so early — or, since the place is Paris, shall we say so late? — into the Café des Oiseaux. He was a prudent bourgeois.   Since there lay the earnings of a lifetime in that shop, M. Duclos wished it always under someone's eye.   And he had managed in this fashion:  Until midnight there was no danger; then until half-past four his friend, the gendarme Jacques Fuillon, watched over the Rue des Petits Champs.   One found him always, like a gigantic Cerberus, before this shop.   And at half-past four M. Duclos came, always exactly on the hour; for the gendarme, a cog in the police machinery of Paris, controlled his movements by the hand of the clock.

" It was the custom of M. Duclos to enter the Café des Oiseaux for his cup of black coffee before he went on guard; and as he waited for the day to open it was his custom also to read romances. He carried one always under his arm; he opened it in the Café des Oiseaux before his cup. M. Duclos preferred tales in which tragedies were accustomed to happen — wherein a mystery seized one in the opening lines and one trailed it through with one's nose against the page. M. Duclos had about exhausted the literature of Parisian mystery. He had come to the last of the intricate adventures of M. Lecoq when, by accident, a new door had been thrown open to him.

" In the Café des Oiseaux — as sooner or later it must have happened — he had chanced upon the author of Hugette's advancing fortunes. This elegant young man had bowed to M. Duclos as he sat over his coffee, and from the bow he had advanced to a word of comment upon the literature that M. Duclos affected.

" ' Ah, if one admired tales of mystery, then one should by all means read those of Monsieur Poe, the American. He was the master of such tales; the others, all the others — Gaboriau, Monsieur le

300

Docteur Doyle — these were mere imitators of him.'

" M. Duclos had inquired where the tales of this Monsieur Poe could be had; and, having been directed, he had found them. He came now, on this morning, with a volume of them tucked under his arm.

" As M. Duclos entered from the Rue des Petits Champs he observed that his elegant preceptor in the literature of mystery was already there. He stood at the back of the café before the clock, as though he came at this moment from a bandbox. His fair hair was curled and perfumed under the silken brim of his English opera hat; there were double pearl studs in his shirt front; his immaculate hands were loaded with rings; he wore a jeweled bangle on his wrist beneath the cuff. Before him on the table were his gloves, his cane and a glass of liqueur. But for the moment he stood with an evening journal extended in his hands, idly glancing down its columns like one who performed a certain habit with but little attaching interest. M. Duclos thought that the elegant young man had been facing the other way and had turned swiftly as he entered, but if so, he did not advance toward M. Duclos — he bowed slightly, as to a chance acquaintance, and returned to the columns of his journal.

" M. Duclos crossed to his table; the rotund *veuve,* Consenat, who maintained this Café of the Birds, brought his coffee.

" ' Monsieur is early to-night,' she said.

" M. Duclos, who was never in his life either late or early, bowed, congratulated Madame Consenat on her excellent coffee — as he had been accustomed to do every morning for two years — tasted his cup and opened his book. He sipped both the coffee and the tale. At length, when he had come to the bottom of the cup, he closed the volume and looked up over the rim of his noseglasses. At this moment the elegant stranger, with an air of ennui, folded his journal, tossed it on to a near-by table, and moving forward took up his cane and gloves as though about to depart. It was then that the café clock came into view and M. Duclos observed that by this clock Madame Consenat's words were verified — it was but three o'clock and thirty minutes; he was early by half an hour.

" The elegant stranger, sauntering out of the Café des Oiseaux, paused by M. Duclos' table as he had been accustomed to do. He bowed with a trifle of condescension. Had monsieur found the great Poe to his liking?

" M. Duclos replied profusely, like one who has received a benefit that he cannot measure. He was wonderful — this Poe! Gaboriau — the great Gaboriau — could not approach him; and that *docteur anglais* — what did one call him — Doyle? Pouf! He was an echo. What was Lecoq! What was Sherlock Holmes beside this Master Dupin! These were the successors of Alexander! . . . And when he wrote weird tales one's blood chilled. That German, Hoffman, whose head was full of horrors! He could not make one hear the piercing cry, or feel the awful suffocation, or see the ghastly dead face, like this Poe! The German told like one who had heard of such hideous tragedies, but this American like one who had survived them.

"The elegant stranger was charmed. One takes a certain merit from merely discovering a pleasure to another. He became more friendly. M. Duclos read with a discriminating taste — it was so rare a thing! His opinion, then, would be most interesting to hear. Monsieur had observed the great Poe's tales to lie in two separate zones. In which of these did M. Duclos believe him to excel?

"M. Duclos was certain upon this point.

"'Monsieur,' he said, 'the tales in which M. Poe unravels his mystery from some tiny incident are his greatest. They seem to me to move along the lines of a profound truth — that is to say, there are always evidences which, if one did but observe and correctly interpret, would presently disclose the whole mystery. It is not upon some elaborate theory that one must depend; it is upon the tiny evidences — the crook of a letter in a written word, a scratch on a table, a bit of paper. It is the value of these trivialities that M. Poe brings so forcibly before us. This, monsieur, is a great truth, a valuable truth, a useful truth — one to remember and apply, monsieur.'

" Did M. Duclos think so? The elegant stranger was of a different opinion. Now, he would select the great Poe's weird tales as the most excellent of his writings. These were cups of opiate, which one tasted and forgot the place in which he sat; tasted and forgot his anxieties; tasted and forgot the flight of time. The interests of men in their affairs were so consuming, their anxieties so keen! To make them forget! Ah, this was the test!

" M. Duclos protested. But such tales were false; the incidents of them were things that did not happen. But those of M. Dupin — they rested upon a truth to be verified in one's experience. They were didactic; the reader learned a thing which he might convert to his use.

" The stranger slipped into a chair beside M. Duclos at his table. In the interest which this discussion had inspired he forgot that he was going out.

" But were those tales false? Did they not happen? For himself, he was not so certain. Of course, it was in the genius of M. Poe so to stage them that one could not say: Ah! That was a trick that only a master could turn. To present the weird, the ghastly, the tragic, with such cunning that one could not say whether they happened in the narrator's mind or in the world outside. But — and M. Duclos should mark it — men, in fact, sometimes had experiences like this. Strange, incredible adventures came to them now and then in such a manner that afterward they never could be certain whether or not they had happened. . . . M. Poe was not off the ground here. He was dealing with a certain order of human experience in these tales. True, they were experiences that men rarely spoke of, since they were things one could not verify. M. Poe had not exceeded those experiences. One had adventures on this borderland as strange as M. Poe had dreamed of. Did M. Duclos doubt it? The stranger knew a certain case in point. He put his cane and gloves upon the table.

" Had M. Duclos ever, by chance, heard of Monsieur le Docteur le Duc de Borde? He was young. Perhaps his fame was local yet. M. Duclos had not? Well, a weird, a strange, an incredible thing had befallen this young man. In Paris? No. In the very land of this M. Poe — in the city of Washington, in les Etats-Unis, when M. McKinley was le Président, shortly before the Spanish-American War.

"'Monsieur le Docteur le Duc de Borde had been attached to the French legation there. He was a gay dog, this Monsieur le Docteur le Duc de Borde. Ah, one may find companions who dine late in other cities than Paris. And the good wines! They are not all poured out in France. . . . Well, it was about this very hour of the morning, after a dinner of the best, that Monsieur le Docteur le Duc de Borde was returning to his lodging. The good wine was in his head and he had dismissed his carriage and gone afoot to get the air. It was a bit cold and monsieur walked briskly.'

"Did M. Duclos know the city of Washington? He did not? The elegant stranger traced an imaginary map on the table with his finger. It was traversed by a great boulevard l'Avenue de Pennsylvanie, running from la Maison Blanche to le Capitole, and then, turning sharply, it passed la Bibliothèque Congressionale.

"'As Monsieur le Docteur le Duc de Borde traversed this boulevard a hansom cab such as one sees in Londres, going at a slow jog, turned in. As the cab passed it seemed to Monsieur le Docteur that a woman thrust her arm out of the window and waved a handkerchief, as though to attract his attention. Now, Monsieur le Docteur le Duc de Borde is very gallant. He began at once to run after the cab, shouting to the driver to pull up and waving his walking stick. The cab horse proceeded leisurely down l'Avenue de Pennsylvanie and turned out toward la Bibliothèque Congressionale. During all this time a woman's hand remained thrust out of the cab window and a tiny white handkerchief fluttered in her fingers. Monsieur le Docteur followed.

" ' In American cities there exists an inconceivable custom, when repairing a street, of digging a trench half across it, setting up a red lantern at each end and leaving Providence to care further for the traveler. In front of la Bibliothèque Congressionale there was such a trench to lay a water main cut half across the street, a red lantern marking its limit. As the cab passed, one of the wheels struck the lantern and went suddenly into the ditch; the cab lurched heavily to one side and, to the horror of Monsieur le Docteur — who was close behind — the woman plunged out, striking her head on the asphalt pavement. The cab righted itself and went on, the heavy wheel rolling over the woman's coat.

" ' Monsieur le Docteur le Duc de Borde ran to the woman and bent over her to lift her up. To his utter amazement, he found that the woman was not only dead but that she was cold and her limbs set in *rigor mortis,* showing that she had been dead for hours.

" 'She was a very beautiful woman, perhaps thirty, of a decided continental type, black hair, heavy brows, long black lashes and a low oval brow. She wore a magnificent sealskin coat, trimmed in ermine and reaching to her feet. M. le Docteur noticed that her hands were small, with delicate, tapering fingers; in one of them a handkerchief was tied; there was also a broken leather strap around the waist. Monsieur le Docteur le Duc de Borde shuddered with horror. The dead woman had been tied into the cab!

" 'He had been flirting with a corpse!

" 'Monsieur le Docteur sprang up to call for aid. He had hardly got to his feet when a hand seized him by the shoulder; he whirled around to find himself in the grasp of a powerful man, wearing the uniform of a naval officer. The man's breast was covered with decorations; his teeth gleamed through a tangle of black beard and he growled in a hoarse guttural tongue, which Monsieur le Docteur recognized as Russian.

" 'The man held Monsieur le Docteur with one hand and thrust the other into the bosom of his own coat. Monsieur le Docteur instantly divined that his adversary hunted a weapon and he seized the arm with both of his hands to wrench it away before the weapon could be got. The two men began to struggle desperately. The Russian cursed in that unintelligible Slavic jargon which is like the chatter of an engine. He shifted his hand from the shoulder to Monsieur le Docteur's throat and began to choke him. The two men were now in the middle of the street and Monsieur le Docteur was facing le Capitole, in the direction from which he had come. He could not breathe; his eyes protruded; he felt that he was dying.

" ' At this moment, across the Russian's shoulder, he saw a huge motor car coming swiftly down the street toward them. It seemed to pull up a bit as it approached; then, when it was nearly on them, it came forward as though all the power were suddenly applied.

" ' The car held only the chauffeur and carried no lights. It struck the Russian a frightful, crushing blow in the back and both he and Monsieur le Docteur le Duc de Borde were flung far down the street.

" ' The first impression of returning consciousness that came to Monsieur le Docteur le Duc de Borde was that of a heavy cloth lying over his face and body. He raised his hands, pushed it back and sat up. He saw that he had been lying on the floor of a dimly lighted room, under the corner of a great silk Oriental rug, which remained spread out as though covering other persons asleep on the floor.' "

## CHAPTER XVI: *A Critique of Monsieur Poe*

THE room, which seemed to be a library, was lighted by a lamp somewhere behind him. He turned his head to see. A large table stood in the center of the room, littered with books, papers and various articles. Over it leaned a man holding a small copper coffee-pot in the flame of an alcohol lamp. At the sound of Monsieur le Docteur's turning around on the floor the man looked up. He was tall, thin, dark and apparently Spanish.

" ' " Ah! " he said, with a curious lisping accent, " One of them returns! "

" ' Then he came swiftly over to Monsieur le Docteur, took him by the arm and helped him into a big leather chair directly before the table, poured out a cup of coffee and held it to his lips.

" ' The coffee was thick, strong and black, and Monsieur le Docteur le Duc de Borde at once began to feel the effect of it. He could sit up by holding on to the arms of the chair, but his head ached frightfully and his senses were dazed.

" ' " Perhaps," said the Spaniard, as though speaking to himself, " I would better see if the others are intending also to return."

" ' He seized a corner of the great rug and threw it back, revealing the body of the woman which Monsieur le Docteur had found tied in the cab and, beside her, lying at full length, the body of the man in the uniform of a naval officer — his black beard clotted with blood where it had dripped from his mouth.

" ' " Ah," he said, " these are more courteous; they prefer to await our arrival."

" ' Then he poured out a cup of coffee and drank it.

" ' " It is in all countries the same," he continued; " the coffee for the last course — no, the cigarette; and then — the end. A word of explanation, señor, before the cigarette, that you may feel less among strangers when we presently join madame and the admiral.

" ' " Madame and I are rather famous specialists of a certain order, usually employed by a Government when its diplomatic corps proves a bit inefficient. Our mission here was to determine whether, in fact, it is the intention of les Etats-Unis to attack the Kingdom of Spain.

" ' " One does not fail when one's country is in

peril — and when one is paid enough. To-day we have learned the truth — there will be war ! "

" ' The Spaniard smiled; then he went on:

" ' " Ah, señor, madame is a charming woman. You yourself will say it when you come to know her better — exquisitely charming ! The admiral here could not fail to mark it. And madame ! She has a heart so tender ! So susceptible ! Alas, I alone remained to mar this happiness ! And what am I, señor, to stand in the way of Paradise ? A drop or two of a drug in a cup of coffee and my interest in events would cease. Unfortunately I have made it a custom never to drink anything over which the hand of another is unnecessarily placed; it is not hygienic. And so to-night at dinner I tip my coffee out on to the floor. A little later I pretend to sleep. Madame leans over me, doubtless to secure some articles which I should no longer need. I seize the hands. I tie them behind the back with a silk stocking — an excellent thing a silk stocking, señor ! and more excellent, since there are always two. The other I tie around the throat. Then, with a riding crop thrust through it, I have a beautiful garrote." He moved his hand among the books, took up a twisted silk stocking and tossed it over into the chair beside Monsieur le Docteur, who, still dazed and hardly knowing what he did, put it into his pocket.

" ' The Spaniard paused and drew a cigarette-case from his pocket.

" ' Monsieur le Docteur le Duc de Borde noticed a little black line of something resembling ashes, running from the leg of the table around the chair in which he was seated. He put down his hand and brushed a little of it into his palm. It was gunpowder!

" ' The Spaniard sat down on the corner of the table and began to roll his cigarette in his hands.

" ' " In madame's bosom I find a delicious little note from the admiral asking her to come on this night to the rendezvous. Ah, the rendezvous! I faithfully kept it for her. I excellently kept it for her. She was to wave her handkerchief from the cab somewhere between this house and la Bibliothèque Congressionale. I do not know where — but I do not disappoint the admiral. I get a hansom from the stable beyond the library, I dismiss the driver. I tie her in. I put the hand out of the window. I tie the handkerchief in the fingers. I send the horses home. So the rendezvous was beautifully kept after all." He nodded to Monsieur le Docteur le Duc de Borde.

" ' The Spaniard leaned over on the table to get a match for his cigarette.

" ' " Afterward," he said, " I bring the three of you comfortably home in the motor car."

" ' He sat up and puffed his cigarette for a moment; then he said softly:

" ' " If you quite understand we will not keep the others waiting."

" ' The full import of the man's plans came suddenly to Monsieur le Docteur le Duc de Borde and he sprang up shouting. Instantly the Spaniard leaped to the floor.

" ' " Let us be going, señor! " he cried.

" ' Then he jabbed his lighted cigarette down on the table. A flash of light ran to the leather chair. Monsieur le Docteur rushed into the hall and tried to open the door to the street, but the hall was dark and he was unable to find the bolt that held the door. Each moment he expected the house to be blown to atoms. Fortunately, for an instant, the light was switched on, illuminating the hall and the great library. Monsieur le Docteur le Duc de Borde saw the Spaniard on the floor, groping for his broken powder train. He also saw the bolt holding the door and in a moment he was outside, running down an old garden path. He broke through a hedge into the street and continued to run madly, with his head down. Finally, running thus, overwhelmed with terror, Monsieur le Docteur le Duc de Borde collided with a gendarme.

" ' Monsieur le Docteur was incoherent then.

The gendarme took him to the Department of Police. It was morning when he came before the prefect. That official laughed at the story of Monsieur le Docteur le Duc de Borde. Wine had carried monsieur into the region of the fancy! Since Monsieur le Docteur le Duc de Borde was of the French diplomatic corps he was at liberty to go. But the story! Monsieur must pardon his incredulity. And, in fact, what proof had Monsieur le Docteur le Duc de Borde of this adventure? True, there was the silk stocking in his pocket! But, monsieur '— the speaker made an elegant gesture —' I ask it of you, what does a silk stocking prove on the morning after?'

. . . . . . . .

"The consuming attention of M. Duclos, set on the interest of the tale, relaxed. The elegant stranger arose with a laugh that rippled through the Café des Oiseaux. He pointed to the clock.

"'Ah, monsieur,' he cried, 'have I not proved my point? Here is a tale infinitely below the genius of M. Poe, and yet, see what it has done! It has held Monsieur Duclos, a dealer in jewels of the Rue des Petits Champs, for some thirty minutes in the Café des Oiseaux. And it has held him against his anxiety to guard his shop — against his fear for his thirteen diamonds. Observe, monsieur; it is late.

The gendarme Jacques Fuillon has gone out at the end of the Rue des Petits Champs for some thirty minutes by the clock! '

" He took up his cane and gloves from the table. He lifted his silk English opera hat from his curled and perfumed hair.

" ' I bid M. Duclos good morning.'

" M. Duclos did not rise.

" ' A moment, monsieur,' he said.

" The stranger paused. ' Does not M. Duclos hurry to his shop? '

" The dealer in jewels shrugged his shoulders. ' What is the use, monsieur? ' he said. ' I am already late and there remains this question of M. Poe's tales to settle. And, besides, monsieur is charming. And this I must charge against this argument: told by another, monsieur's tale might not have held one so well. Such a quality goes very far. What one among us could resist monsieur? Not *la petite* Hugette, nor yet *la veuve* Consenat. Monsieur takes his liberty with the heart of the one and the clock of the other.'

" The elegant stranger regarded M. Duclos now with a certain interest, but his gallant manner remained. He bowed.

" ' Monsieur does me too much honor.'

" Not so. M. Duclos did but recognize a merit.

But this question of the tales: he must be permitted his opinion.

" ' Monsieur,' he said, ' those concerning M. Dupin I continue to regard as the masterpieces of M. Poe; and, for the following reason, which monsieur will himself deem excellent when he has heard it.'

" M. Duclos leaned forward on the table.

" ' Monsieur,' he said, ' on yesterday morning I noticed a crumb of plaster on the floor of my shop, in the Rue des Petits Champs.  Now, monsieur, what is a crumb of plaster?  It is nothing.  But for these tales of M. Poe — but for these warnings of M. Dupin — I should have passed it over.  But having, through the courtesy of monsieur, read these tales, I reflected.  Whence came this crumb of plaster? Why, obviously, monsieur, from the ceiling above. I examine that ceiling and I find there a tiny crevice. I go into the shop of Hugette above.  I remove the carpet.  Ah!  I find a hole cut in the floor!'

" M. Duclos paused.  The elegant stranger had taken one swift stride, stopped abruptly and now stood, very pale, his gloves clutched in his fingers, his eyes on the door of the Café des Oiseaux.  Something moved out there in the Rue des Petits Champs.

" M. Duclos continued softly:

" ' Ah, monsieur, that is not all.  To point out how the gendarmes could take the poor creatures

"The Café des Oiseaux was filled with gendarmes."

who were to execute monsieur's design was an unpleasant duty; but to entertain monsieur until they should come for him — that has been a pleasure.'

" M. Duclos did not finish his discourse. He was interrupted by a cry. The Café des Oiseaux was filled with gendarmes."

The judge had hardly ceased to speak, when a servant entered with a telegram.

" For Mr. Flint," he said.

The judge tore open the yellow envelope and glanced at the contents.

" Gentlemen," he said, " this confirms the investigation which I set on foot last night. From what I have learned, I am now able to give you the history of this man Druce."

He turned toward the doctor.

" If Lennard has ready the result of his experiment, we can now try to put the pieces of this puzzle together."

" I have sent my coachman to the village chemist," replied the doctor; " he may return at any moment; in the meantime, you might tell us what you have learned."

CHAPTER XVII: *The Low Door*

F ROM this photograph," began the judge, " the name Wilfred Druce, and the servant's story, it was fairly certain that the man was English; from his notes referring to some occurrence on the *Victory*, I concluded that he may have been, in some way, related to the navy. I, therefore, called up one of our clerks in New York and had inquiries cabled to the English Admiralty. I was right. To-day I have received the history of the man in reply, and a reference to certain old copies of the *London Graphic*. These copies my clerk was able to obtain in New York and sent up to me this afternoon. Now, with the reply of the Admiralty, and the copies of the *Graphic*, I have been able to interpret these penciled notes which Druce left in his iron box. Let me first give you the story which these notes and the copies of the *Graphic* tell, and after that I will explain the tragedy, to which these events refer. But, first, I bid you observe that we were right to conclude that the *Victory* meant Nelson's flagship, but we were wrong to assume that Druce's relation to it must have extended back over a period of one hundred and seven years. The fact is that the *Victory* is now anchored in Plymouth Harbor and for a number of years has been used as a place for the sitting of naval court-martials. Wilfred Druce was tried by a naval court of inquiry aboard the *Victory* in Plymouth Harbor, a few days before he came to America. Let me give you the vivid story as it arises out of these undated fragmentary notes. . . .

"The canvas screen stretched taut across the main deck of the *Victory*, barred out the marine guide and his flock of tourists, but it admitted his lecture with distinctness. The man, walking up and down behind this canvas, caught every word. The description of the ship, the history of Trafalgar, the last words of the immortal admiral with his captain, set out in cockney, ''Ardy, I am wounded,' and the answer, 'Not morshally, I 'opes.'

"It was doubtless the high nervous tension of the man, pacing the length of the sail cloth screen, that made him conscious of every sound. His body, his moving fingers, showed this tension. The pupils of his eyes were distended as from loss of sleep. His skin glistened with sweat. Now and then, he stopped, wiped his face with a handkerchief already wet, crushed in the palm of his hand, and continued up and down across the deck of the ship.

"He was a young man, under three and twenty,

in the uniform of a naval lieutenant, except that he wore no sword. The straps of the belt were hooked up. Now and then, as from unconscious habit, as he walked, he put down his left hand to these straps. The hand would grope for a moment, and then come up with a jerk of the elbow.

" Opposite this canvas screen, at the door leading aft, stood a naval master-at-arms, with a drawn sword. Presently that door opened, and the naval master-at-arms stood back. The young man stopped abruptly, turned sharply on his heel, crossed the deck and entered the cabin. The guard followed, closing the door after him.

" Nelson's *Victory*, anchored in Plymouth Harbor, is now subject to two uses — that of the tourist, and that of the naval court-martial. This latter use was not contemplated when the old ship was opened as a museum. A court-martial room was provided in each of the new naval barracks, but when they were all fitted, someone pointed out that the Naval Discipline Act required a court-martial to be held ' on board one of his Majesty's ships or vessels of war.' The old museum ship, attached to the harbor, came within the Act, and Nelson's quarters were pressed into a modern service. The big cabin, running the entire width of the ship, remained empty and bare, as the great admiral had left it, except for a rather disreputable stove, a black iron box, with 'court-martial papers' painted in white letters on its lid, and a long table.

"This table was now the point of exclusive interest. Ten persons in the service of Great Britain on the high seas, sat about it. A rear admiral, acting as president of the court, at the end nearest the door; the deputy judge advocate at the farther end, and the others at either side. The lieutenant, and the master-at-arms, now acting as provost marshal, crossed the cabin and took a place beside the judge advocate; the provost marshal on the right of the lieutenant, with the sword in his hand.

"The court sat uncovered; now, as the deputy judge advocate arose to read the sentence, the members of the court put on their hats. But the sentence was already indicated. When an officer is brought to trial before a court-martial, he is visited by the provost marshal, put under arrest, and his sword taken away. When the court convenes this sword is laid across the table before the president, and there it lies in sequestration until the deliberations are concluded. Then, when a finding is arrived at, and before the prisoner is called, it is laid along the table with the hilt toward the place where he will stand, if the finding be in his favor, and the point, if it be against him.

323

"It is the verdict lying naked to the eye — the prisoner's destiny, indicated by a sign. The human mind, when all of fortune is in hazard, strangely abhors an abrupt announcement of the issue, and, for as long as he may, one will keep himself in doubt. No man, drawing lots for his life, was ever known immediately to open his hand and look. It is in nature to palm the ball, to wait, to peer fearfully through the fingers.

"The lieutenant, entering with the provost marshal, did not at once look for this sign lying on the table. He kept his face lifted, his eyes above the court, until he came to his place beside the deputy judge advocate. It was not until that officer began to unfold the paper in his fingers that the young man looked down. The sword was lying along the table, with the point toward him. The light entering the cabin behind the deputy judge advocate, twinkled on this point. It held the man's eyes like the crumb of a jewel.

"That which followed seemed to the lieutenant a thing acted in a play — of no concern to him, and lacking in interest. The rising of the court; his discharge from the custody of the provost marshal; his going out alone through the door, were in keeping with that fancy. And it was a fancy not wanting truth. For him, indeed, the curtain had descended. He was dismissed from his Majesty's service.

" He went out through the quaint door and down the gangway, over the ship's side. Below bobbed the naval steam pinnace and some scattered boats waiting for the tourists. He called one of these boats and returned to the *Mercury,* lying a little farther down the harbor, with a flock of submarines nestling against her, wallowing low in the sea, their dingy turrets, their lean steel backs crowded together, like some uncanny brood hatched out by the war-ship.

" The young man went aboard to his cabin, put on a suit of civilian clothes, strapped up his luggage, and returned with it to the boat. No man on the ship took any notice of his presence. The finding of the court, with the incredible swiftness of a rumor, had preceded him. He sat in the stern of the boat among his boxes, while the boatman pulled across the harbor to the railway station, in silence, except for the grinding of the oar against the pin. The boatman, like the others on the ' Depot Ship,' understood that this man was now a sort of outcast.

" The noon sun lay on the harbor, on the loopholes of the *Victory,* on the ungainly tugs churning through the bay, and farther out on the dirty, looming bulk of that third-class war-ship, called by the common sailor the ' Bully Ruffian.' "

## CHAPTER XVIII: *The Coward*

AN hour and forty minutes later the man was in London. The train raced north, over Hampshire, Surrey, and finally, over that vast Sahara of chimney pots, leading into Waterloo Station. Here he took a hansom, heaped his luggage on the top of it, and gave the driver an address in Pall Mall. The hansom turned down one of those huge, dirty alleys that end in this train shed, crossed Waterloo bridge, entered the Strand, packed with traffic, threaded its way into Trafalgar Square, and turned westward toward Pall Mall. In the meantime the man, sitting in the hansom, had not moved. He sat forward, his elbows resting on the doors. Now, as the hansom passed that curious statue of King George, riding in the Roman fashion, on a rather frisky bronze horse, the man tapped on the window. The cabman pulled up by a building that is an apex between the two streets, joining at this bronze. This building is decorated with many flags in enamel on its windows, and is the London office of one of the great transatlantic steamship companies.

"The man did not immediately descend when the

hansom stopped. He sat for a moment, as if in doubt, then he got down slowly and entered the building. The office was crowded. Diagrams of various ships lay on the long counter, running the length of the room, over which groups of persons stooped. It was some minutes before the man could find a clerk who could attend him, and then he came in for a disappointment. The next liner to New York sailed in five days, but there was no vacant cabin. The flood of American travelers was turned homeward. The ship was booked. However, if he wished it, he could have a berth in the second officer's cabin for twenty pounds. He paid down the money in gold and came out with his ticket in his pocket. The hansom was waiting. He got in and the driver turned west, past the bronze of King George, into Pall Mall, and presently drew up before the massive columns of a club. The quarter of London about this club is visibly historic. In the square adjoining is the bronze to the Crimea; below is the wide Plaza Napier, and behind him, at the park steps, the Duke of York's column.

" The man got out of the hansom here, took off his luggage, paid the cabman, and entered the club. He stopped at the desk and asked to have his account made out. The clerk immediately produced it, enclosed in an envelope. The suggestion was pointed, his fame had come on some hours before. He gave the clerk the amount indicated, put his luggage in charge of the hall porter, and went on into the club.

" The interior of this club, and especially that part about the stairway, is a monument to the prowess of England on the sea. Along the wall are marbles running from Nelson to Keppel. At this hour of the afternoon the corridor of the club is apt to be deserted. The man hesitated, then he went slowly up the stairway. Here at the top are two famous paintings — Waterloo, on the right of one coming up, and on the left, Trafalgar. At the end of the second floor is a writing room, running the whole length of the club.

" As the young man approached the door of this room, the greatest sailor now living came out of it. The old man started like one struck across the face, threw up his head, and passed on. The blood mounted from the young man's collar upward to his hair, and he went on swiftly into the room. A few elderly men sat about in whispered conversation over the evening papers. They paused for the fraction of a second when he entered, and then continued with their talk, as though he were not there on the sill of the door.

" He went down the long room to a vacant table, took a sheet of paper out of the rack, selected a pen and dipped it into the ink. Then a newspaper lying

over a chair caught his eye, and the red in his face
began to burn. The press had been merciless. He
was given here no benefit of any doubt. Here were
words in print, in headlines, that he had lacked the
courage to say, even to himself. For the moment he
was glad for the screen of the desk. He sat with the
pen in his fingers. The inanimate things about this
room seemed vividly to scorn him. This place was
a patriotic shrine,— there was a full-length painting
of Queen Victoria above the fireplace, of the king, of
Queen Alexandria on the wall, and beyond the cover
of the desk top, old men whose names headed fragments of history.

" He put down the pen, got up abruptly, and went
out. On the side looking down into Pall Mall, there
is a smaller writing room, usually vacant. At the
door of it, above the well of the stairway, is a famous
painting of Nelson, and under that portrait, in a case
with a glass lid, is Nelson's sword. The young man
went along the corridor past this picture into the
room. This room was empty; he closed the door and
sat down here to write the thing he could not write
in that other room. The pen was hardly running on
the paper when the door opened, and the servant
entered.

" ' Mr. Druce, sir ? ' inquired the servant.

" The man replied with an inclination of the head.

329

" ' There is a parcel for you, sir,' said the servant —' arrived by this post. Shall I bring it up, sir? '

" ' If you please,' replied the man.

" Then he waited, with the pen in his fingers, the ink drying on the point.

" In a moment the servant returned with a long parcel tied up in heavy paper, put it down on the table, and went out. The man sat for a time looking idly at the parcel, and tracing indefinite figures on the cover of it with the pen; then, as though uncertain of its contents, and moved by some vagrant curiosity, he began to untie the parcel and pull off the heavy paper cover. His sword fell out on the table.

" The sword of an officer, as a physical thing, is a piece of private property. It is always returned to its owner. The man sat as though struck, by some sorcery, into wood. The Admiralty had been prompt. The thing had come, at his heels, off the *Victory;* it had traveled with him on the train to London.

" For perhaps twenty minutes the man sat unmoving before the table, then he took up the pen which he had put down, dipped it again into the ink and finished his note to the governors of the club, surrendering his membership, and signed it ' Wilfred Druce.' Then he arose, took up the sword, broke the blade over the corner of the table, laid the pieces on the cloth beside the paper that he had written, and went out of the room."

The judge paused.

"That night," he continued, "the old drunken butler found Druce crossing the embankment toward the Thames, and you know the remainder of his history."

Flint relighted his cigar.

"Now, what had this man done? . . . I will tell you. At this time the English Admiralty was experimenting with submarines. The experiments were tremendously dangerous. The Admiralty was loath to detail sailors for this work, and a number of young Englishmen in the navy volunteered to undertake it. . . . Yes, you have their photographs in that box — Druce was one of them. It is said that these young fellows had some sort of pact, which, after a dinner in London, they solemnized at midnight in a cathedral, to the effect that no one of them should, under any circumstances, avail himself of an opportunity to save his own life, unless that opportunity were available to all, under penalty of an invocation to God to permit the dead men to destroy the survivor.

"Remember, the *Graphic* gives this as mere gossip — a vagrant, and doubtless an idle story, grown up out of some nonsense of young men in their cups.

Aristotle says that we all so love something strange that every man who tells a story, adds a bit of the wonderful out of his own fancy. And this is the very sort of thing that an old wife would tack on.

"Well, at any rate, what did happen is certain. These eight men, under the command of Druce, were experimenting with the submarine A7 in the open sea off Portsmouth Harbor. In coming to the surface the conning tower of the submarine was struck by a passing liner; the heavy casting was bent slightly on the port side, and the rivets where it is joined to the hull of the submarine sprung; the water entered and the vessel began to sink. The pumps were started, but the submarine continued to sink, and the ballast tanks were blown. The submarine then arose until its conning tower was at the surface, or perhaps barely above it. But, in order to bring the vessel up, all power in the motor had been put on and the pumps stopped, and now, so much water had entered through the leak that the submarine began once more to sink. The vessel was filled with chlorine fumes, generated by the salt water. Druce realized that the submarine was about to descend, and in a funk of terror, rushed to the conning tower, opened the hatch, which is operated by gearing, and jumped out just as the conning tower top disappeared below the surface. The submarine filled and sank. No one escaped but Druce, and he was picked up swimming in the open sea, by the liner. Druce was tried by a naval court of inquiry, sitting aboard the *Victory* at Plymouth, and dismissed from the service.

" Now," continued the judge, " here was enough to drive any man into exile. The thing doubtless preyed on his mind and developed these fears and precautions. I can now understand the man's strange acts, even this will. Druce's antecedents were of the Catholic faith, and he devised his estate here to Father Jerome, since he had no family to inherit. This clears up the mystery of the man's life."

" And also the mystery of his death," said Father Jerome.

Dr. Lennard shook his head.

# CHAPTER XIX: *The Assassin*

YOU men of science," continued the priest, " deny the supernatural, but the supernatural are the forces back of life. The dead, as well as the living, are instruments in the service of God's Providence. I have seen men die, threatened by the invisible presence of their victims. Who can say what the dying see, or those come at last into the presence and danger of death? The thing is clear before me. Druce was in deadly fear of these men whom his selfishness had murdered. They had sworn a vow in God's house. It is not idly that men enter into vows before the Lord. Has this man not written that he knew the ' design ' that would destroy him, and does not every act and aspect of his life show the presence of this fear? . . . Ah! the vow! Did not God's Providence awfully fulfill it? Druce saw these dead men at his windows. . . . That was water, and not blood, on the cement walk. He saw them, ghostly and dripping, come at last, and he fought madly with a weapon, but of what avail is a weapon against the disembodied dead!"

" Father Jerome," said Dr. Lennard, " you have touched precisely the point. Your disembodied ghost can neither receive nor do a violence. Believe me, if Druce could not inflict a physical injury on his ghostly assailants, neither could they inflict a physical injury on him. It is here at this cross road that Science bids you adieu. She admits all your human testimony to ghosts and apparitions. Nay, more, she knows that men see these things — the clinic and the mad house show her innumerable cases. They are crowded with men who see the ghostly and the dead as vividly before them, as are the living before the sane.

" She will go with you to this point in the case of Druce; will agree, that brooding on a fixed idea, this man came to develop all the peculiarities which we have observed, and to accomplish all the acts which have puzzled us; and she will agree that this mania finally dominated and possessed him until, on the night in question, he saw these dead men climbing through his windows, and that, in terror, he resisted them with cries and shots. All this she will agree to, nay, more, she will tell you the very form of mania that he had, and she will show you innumerable cases like it. But she will never admit that these apparitions dealt Druce a death blow that fractured the occipital bone."

" But the testimony of the butler," said the priest, " the water on the cement walk? "

The doctor smiled. " You fix the value of that evidence," he replied; " the man said blood, you correct it to water; of such account are the delusions of the drunken."

The judge interrupted.

" Did Druce kill himself? "

" He did not," answered Dr. Lennard; " no man living could have given himself that wound."

" What killed him, then? " said the judge.

There was the sound of a wheel on the gravel outside.

The doctor arose.

" If this is my coachman returned, I may be able to answer that question."

A moment later the butler brought in the iron box and a note.

Dr. Lennard set the box on the table, then he glanced at the note.

" I was right," he said. " I can now tell you what killed Druce. It was neither the hand of the living nor the dead. . . . Listen! You will remember that Druce was found lying in a corner of his library, near a bookcase. This heavy iron box sat on the floor beside him in a pool of blood; that blood had dried on the box, coating it with a heavy border. Well, yesterday, as I have said, I noticed something that we had overlooked in that room — it was this: the top of the bookcase, which Druce, in his terror, had partly overthrown, was covered with dust, except for a single clean square directly above where he lay. I measured this square, and its dimensions were exactly that of the bottom of this box. An idea occurred to me, and I sent this box to a biological chemist, requesting him to remove the coating of blood from its corners, and analyze what he could find beneath it."

The doctor held up the note.

"He tells me that on one corner of the box, under the coating of blood, he has found minute fragments of flesh fiber, hair and bits of bone. That clears the mystery. This is a heavy box with sharp corners; it sat on the top of that bookcase, and when Druce lurching against the bookcase, in his paroxysm of acute mania, threw the end of it off of its support, this box fell, its sharp corner crushed his skull, and as he went down, it dropped to the floor beside him."

"Ah," cried the priest, "how wonderful are the ways of God! Only the hand of His Providence could have done this thing."

"Only a great impulse," said the judge, "behind mind, behind matter, moving each equally to a common end, could have done it."

The doctor smiled.

"It was accomplished," he said, "by a perfectly natural sequence of events."

Father Jerome interrupted. " Moved by God's Providence ! "

Mr. Flint arose, threw the fragment of his cigar into the fire, and selected another.

" We shall never be able to agree upon our terms," he said. " Let us say that Wilfred Druce was killed by The Nameless Thing."

(1)

**THE END**

www.ingramcontent.com/pod-product-compliance
Lightning Source LLC
Chambersburg PA
CBHW032233010726
47494CB00002B/475